SKORPION'S DEATH

The tradition is to offer a blindfold. It's so you don't look into the eyes of the man who will kill you . . . Why hadn't I been given a blindfold? I closed my eyes.

Footsteps approached. I felt a coldness at the side of my neck under my ear.

'Open your eyes.'

Major Fellah had his pistol against me. What kind of threat was that? I faced a line of rifles. Why should five seconds more or less matter?

He took a fistful of hair and jerked it and my eyes flew open. I glanced sideways at his face. He was mad. I could see that in the eyes that stared at me and through me and into a private vision of his own. One of his eyelids had gone berserk, a wild dance.

Somewhere far off I heard Jaafar cough, dry as a desert breeze.

This is not happening to me. I don't believe it.

I felt the suck of Major Fellah's breath before he shouted his final order.

The world exploded.

About the author

David Brierley was born in Durban, South Africa. He spent fifteen years in advertising before taking up writing full-time in 1975. His previous novels include COLD WAR, BLOOD GROUP O, BIG BEAR LITTLE BEAR, SHOOTING STAR and CZECHMATE.

'Tough, staccato, sardonically witty'

New Yorker

'Fine unflagging stuff'

Observer

This is for Fanny
whose name I borrowed
and for Mike
who gave her a new one

1

The man scarcely bothered to look. He'd seen enough staring eyes and tight-packed bodies.

'It's quick, really very quick.'

Somewhere a baby began crying and the mother made soothing noises. I couldn't see them. My view was of the two men jammed in front of me. One had a cut above his cheekbone like an old duelling scar. As I watched, the blood drained from his face, leaving the skin dead white.

'It only takes forty seconds.'

The steel door slid shut. The hiss could have been escaping gas and the man with the scar on his cheek suppressed something, a gasp, a shiver. Sweat had come along his hairline; seconds before there'd been nothing and now the drops were like the beads of a necklace. He wore a dark suit and carried a black attaché case, one of the builders of the brave new France. I thought he was holding his breath, as if it was the shower room at Belsen, as if it would have made any difference.

The deceleration at the end was the worst. My brain said we were slowing but my stomach said we were falling back down the shaft. The lift doors sighed open and the man with the scar moved out. His companion had his wrist turned, checking the seconds added up to forty. He'd be the kind who counted his change when he bought matches from a blind man outside the metro station. They moved off together, business deals in their slim leather cases. I held back a moment, watching them turn right to the bar where they shake you twenty-odd francs for a *Ciel de Paris* cocktail.

I turned left.

I lost myself in the group that came out of the lift. The baby was still crying. A boy I thought, they cry longer, the whole of their lives sometimes. The mother clutched the baby to her and he was trying to reach her nipple through

7

the thin material of her dress. Definitely a boy, fumbling for a breast. The mother had stopped and was looking round, perhaps for the *toilettes* so she could give the baby a feed. And then I lost interest in them.

I picked out my contact at once. Of all the sightseers who'd come to the fifty-fifth floor of the Montparnasse Tower, she was the only one who'd turned her back on the view. It had to be Ella Borries, searching among the new arrivals, trying to pick me out. I turned aside, walking away from her past the souvenir stall, glancing at the dazzle of the May sky through the plate glass. I looked back. She was leaning against a display case of maps and prints of Paris and her belly was heavy with a child. It set her apart from everyone else. Pregnant women have this look to them, as if they are a whole world to themselves. But she seemed to be marked by something else. She had checked all the newcomers and now she was staring down at her hands, twisting the ring on her third finger. Round and round the ring went, round and round.

I thought of her voice on the phone. She'd been desperate to see me, her voice frayed with anxiety. 'It's because of Bertolt. You must help me. There's no one else I can go to. Please.'

She kept twisting the ring, as if that was all she had left of him. The ring and the baby in her womb.

I kept close to the windows as I came back. She never saw me, too intent on unscrewing her finger.

'Excuse me,' I said, 'can you see the Beaubourg from here?'

'Are you . . .'

'Yes.' I cut her short. Her voice had been unexpectedly loud and I was abrupt, her nerves affecting mine. She was staring as if I wasn't in the least the miracle-worker she'd been expecting. 'We'll go round to the other side. It's quieter there. Not so many sightseers.' And not so many ears to overhear. I didn't know what nightmare she was going to bring out.

'Is there somewhere to sit down?' she asked, laying both hands on her belly. She might have been as much as eight months gone. Certainly she was near the end of her pregnancy. We found two chairs and I turned mine so that I was

8

head on to the glass. It was one of those perfect days in late spring that God deals Paris in a forgiving moment: the 747s were on the wing, the Montparnasse Tower was in heaven, and all was well with the Bourse. When I focused on the glass I could see reflections of people wandering behind us. I waited.

'I don't know where to start, Miss . . .'

'Cody,' I said. 'Just call me Cody.'

She came to a full stop. I began to wish I'd never agreed to meet, not been at home when her call had come. We'd already been through the preliminaries on the phone. Her husband was missing; no, he didn't have sticky fingers with the girls, she was positive it wasn't that. She'd hesitated and come out with it: 'I'm frightened.' For yourself? 'For Bert.' Why not go to the police, I suggested. That's what we pay taxes for. 'Oh no, the police would be no good in something like this. In any case . . .' and there had been a pause while she faced the fact that life can be nasty, '. . . I'm not sure Bert would want the police looking for him.'

One of those, I'd thought. Edged on the wrong side of the law and found his new pals didn't play by the Queensberry rules. But there'd been something about her voice, a little-girl-lost hesitation. You felt life had just pulled the rug from under her feet and you wanted to help.

'At least let me meet you,' she had pleaded, because I had gone very silent at my end of the phone. 'Let me tell you about it.' So here we were, side by side, like waking up after a party and finding a stranger beside you in bed. Someone you can trust? Someone you can like? How to begin sharing delights and fears and that skeleton in the cupboard?

There was a scream behind us, cut short. Ella didn't seem to hear, her mind swallowed in her own problems. I turned slowly, puzzled because there were no reflections in the glass. Behind a pillar I caught sight of a girl with a hand up to her mouth, a giggle written all over her face. The sixteen year old by her side had sweet innocence on his face.

'Bertolt is a pilot.' Ella's voice came suddenly loud again, like a boy's at puberty, and she broke off. It was my morning for waiting. It wasn't going to be easy for her, bringing out her secrets in front of a stranger. 'He worked for Lufthansa, flew mostly the west European routes. He's good, really very good.'

She flicked her eyes up to make certain I was suitably impressed. We were as different as two people could be. Her eyes were blue and as guileless as a doll's; whereas mine were brown. She was tall and fair and Aryan; I was half a head shorter and could have passed for French. Her hair was long and straight; mine lay in dark curls. She would stride out with the confidence of an athlete; I moved with my body leaning forward, soft-footing. I was a hunter. That was what Michel said. While Ella was the blonde prize men hunted.

She searched for Bertolt under her ring and in the end I prompted: 'How many hours has he got?'

'Hours?' She seemed puzzled.

'They measure . . .' I'd been going to say: They measure a pilot's life in hours. It wasn't the most tactful way to put it but she picked me up.

'Of course. I'm sorry to seem stupid. He got his certificate nine years ago but he rose no higher than first officer. There's a problem with promotion. Lufthansa don't lose captains through crashes, you see.'

I peered at her, thinking this might be the famous German sense of humour. Her face showed nothing except the secret fears. Her fingers wouldn't let go of the ring, worrying at it.

'He left Lufthansa last winter. Quite suddenly.'

Ella Borries lost her way again. She was wondering for the hundredth time exactly why her husband had left his job so fast.

'Where did you meet?' I asked.

'On a flight to Milan. He was walking down the aisle when we hit an air pocket and he ended up in my lap.' She dug out a brave little smile.

And I thought: Perhaps that's why she arranged to meet me on top of the Montparnasse Tower. Up in the sky, where she'd met her Bert.

'That was three years ago,' she said. 'March 12th. I was working at the time for Mielke. You know, the German fashion house.'

I didn't know. I'd never thought of the Germans having a fashion industry. Boots, uniforms, nothing else.

10

'You were a model?'

Long blonde hair shook round her head. 'No. Even then I wasn't thin enough.' She looked down at the hill which was her belly. 'I was on the administrative side and someone thought I should see how the Italians got their shows together.' She paused again. Like a swimmer who's decided to dive into the cold sea, she took a deep breath. 'Anyway, I moved into Bert's apartment in Frankfurt. After a few months I thought I was pregnant and we got married. It was a mistake. The pregnancy, I mean.'

She gave a silly-me smile and shrugged. And Bert? I wondered if he had felt resentment. A lot of men would feel they had been trapped. It's not that they dislike the idea of being a father or don't love the woman. But inside a little voice whispers: She tricked you. Resentment is a fast growing weed.

'Was he pleased when you did get pregnant?'

'Of course.'

I counted the months back from May. 'You would have known you were pregnant – when, last October, November?'

'I was certain when I missed the second period in November.'

'And when did he leave Lufthansa?'

'December.'

'Did he discuss it with you first?'

'No.'

'Even though you were starting a family?'

She didn't respond. It was another little doubt mushrooming about their life together. She must have been nearly the same age as me but she was younger by several lifetimes. Pregnancy is meant to bring serenity but the glow had gone out of her face. Her mind should have been on motherhood, she should have been full of milk and secret smiles. Instead her expression had turned ugly with the thoughts that hammered inside her head. If I wasn't careful she would start to hate me because I wasn't soothing her but prodding into all the dark corners.

She seemed to have given up the effort of telling me, so I had to prod again: 'Tell me about his freelance work.'

11

'There's really nothing I can tell you.'

'Nothing? He must have talked about it to you.'

Her eyes returned to the ring. It was broad, a band of gold. 'We had other things to talk about.'

'But he can't simply have announced he was leaving Lufthansa and going freelance and that's that. Did he get a dry-wing lease for a cargo plane of his own? Did he freelance with one of the charter companies? Did he get together with other ex-Lufthansa staff?'

'He said a quite exceptional business opportunity had come up. He said he had the chance to make a lot of money. He said it wasn't something he could talk about. He said it was secret and if word got out they'd lose all their profit.'

'Profit? Is that the exact word he used?'

She bit her lip trying to remember. 'I'm not sure.'

I don't speak German so I don't know the force of the word *profit* in the language. Ella and I were speaking French in which it could mean money or it could mean advantage.

'He wasn't working on his own but with other people?'

'Yes.'

'Did you meet them?'

'No.'

'Do you know if they were French? Think, really think.'

She stared at me because I'd put a bit of urgency into my voice. It was essential she told me something useful if I was going to help her. I'm not a magician. I can't make someone appear out of nothing.

'Swiss maybe. Bert had two or three meetings in Switzerland,' she said.

'Switzerland is a cosmopolitan place. The people he saw could have come from anywhere.'

'I'm *trying* to help. It's just you don't understand.'

I understood. I remembered the time with Paul, so long ago it seems like a different lifetime. We'd had the whole summer together, and that was when summers were hotter and sunnier. We were going to get married, have a cottage, hollyhocks round the door, kids. One of each we decided. We planned it all, though neither of us was out of our teens. We had our own secret place, hidden in a copse of aspens that shivered with delight at every breath of air. We spent

12

every afternoon there, in talk and kisses and more of the same. Innocent love. You only ever open your heart like that the first time.

Bertolt Borries's meetings had been in Switzerland. But he and Ella had come to live in Paris, rented an apartment somewhere in the Buttes-Chaumont. I already knew that, and a bit more, because of the brief talk we'd had earlier. She hadn't known my name, just my phone number. I'd asked who had given it to her. It's the most basic security check when you're in my line of work. Again she didn't have a name, just the initials of a certain man. He is a fixer. He's one of those who sit in the shadows and murmur deals with men or organizations who are also known by initials. PLO, OPEC, CIA, those kind of initials. 'Bert said he'd first heard of this business opportunity through this man PDS. And if I ever . . .' I'd stopped her very fast. You don't talk about PDS on an open telephone line.

Borries had been recruited by a fixer in Paris and had a couple of meetings in Switzerland but his job could have taken him anywhere. A pilot's licence opens more frontiers than a passport. I asked her if she had any idea where he had been flying.

'I told you: we never talked about it. He was vague about his flying. He could be away for a week or even a fortnight but when we were together again we never mentioned it.'

Pilots are never vague about where they are flying. This one simply wasn't telling.

'You're his wife. You must have some idea of where he went.'

She thought about this. 'He said once: "When this is over we'll have a holiday in Siberia – I've had enough of sun and sand."'

'Did he bring you presents?'

'This.'

This was a necklace of silver with a pendant of lapis lazuli. For a moment her fingers toyed with this as a change from the wedding ring.

'Anything else?'

'A kaftan. Royal blue with gold buttons and stitching down the front.'

13

'Wasn't by any chance a label sewn in saying: Made in . . .'

'No.'

Hopeless. You can buy a kaftan like that in Anastasia, and that's only down the road from my apartment.

We stayed in silence. Through the glass I could see the Eiffel Tower and beyond that the concrete slabs of Neuilly and La Défense. The heart of Paris is still the slate roofs and soft grey walls of Utrillo; but the twenty-first century marches all round.

I could have got up and walked away. That's what they teach you to do: look on it as a job, keep your emotions out of it. If she had still been at the end of the telephone, perhaps. But she sat like a patient with a doctor, waiting for the pain to be made better. My father had been a doctor. This is how he must have felt when he'd put the stethoscope to some old man's chest and learnt there was no hope. But I didn't walk away. I seemed already to be involved. I asked: 'Tell me what decided you to get in touch with PDS and then with me. What prompted you?'

She'd been looking in my face but now she dropped her eyes and her voice. 'He's been away for four weeks. I've only heard from him once, a fortnight ago.'

She stopped. Even her fingers stopped their compulsive fiddling.

'Yes?'

'Wednesday was our wedding anniversary. Our second. He didn't come back. He didn't even telephone. There's been no explanation.'

There was the obvious explanation and I said: 'He could have forgotten. Men do.'

'Not Bert. You don't know him.'

Can you ever know another? I thought I'd known Paul. I thought I'd known M and Canuck, and Ella Borries thought she knew Bert.

She insisted: 'Something has happened to him.'

Poor love. Poor blinkered trusting love. Husband vanished, child in her belly, and only a stranger to help. My heart went out to her. It still seemed hopeless. I had nothing to go on. But how could I let her down gently? She must

14

have seen something of the doubt in my face because she had a sudden thought. She picked her bag off the floor and said: 'If it's money you're worried about . . .'

'I could spend your money and turn up nothing. Or worse, you might not like what I find.'

'I want you to find Bert for me. I don't care about the rest.'

No, there'd never be any way to let her down gently. The bump would come tomorrow or next year and something would smash inside her and never be mended again. What do you say to such an innocent?

'Listen,' I nagged at her again, 'a couple of weeks ago when Bert rang he must have said *something* about where he was or what he was doing.'

'He said he loved me.' Ella spoke very simply, as if I was the child. 'He said he missed me. He wanted to hear how I was, and the baby. He said he wanted to kiss me . . . and you know.'

Yes, I did know. I'd loved someone and trusted him and wanted to believe his lies. Men cheat us and hurt us and we dry our eyes and smile at them again. Is that what I should tell Ella? Is that all I could do for her?

'He dropped no hint of what country he was in? He didn't say what he'd eaten for dinner or how much things cost or what clothes people wore or what make of car he'd rented or anything?'

'No, I keep telling you.'

But she paused. If you keep prodding long enough they usually come out with something useful.

'It wasn't something Bert said. But when the phone rang, before he was connected, there was an operator who said: "*Ici l'Hôtel Quelquechose à Sfax. Je vous donne Monsieur Borries.*"'

'He was speaking French? "Monsieur Borries" he said? You're sure of that?'

'Yes.'

So a French-speaking country. Where the hell was Sfax?

'I'll need a photograph of Bert,' I said.

'You mean you will help me?'

There was hope in her smile. The shadows were chased away from her eyes.

'I'll do what I can.'

Perhaps because I remembered that summer, long ago, hidden among the aspen trees. I'd cared about nothing else in the world that summer. I'd wanted to hold Paul, hold and hold him. As if you can hold love in your hands, as if you can stop quicksilver slipping through your fingers.

There was muzak. I only noticed it as I walked away from her towards the lifts. Muzak is the funeral march of the plastic age. Someone said that to me once. Why should I suddenly remember it now?

2

---◆---

I got off the metro at Odéon and turned left. The day was still perfect. I saw the *flic* on traffic duty give a flourish with his white gloves and relax the muscles round his lips. It could pass as a smile.

Bertolt Borries thought he'd like to cool off in Siberia. He'd had his fill of sun and sand but I didn't think he meant some beach in Majorca. He meant sand from horizon to horizon, sun that was a brute. That was the first indication of where he had been flying to.

The sun today was bright but it was only Paris in the spring. I felt it warm on my cheek as I continued on past the turn-off to my apartment. The smells of Paris when it heats up were in my nostrils: exhaust fumes and damp stones and urine. And the smells in Sfax – what were they like? That was the second nugget of gold. Borries had spent at least one night there, wherever Sfax might be. That was the least of my problems; thirty seconds with the index of a good atlas would tell me.

What sort of plane was he piloting? It wouldn't be his own, purchased with a bank loan. To own a plane would be ten times more potent than buying a new car. To hell with the need for security, he would have *had* to show it off to Ella. So someone else's plane, someone else's plan. And tight security with a big pay-off promised. Ella was right to be worried: if Borries had been promised a pot of money and his employers were sure he'd told absolutely nobody, they could guarantee their security and keep their money by killing him.

So her worry had driven Ella to PDS and he had pointed her at me. PDS – that shook the dust out of a lot of memories. There is something about initials that is more chilling than the full name. The Central Intelligence Agency suggests a benevolent institution, supported by bequests, rich in aca-

17

demic honours. But the initials strike some people pale. Just as over the years others have trembled at the mention of the SS or SAVAK or BOSS, and strained to catch the squeal of brakes before dawn and the thunder of boots up the stairs.

For me it was PDS. Not the man himself. I understood the type too well and, though others might be frightened of him, I had good reason not to be. Yet there was ice in the man and when you were close you felt the cold down your spine. I was going to have to speak to PDS now and that was why I felt a tingle. I couldn't make use of my own telephone; that wasn't secure, not in Paris. I had to use a public phone.

It was the café just before the corner of rue de l'Eperon that stopped me dead. There among the tables and chairs outside were a pair of palm trees in wooden tubs. I'd never noticed them before. Perhaps the perfect day had brought them out on the pavement to entice the tourists. Come and take your ease, the palm trees sighed, sip your pastis and dream you're in the lazy south. I gazed at them as two years of cobwebs cleared away from my memories. Borries had talked of sun and sand but left out palm trees. I wasn't staring because of him. I remembered other palm trees: death staring me in the face: my first encounter with PDS.

He had said he'd pay me twenty thousand francs. My 'fee' he called it. I replied that twenty thousand francs was either too much or too little, simply to deliver a bag to a villa on the coast in Corsica. Yes, he'd agreed, it was either too much or too little, but he didn't know which. And we'd stared at each other in silence, taking one another's measure. PDS looked to be in his mid-forties and wore a banker's suit. Nothing unusual about that in the Sixteenth *arrondissement*, except he was worlds away from being a banker. His short hair was tousled, there was purple bruising under his eyes, and stubble on his chin. He'd had two nights without sleep, he said, and I could believe it. He'd flown back to Paris to raise half a million dollars in used notes. That was the price of getting his son Carl back. Don't go to the police, the kidnappers had warned, as they always do. PDS hadn't gone to the police; he'd got hold of me. He had a contact in West German Security and the computer at Wiesbaden had spat out my name. I could believe that too.

It turned out that I was part of the demands: a woman had to bring the money. It was to be in a red and yellow nylon grip. The woman must come on her own. The woman must be unarmed. The woman must not carry a radio or make contact with any person or young Carl, eleven last birthday, would not see his twelfth birthday.

At that time I knew nothing about PDS except that he was some kind of international fixer. He'd murmured to me: 'You're to pay over the ransom and see my boy is safe.' The words had not come easily out of him and I thought a lot of his sleep had been lost agonizing over whether to meet their demands at all. 'And then,' he continued in the same soft voice. 'I'm going to nail them to the wall.' He never swore or raised his voice: that impressed me.

He flew back to Corsica, where he'd been holidaying with his family, via Marseille. I flew directly from Paris. That way we didn't arrive together. It was a funny feeling walking out of the Air Inter 737 at Ajaccio with half a million dollars in my luggage. I'd packed the red and yellow nylon grip inside my suitcase. I wasn't going to walk round the airport to the baggage claim and the Avis counter and the carpark carrying the grip. I was certain the kidnappers would have someone watching the incoming flights. I didn't want to have my car rammed along the route.

Take the road to Propriano, had been my instructions, and then swing inland on the Sartène road. Take the turn-off down to Campomoro on the sea. It's a small place, nothing much happening there out of season. Follow the road to the left all the way round the bay. There is a rash of holiday cottages and then, set apart and protected by a bamboo windbreak, you come to the Villa Nova. I drove past the Villa Nova, just to get the lie of the land. Beyond was a promontory with weird rocks carved by the sea into lunar landscapes. Alongside the villa a dirt track twisted inland and ended in a shabby field where a mule was tethered. There was no sign of the mule's owner but I doubted anyone made a get-away by mule clutching half a million dollars. So I returned to the villa.

It was past five o'clock and the sun had lost its strength. The villa didn't belong to PDS and I thought the kidnappers had chosen it because it wasn't in use yet that year. The shutters were closed, all except for one upstairs. I hated that. I stared and stared and saw no shadow move. Winter storms could have broken the catch. But I couldn't get it out of my mind that eyes were on me. It wasn't nerves. It wasn't a woman's intuition. It was professional instinct. I should have trusted it. If professional instinct saves your life once, it's worth it.

A stone terrace ran the length of the villa and at either end was a palm tree. There was an afternoon breeze and the dead fronds that hung down rustled. It was a noise like rats in an empty house at night. I wedged my back against the trunk of a palm tree to wait. The fronds were never still.

Stay outside, keep in full view. That's what I had been told. At six o'clock contact will be made. I didn't know if they'd come by car or by helicopter or by Chriscraft across the bay. Perhaps, I toyed with the idea, they'll come by mule after all. The hand-over of money will take place and young Carl will be released.

The hour came and went. I heard the occasional car across the bay in the village. Nothing closer. No speedboat, nothing descending out of the cloudless sky. At seven I made my move. Shadows were growing long. I didn't want to go into the house in the dark.

The front door was locked. I walked along the terrace, trying the shutters. They were all locked from the inside. All I could make out through the slats were ceilings and odd patches of wall. I walked to the rear and the kitchen door pushed open. I knew where I had to go. I had to go to the left-hand front room on the first floor, where the shutters were open. Something had gone badly wrong with the exchange agreements. And when something comes unstuck you check what is out of place. But first I had to go through the rooms on the ground floor.

The electricity hadn't been cut off. The rooms were in three-quarters darkness because of the shutters and the coming dusk. I switched on the lights in the kitchen, the dining room and the living room. On the walls were canvases of local scenes done by a holiday painter. At the back was a games room with a *billard* table under a dust cover; a ping-pong table had been brought in from outside and stood folded against one wall. There was a hall with a staircase up to the first floor and beside the stairs was a toilet. I opened the door and it was then I found him. The smell hit me first. I thought the plumbing had ruptured. But then I touched the light switch and there he was, jammed in under the basin. Carl had only been eleven and boys haven't made their spurt of growth by that age. He had been squeezed in with his knees up to his chin. He could have been a bundle of last year's dirty clothes, apart from his staring eyes and the bullet hole above his ear.

I backed out into the hall. I stood a moment, trying not to think about what I'd just seen. But the images of death pressed in. How could any human being do that to a boy? Hate rose inside me at men who squeeze a father's emotions until he pays, and kill his son anyway. The kidnappers were worse than animals. No other animal behaves like that, only the human animal. I tried to put the dampeners on my feelings but I found myself whispering out loud: 'For the love of God, why?' I had half a million useless dollars in my hand. I dropped the grip on the floor and went to find a phone. You'd better come at once, I told PDS. You've got him back? Carl's safe? Can I speak to him? Come at once, I repeated.

PDS had been waiting for a signal at a café back in Sartène. It took him thirty minutes to reach me through the dusk. In full daylight I had taken forty-five minutes on that route. I unlocked the front door when I heard his car draw up outside.

PDS looked at my face and asked: 'Where is he?'

I nodded at the open door to the toilet and didn't follow for a minute.

'At least it was quick.'

'My son,' he said, as if he couldn't take it in.

'I'm sorry, truly sorry.' I should have said more. Words of comfort wouldn't come. I felt angry and sickened. 'His skin is absolutely cold. He must have been dead for two days. Perhaps they shot him right at the start. Or maybe they panicked. They must know what your business is to make you worthwhile as a target. When you flew up to Paris, they might have got cold feet about who you'd get in touch with.'

21

PDS had looked at Carl a long time and then he raised his eyes to mine. 'I want you to find them. I don't care how long it takes or how much it costs. When you've tracked them down, I want you to kill them.'

I have only once been to PDS's office. It was that time when his son had been kidnapped. He has the sort of secretary you'd expect: competent, middle-aged, with a bun held together by a tortoiseshell comb on one side of her head. She ran the front office, typed the letters, filtered the phone calls. But the number I have doesn't pass through her; the phone rings directly on his desk. I used it now.

There was silence for a moment. He'd picked it up and must be listening for a tap. They've grown sophisticated in France recently and you don't get clicks coming down the line like a flamenco dancer. But the call could have been coming from anywhere and so PDS listened for taps before he spoke. I heard from someone – Duraine, I think, back in my former life – that in Bulgaria he was once talking to a contact when a third party came on the line and told him to speak more slowly.

'*J'écoute*,' he said softly, and waited.

'I was trained by the Company,' I replied, 'but I'm not on the Company payroll.'

He thought about this and about my voice and said: 'Tell me about the palm trees.'

It was like a code, going back to that time in Corsica, something only the two of us would know. He wanted to be sure it was me.

I said: 'There were two palms outside and they had dead fronds hanging down. These rustled in the breeze and tapped against the trunk. It was because of the noise of the palm trees we didn't hear them.'

'How many were there?'

'Three. Three men. They didn't even bother with stocking masks over their faces because they had come to kill us.'

'All right,' he said, 'that's enough.'

Enough? Did he imagine you could wake up memories and put them back to sleep just like that? I remembered how PDS had glared and glared when I said: No, killing was never part of any contract I made. He wouldn't accept my answer was final. It was a new contract he was talking about, a hundred thousand dollars. I was shaking my head. Plus all expenses. I was shaking my head and repeating 'No', while the wind played with the palm fronds. We were so intent on each other we never heard them come down the stairs into the hall. They wore jeans and tee-shirts and one of them had a leather jacket to bolster his toughness. All three had pistols. They were going to use them straight away until the leader calmed them: 'First I check the money is all here. Keep your guns on them. If they move even one centimetre, shoot them both.'

It was only two years since that moment. Did PDS think I would have forgotten the hungry look in the eyes of the killers? He was saying something to me, repeating a question, and I had to concentrate.

'How much do you know?'

'About Borries?'

'Yes.'

'Only what his wife told me. Very little. Her husband has vanished after you fixed him with a job. He was being paid danger money from the sound of it. I don't know how much. Maybe it was like me two years ago: too much if the job was straight, too little if it was the wrong side of the sky.'

'Now wait a minute,' he began.

His voice had lost a good deal of its smoothness. I'd caught him on a raw nerve. But I'd been under big pressure because of him two years ago. Why shouldn't he be under pressure now?

'Listen to what I have to say,' came down the phone. And I knew I was going to be treated to the morality of an amoral man. 'It was back at the beginning of last winter. I was approached by some people – Arabs with the smell of oil money – who needed help in setting up an operation.'

'What sort of operation?'

'I didn't ask. That is a principle with me.'

'But you could guess.'

'People come to me because they don't like questions being asked. If they are in search of certain commodities – it could be arms or documents or aircraft or blind-eye customs

23

or pilots or votes at the UN – well, there are cheaper sources than me. You know that. But sometimes people prefer to come to a quiet back office in the Sixteenth *arrondissement*. No awkward questions, no publicity, no newspaper headlines, no trouble.'

PDS paused here and I added: 'No comebacks.'

'No comebacks?' His voice hardened. We had switched to English. Perhaps that was an expression he hadn't heard before. 'Take note of this. I have another obligation, and that is to the people I provide to my clients. That person may be required to do irregular work or dangerous work but he must not be tricked into going on a suicide mission. That is an absolute principle with me. You're listening?'

I was listening. What I heard was an even more important principle: that if ever he got the reputation for sending people out on dead-end missions, that would be the end of his business. I asked PDS what his definition of a suicide mission was.

'Carrying out a bombing raid on Jerusalem on the false claim that the Israeli air force was neutralized. That sort of thing I would never do.'

'So Borries was not hired to fly against Israel?'

'Definitely not.'

'Even though they were rich Arabs?'

'I need to protect myself. I made certain enquiries, very discreet. I was satisfied.'

As long as his principles weren't bruised, everything was shiny in PDS's world.

'Their specification for a pilot,' PDS continued, 'was someone good enough to land a plane on a goat track in the middle of a sandstorm.'

'Was that all they said about the pilot's job?'

'That's all that is relevant for you.' He had recovered his cool.

'Have you seen them again, these Arabs with the smell of oil money?'

'No.' He paused and added, 'But I wasn't expecting to. My business with them was concluded.'

By which I suppose he meant he had been paid.

'Ella Borries says she contacted you this morning.'

'Very early,' he said. 'Her husband apparently left her my number to ring in an emergency. That is not a habit I encourage. But anyway I was perturbed at what she said. Sufficiently so that I gave her your number.'

'Why me?' After two years, why should PDS have gone through his files and dredged up my name? Because I was a woman and could comfort Ella Borries? Because I was the resourceful kind who could look after herself? Some other reason?

PDS said: 'I'm putting a job your way and charging no percentage. Aren't you satisfied?'

I should have been grateful. I should have said thank you.

PDS knew much more about Borries and the people who employed him. He just wasn't telling me. That was his style. If I was smart, I would find out anyway; if I couldn't find out, I didn't deserve to be told.

PDS was efficient on the telephone, persuasive with money, good at reaching out and putting a finger on the right person. Do this, he would say, and the rewards are yours. He himself would never dirty his hands. Except there'd been this one time when we'd been together.

There'd been the three *pistoleros* in the villa in Corsica. The one who checked the money seemed the boss. He came back, nodding. 'Correct to the last dollar.' He waved the pistol round the hall as a possible place of execution. 'Here? Would it be better upstairs in a bedroom?'

Three of them and only one of me. PDS I couldn't count on: he was a deskman.

I'd felt the moments of my life ticking away very fast. It was now that I should make my move. Except there was no move I could make. One of the bandits had his gun targeted on my stomach. I didn't dare move so much as a finger. *Use your brain*, I'd been taught at the place in Virginia, *you can think your way out of any situation*. But my brain was paralysed. Even if my brain began to work, the thug would notice and shoot me. His gun and his eyes were very steady. He would shoot me now or in two minutes. I thought he could hardly wait.

PDS spoke: 'You've got the ransom money and you want

no witnesses alive. You're going to kill us. Is that your intention?'

'Take your clothes off,' the gang boss said. 'Both of you.'

So that was it. They intended it to look like some sex murder. *Orgy in holiday villa ends in death riddle.* I could see the headlines now. Maybe the police would believe it, maybe not. Maybe the police would query why there was also a shot eleven year old boy. But the sexual connection would certainly confuse them.

PDS said: 'I want to bury my boy first. I will not take a single thing off until I've done that. A man has a duty to bury his son.'

Were the gang Corsicans, Sardinians, Sicilians? They argued fiercely for a few moments and I understood nothing of the patois. Finally the boss said: 'You will be permitted to bury your son before you are killed.' Perhaps some kind of masculine pride was involved. It shows itself in bizarre ways.

The soil was sandy. We had chosen the palm tree to the left as a burial ground and we dug under the guns of two of the gang. The boss had returned to the house, in search of a bottle or a telephone, I didn't know. All I knew was that this was the only time, while the odds had shortened, darkness surrounded us, the thugs were dulled by waiting to kill, and I had a weapon in my hands.

They had made PDS and me do the digging. A spade apiece, found in a shed at the back. We'd been digging twenty minutes, the earth was sandy and easy going, the grave was deepening. It was now, I decided, now while the others were lighting cigarettes.

A spade is a superb weapon. With a spade you can chop off toes, break an arm, fling earth into eyes. The action of digging quite naturally puts the spade into an offensive position. I lifted it high as if to gain force for a downstroke into the ground. At the last moment I altered the angle so I drove it across the grave. I struck the nearest one in the knees. All my strength was in that blow. The kneecap is a relatively thin bone and would have shattered under the impact. He screamed. The pain was acute enough for him to drop the gun and the lighter he had been using. He staggered a pace into his companion, knocking his gun-hand. The second man shot, but he would have shot wild anyhow. After the brightness of the cigarette lighter he must have been half blinded.

The palm tree was at my back. The noise of it, restless in the breeze, had disguised footsteps coming down the stairs in the villa. That had almost cost me my life. Now the palm would have to save it. I reached up and wrenched off the dead frond that never kept still. It was hard and sharp and I could feel it cutting into the flesh of my hands. I used it two-handed, swinging it across the face of the second man, knowing it would be like twenty razor blades slashing his skin. He cried out, part of it a scream, part of it words I didn't understand. All thoughts of fighting were driven from his head.

Which left the third man, the boss who'd disappeared into the villa.

Except he was in the villa no longer. Alerted by the screams and the gunshot he came bursting out of the front door, jumped over the edge of the terrace and stopped. He raised his pistol, aiming it towards me. Six or seven paces separated us. The night was dark but I wore a white shirt and at that distance I would be a shining target for him. I launched myself in a roll across the ground, aiming to hook an ankle, when the shot came. It came from behind me. When I looked up I saw the gang boss slip to his knees with his hands clasped to his chest. When I swung round I saw PDS who'd picked up a gun one of the others had dropped.

The position was now reversed and the gang knew it, and even the screams fell away. This garden with its palm trees was the jungle. No other word describes it. The law of the jungle demands: kill or be killed. These were not men but beasts which had come out from the undergrowth. They had snatched PDS's son and murdered him. They had stolen his money. They were minutes away from killing him in his turn. That is why PDS took his time, looking into each man's face before he squeezed the trigger. The one in the leather jacket pleaded. PDS listened to a few babbled sentences and shot him twice. The boss, who'd got a bullet through the lungs, he saved to the last. PDS had offered me one hundred thousand dollars to do this. I had refused. So he did his own dirty work.

Before he pulled the trigger for the last time, PDS said to the gang boss: 'It's because we no longer have the guillotine in France.'

The light coming through the open door showed up his face. No one should have such an expression as he did what he did. After the shots the night was still. Then my ears picked up the sigh of the palm trees in the breeze. PDS let the pistol drop on the ground. He'd no need of it any longer.

No, I'd said to PDS, killing was never part of any contract. It explains why I was in Paris today. I'd been recruited in my eager years by the old boys in Britain. SIS, SOE, DI6, the initials change but the tune remains the same. I was part of an experiment which I doubt has been repeated. I was sent to the Agency in America for training. Lend-lease in reverse you could call it. The theory was this would avoid more embarrassing red moles burrowing under England's green and pleasant land. I had four years hard labour. I learnt all the tricks of the trade until I could stomach no more. I quit. I refused to swear blind allegiance, would not destabilize, wouldn't bed down to order, wouldn't dehumanize the human race. Which was why I told PDS I'd been Company trained but wasn't a Company woman.

Dear Lord, how they'd hated me for going freelance. The megabucks spent on me, all those secrets learnt, all the dirt I'd seen.

PDS was on my mind still as I walked away from the telephone. I had to pass the café again with its pair of palms in tubs. They no longer whispered a siren song of pastis and the warm south. Palm trees had a different message for me: of money, violence and death. That was the chill I felt when I thought of PDS.

I wondered about the job he'd pushed my way.

He was prickly, as if he had a conscience about it. He'd had no conscience about killing those men in Corsica.

3

Why do I live in rue St-André-des-Arts? I suffer from noise, the blood money called rent and Madame Boyer. Still, it's home.

After you pass the Café Charlot, there's Anastasia. It's not so much a boutique as a window into the soul of Paris. Two skinny girls stood behind the plate glass, barefoot, cigarette smoke twisting their faces. They were draping the new holiday fashions over equally skinny models. This summer it was fishnet tee-shirts. Where the plastic models' breasts should have been, there were hand grenades. Satire, surrealism, sexploitation – take your pick. Next to the boutique is an alley where cats romance at night. Then there's the entrance to my building.

Madame Boyer was standing in the open door to her lair. When I first moved in she had a geranium, with flowers the pink of a baby girl's clothes. She used to carry the pot from one window to another to catch gleams of sunlight. This winter it died. She replaced it with a cat, a marmalade thing with one black ear. She was clasping it to her. The cat's face seemed lopsided because its black ear was lost against the black of her costume. In honour of the perfect day she had changed into her summer dress. It was the same as her winter dress but with short sleeves. A dry cleaner could starve to death waiting for business from her. I could see last summer's sweat stains; they were like oil slicks in her armpits.

She has a particular way when she loiters, her head tilted to one side, her beak of a nose in the air. She was like a blackbird listening for a worm. I'd seen her smile once. I can still picture the grey of her teeth, the rottenness spreading from her heart.

'No visitors, Madame Boyer?'

We don't spend words on each other. She answered me with a sniff. In her code that means Michel has gone up.

29

He keeps a bookshop off Boul' Mich' that specializes in English paperbacks. One day back in January Madame Boyer had chanced to walk past and through the window seen Michel surrounded by hundreds of volumes from Pan, Fontana, Coronet, all the rest. She was aghast. Every cover showed a woman in a state of undress: if the woman wasn't being ravished, she was being wanton. That a man who sold such trash had a key to my apartment! We might all be murdered in our beds.

Within days of this discovery her pink geranium had taken sick and died. She hated me for that. If I hadn't done it to death, Michel had. He was a profligate and a pornographer, and now a molester of geraniums.

As I passed she murmured: *'Viens ici, minou.'* The cat was already in her arms. She grasped the beast a little tighter to her black bosom until it growled. *'N'aies pas peur,'* she crooned. Her eyes were intent on me. She spies for the police, of course. All of them do, all the concierges in Paris.

He said as I opened the door: 'Bang, bang, you're dead.'

He held a *baguette* to his shoulder, squinting with one eye closed as he aimed down the length of it. He must have heard my feet on the mat outside.

Why do men play war games, even Michel? The gospel according to Freud talks of guns and penises being a source of power, about the glories of conquest. But there's damn little triumph if you end up dead. Perhaps men don't imagine they will be defeated or killed; perhaps they really want to be wounded so they can lie in bed and be nursed by women.

The next thing Michel said was: 'Kiss me.'

I went to him and took the bread out of his hands, because there were better things for them to do.

He said through a mouthful of hair: 'Have I told you recently that you're beautiful?'

'No,' I told him, 'not since yesterday.'

But he hadn't had time to look at me. His mouth kissed my mouth and his hands smoothed and pressed at my body and he was too preoccupied to look into my face. For there would be lines and shadows that weren't there this morning. Ask a grandmother about her wedding and see her wrinkles fade away as she relives that shining morning. Ask a refugee how he survived the Nazi holocaust and watch fear and anger chase each other across his face. So with me. If Michel had looked, really looked, he'd have picked up the echoes of my day.

He said: 'I don't think you should wear a bra.'

'Take it off then.'

'I'm trying. I can't unhook the damn thing.'

'You've had enough practice.' I nibbled at his earlobe. 'Or didn't any of the others wear bras?'

'What others?'

'Anna and Arlette and Anouk and Annabelle . . .'

His tongue slipped into my mouth and I couldn't go on with the roll-call. I hadn't finished with the As. A is for *amour*. He was my Michel, the profligate, the pornographer, the molester of geraniums, fierce and tender lover, mine alone. There was no one else. I was sure of it. He came to see me every day. Sometimes he went home, sometimes he spent the whole night. There couldn't be anyone else. There couldn't be.

I always told myself that.

He had the hook of the bra undone. His hand cupped my breast, his fingers pinching the nipple. That started the fire in my belly. There was only one way to put it out.

'Here,' he urged. 'Right here on the carpet.'

'Let me close the curtains.'

'No, leave the curtains. Let the neighbours see. Let them be aroused to make love and pass on the desire to their neighbours. Let the whole of Paris make love right now.'

He wore a medallion round his neck. I've always detested men who did that. But Michel's medallion was Turkish. He said it was to avert the evil eye. When we moved together I could feel it between our bodies, sweat making it slip against my skin.

'Let everyone make love,' he whispered in my ear. 'It will be a better world and it will have started here.'

And when he said *here*, he entered me.

'Are you hungry?' I asked him.

'I shall recover my appetite in a little while,' he replied in the grave tones of a university professor.

'Idiot, I meant food.'

31

He shrugged. 'I read somewhere that to make love burns up one hundred and twenty-five calories.'

'So?' I asked.

'So why are so many prostitutes fat?'

'Their heart isn't in their work.'

He looked all down my body. 'Co, you're getting thin. You're being worn away, burnt up.'

'We've known each other eight months. That's eight times thirty times one hundred and twenty-five calories.'

'Times two,' he said and pulled me so I lay on top of him. Oh God, there was no one else. I was sure.

He kissed me again. Why do we close our eyes when we kiss? What reality don't we want to see?

Sometimes we eat out. Tonight we ate in the kitchen. He'd bought ready-cooked artichokes and I made mayonnaise. He tore off each leaf, dipped it in the sauce, and scraped off the fleshy part with his white teeth. He stared at me the whole time.

I remember that evening. I remember the details with absolute clarity. There had been nothing remarkable about it until now: it was just my life.

I said: 'All I've got in the fridge is frankfurters.'

'I thought you said you'd been shopping.'

'I bought clothes.'

I'd dropped the packages inside the front door. Shopping for clothes fitted with Michel's idea of my life: that a rich daddy had died and left me an inheritance.

'What did you buy?'

'Just things to wear. Slacks, shirts.' Because early in the afternoon I'd looked at an atlas. I knew now where Sfax was.

And then the telephone rang. I left Michel in the kitchen and went through to the living room. The phone sat on the desk against the wall. Through the window I could see a haze softening the streetlamp. I said hello and a man's voice said: 'It was dark and we were digging with spades under the palm tree. Do you remember which side of the house it was?'

So it was PDS, ringing me back at my apartment. I told him: 'The left.'

At my back I sensed a stillness. Michel had followed in

from the kitchen and been alerted by my couple of words. They made him curious because I hadn't hung up, I said no more, I simply listened to the fixer calling from his quiet back office.

'It's about the talk we had this afternoon. I feel you should know there is an official interest in the matter. These officials are sharp, I would even say angry. I am not accustomed to threats of an official nature. With a person such as yourself who is following a parallel track, they could be unscrupulous. Do I make myself clear?'

The warning was plain enough. But there were questions I wanted to ask and couldn't. You could never tell who might be listening on the line. Also in this room Michel was all ears.

'Yes,' was all I said.

'Be careful,' he said. 'But then, you can look after yourself.'

He was gone. I was left with a buzz from the receiver and the strange sensation that PDS felt a measure of guilt. That was not something he was used to dealing with. I turned and Michel was staring at me. His eyes looked serious.

'Who was that?'

'An acquaintance.'

'Oh,' he said, 'just an acquaintance.' There was pride in Michel. He didn't accuse me of anything. But how he stared. 'Perhaps it was the same acquaintance who rang earlier. A man.'

'Another one of my admirers. Damn, how am I going to fit him in? Not the mad monk, I hope . . .'

I trailed off. It wasn't much of a joke anyway and Michel was frowning.

'He didn't leave a name. *Wouldn't* leave a name. He knew you quite well because he said: "Can I speak to Cody?" Just like that. He didn't call you "Mademoiselle Cody". This was only about fifteen minutes before you got back, though of course I didn't know how long you'd be. When I asked if I could pass on his name to you, he just said: "No, there's no message." He hung up. He can't have been a proper friend. He didn't call you "Co". Yet he knew you. What kind of man was that?'

It was the end of the perfect day and I felt cold. Sometimes

33

the nights in May can make you feel like that. Sometimes after you've made love very passionately you shiver. But tonight the chill in me came from the phone calls. The man who'd spoken to Michel couldn't have been PDS because PDS was infinitely cautious. I didn't know who it was. But I wished Ella Borries hadn't blurted out the initials PDS on my phone that morning.

It wasn't long after that when Michel left. Our evening had gone dead.

'Oh,' he said, 'I have to go home at the week-end. Raoul is getting married.'

Michel said it as if it had only just occurred to him. Perhaps it had. Perhaps it was a punishment for my phone calls.

'Another cousin?'

'Another cousin.'

Michel came from Alsace. The cousins seemed to spread out over every hillside. I got bored with his family. Last time he disappeared he announced he was going to exhume his grandmother and I never noticed anything amiss. He lives off boulevard de Magenta, which I can't understand. He explains that it's round the corner from the Gare de l'Est, where the trains from Mulhouse come in. Convenient for the cousins, I suggest. For the cousins, he agrees.

I thought he wanted to say something more before he left, to ask me straight out if there was another man coming into my life. He stood in the middle of the room, staring at the floor. He was frowning, but then he changed his mind about whatever it was.

'I'll see you tomorrow evening.'

'Yes,' I lied.

The street outside was unnaturally quiet for that time of the evening. The only noise came from a gaggle of foreign tourists who cavorted on the street corner waiting for the lights to change. Michel came out and looked up at my window for a moment. He raised a hand and went off into the night. He was an Alsatian. He even loped like one.

I could still feel the imprint of his lips on mine. We never know when it'll be the last kiss. But with Michel, that was the one.

4

You can feel a city round you. It is like a big animal. Paris was a black jaguar that night, a jungle beast.

The light was out in Madame Boyer's lair when I went downstairs. I let myself out into the street and pulled the door shut. It has a Yale-type lock, the kind burglars prefer. I had opened it myself with a hairpin one night when I lost my key.

In the Café Charlot I ordered a *café-crème* and asked Guy if I could use the phone. It stood on the far end of the bar next to the stand with the hard-boiled eggs.

'Sure, help yourself,' Guy said in passable American. He was built on the lines of a basketball player and came from Martinique. He was working on the accent so he could return home and open a bar and grow rich on the cruise trade. I stood at the counter while the coffee steamed at my elbow. The Café Charlot has good old-fashioned pinball machines and I listened to the thwack of the metal balls and the ringing in the receiver clamped against my ear. I counted the hard-boiled eggs, one to each ring of the phone. Six, seven, eight. Why were there always eight eggs? Even when one was eaten, eight eggs remained. Ten, eleven, twelve. I read somewhere that hard-boiled eggs require more calories to digest than they contain in food value. There should be hard-boiled egg clinics where the greedy were stuffed like Strasbourg geese and the flab melted away. Fourteen, fifteen.

'What's the trouble, honey?' Guy leant over with a confiding eyebrow. 'Your Romeo on the loose? You wanna be fixed up? Listen, I finish at one. That's not long to wait. Not for me.'

Eighteen, nineteen. That phone wasn't going to be answered. I dropped the receiver back in the cradle. The steam from my coffee rose and I stared into it. Sometimes you make out snakes, a belly dancer, a leering mouth. Tonight it was just mist in a graveyard. It wasn't unreasonable for PDS to have left the office by this time. His living quarters were on the floors above but I had no number for his home phone. I wanted to ask what officious nose was sniffing after Borries and what questions they'd put and how they'd known to go to PDS. There were a heap of questions I wanted to ask him. I might even be given some answers.

I patted Guy on the cheek and in my best American said I'd take a rain-check on his kind offer.

'Hey, is that a promise, man? Hey Co?'

Promises, promises. I waved to him from the door.

There's a place close by Pont St-Michel where the taxis wait. I got a driver who stared at me in the mirror as if I was a high class *poule* with an urgent summons to a client in the Sixteenth *arrondissement*. On that fine May night the whole of the city shimmered with sex. Of course there are those who imagine Paris is always like that. But this wasn't the tinsel of Pigalle. This was in men's eyes and women's breath, in the blood. Everybody had paired off. Even the groups were made up of couples. We raced along the *quai* in the way taxi-drivers adore, with a foot stamping on the brake for the traffic lights. While we waited for the red to turn to green, the driver's eyes studied me in the mirror. If I was a *poule*, where were my cigarette holder, my cherry red lipstick, my frilled umbrella?

We turned off avenue Victor-Hugo into the street where PDS had his office and home. The driver slowed and growled: 'What number did you ask for?'

His eyes frowned at me in the mirror and then dropped to the road ahead. I sat forward on my seat and saw what he saw.

'Pull in here,' I told him. 'Behind that Mercedes.'

'And then?'

But I had no more instructions. He stopped the car where I told him. We were under a tree that blocked the light from the streetlamps. I didn't open the door but sat staring diagonally across the road.

'Is that the number?' he asked. 'Forty-two?'

It was the number. I said nothing. I sat staring and the driver gave up on his questions. When I made no move to get out he switched off the engine. There were sounds of metal cooling and the distant roar of traffic.

Even the police cars were in pairs that night. They were parked carelessly, one at an angle with its rear half blocking the street. They'd switched off their flashing lights, their sole concession to the posh folk's quarter. It was only a kilometre to the night-time flesh trade of the Bois de Boulogne, where the transvestites did it for love and the others did it for money. But here lived bankers and diplomats and deputies and they shouldn't be disturbed in their virtuous homes. Here also lived an international fixer and I couldn't understand why his front door stood open with a uniformed cop on guard outside it and why the lights shone from every window from top to bottom.

'Just as well you weren't here an hour earlier,' the driver said. For the first time he turned in his seat to inspect me. 'You'd have been caught in the net. The cops come for the big fish but they scoop up the little fish too and stamp on their faces to teach them a lesson. The police are bastards, worse than the politicians and the pederasts.'

Having delivered this judgement, he faced forward again. Your profession had to begin with a 'p' to be in his hate list. If he believed I was a *poule*, where did that leave me?

There was the beginning of a crowd: a middle-aged couple out with their poodle, half a dozen young toughs in black with studs on their leather jackets and motorbike helmets on their heads. A man smoking a cigar appeared from a door across the street. A buxom blonde woman – assuming it was a woman – came teetering from the direction of the Bois. The cop on the door swung a truncheon in his hand as he came down the steps. I could see his mouth moving but couldn't hear what he said to the toughs in black. Move on, keep your distance, something on those lines.

'Law students,' my driver said. 'They've all got rich daddies and think Klaus Barbie was too soft on the Jews.'

This was the year the law students and the medical students rioted. They'd been doing it for weeks, hurling cobblestones with the occasional petrol bomb to hot things up. I don't know where these were coming from: there'd been nothing brewing in the student quarter today. They must have been

37

feeling frustrated for suddenly the night went wild. The cop had gone so far as to prod one of the leather-jackets in the chest with his stick. They yelled abuse and set on him, punching him in the face and the stomach, aiming kicks at his shins, sending his cap in one direction and his stick skidding under a car. The poodle yapped and snapped and the flashy blonde hoisted her skirt and legged it for the corner.

'*Allez, allez,*' my driver encouraged, as if it was a football match.

Three more cops burst out of the house and the leather-jackets put in the boot once more for fascism and freedom and sprinted away down the centre of the road. One cop came and stood with his legs apart and his pistol held in both hands aiming after them. It was tomorrow's headline I was witnessing. I waited for the explosion. Slowly the gun came down. There were too many expensive cars parked along both kerbs and holing one was the kind of mistake that could have you posted to a coal-mining town in the north.

'What did I tell you?' my driver said. 'Bastards.' He started the engine again. It was his insurance in case the police came our way, that was all. We didn't go anywhere.

I couldn't make sense of any of it. PDS was a fixer and seemed to have ended up in a fix himself. If this was a raid, he'd not bought the right protection. The lights blazed from his house and on the ground floor was the office where I'd been once and PDS had hired me for a sum that was either too much or too little. A figure was at the window, pulling the shutters closed. It wasn't PDS, nor was it someone from the uniformed branch.

A klaxon had been fading in, something you pay no attention to normally in Paris. An ambulance pulled up behind the police cars and its back doors were swung open. Two men unloaded a stretcher. It wasn't for the savaged *flic* because he was back by the door with his cap perched on his head and calming his temper with a cigarette. He gestured over his shoulder with a thumb and there was no particular urgency about the way the ambulancemen entered the building.

Another klaxon, another car. It stopped alongside the ambulance, entirely blocking the road. With that official disdain for the convenience of ordinary citizens, two men got out and simply abandoned it. One carried a black bag of the kind medical men favour. It was the other who made a chill sweat start in the palms of my hands. He carried a shiny aluminium box and round his neck was slung a camera. He wasn't press; they don't come with a klaxon blaring. He was the official photographer they send to record the position of the corpse when there's been a violent death.

'If we stay any longer,' my driver said, 'that cop on the door is going to come over and exercise his right of interrogation. He's good and angry, that one. He'll ask questions with his fists.'

'Let's go,' I said. There was no damn point in waiting. When PDS came out, it would be feet first and with his face covered.

The fountains must have been playing earlier in place St-Michel. Spray had drifted on the breeze so that the pavement was damp. Not so much as a summer shower, nothing to spoil the perfect day. Unlike across the river, inside a building where virginia creeper ran riot up the walls. The perfect day had ended there for someone and the long night begun.

I wandered along rue St-André-des-Arts, past the Tunisian snack bars, the hamburger place, the chemist, the boutiques. The little bars had closed. The Café Charlot was open but I didn't want to go in. Guy would think I was cashing in my rain-check. I walked slowly trying to sort it out. PDS had telephoned and warned me the authorities were turning nasty. Obviously nobody had been with him at the time. An hour later when I telephoned back, nobody answered. Either he'd left his office or he was already dead. Half an hour later I'd seen the police swarming in force. A neighbour must have heard a gunshot or there'd been an anonymous phone call. The police had got there before the ambulance, which was the way of things in Paris.

I walked past my building, past Anastasia with its chic hand grenades, as far as the carrefour Buci. I walked just to get fresh air into my lungs. With luck it would reach as far as my brains. I hadn't seen PDS's corpse but the taxi driver and I had both read the signals and reached the same conclusion: he was dead. I didn't know the whole story of PDS's life but he had had a complete absence of scruples, no doubt about that. I had only had a single deal with him and it had ended with his killing three men. That wasn't his usual style. Let others do; he would organize. On that one occasion he'd had a personal score to settle. Over the years the Americans and the Russians would have made use of him. I'd heard that the East German lawyer Vogel had contacted him at one time about spy-swaps. Mercenaries in Africa, opium smugglers from the Far East, cocaine runners from Colombia, the Marseille gangs, the tax evaders, the communist millionaires – he knew names and telephone numbers and prices. PDS would say he was providing a service, no different from hot croissants for breakfast. People were buying, he was selling. Except it wasn't croissants he provided. In a life like his you made enemies. Somebody somewhere had found himself at the wrong end of a gun or the sharp end of a deal and sworn vengeance. That somebody had finally settled the account, drawing a fat red line through the initials PDS.

I turned for home.

It could be anyone. It could be the CIA, the KGB, the MfS, the Mafia, the gun boys, anyone at all from the muddy pool he fished in. There was just this one thing: on the day when questions began being asked about the pilot Bert Borries, PDS was killed.

It could be coincidence. But if you put your trust in coincidence, you shouldn't do what I do.

Oil money has a rich and powerful smell. Certain men were tainted with it and I could catch the whiff in the night air. If they had silenced PDS because he knew about Borries, they must be frightened he would talk. To me?

That wasn't a thought to give me sweet dreams.

I was coming past Anastasia for the last time before turning in and then I stopped dead. I saw something that drove all thoughts of dreams and sleep away. *Leave the curtains*, Michel had said. *Let the neighbours see. Let them be aroused to make love.* It didn't matter that the only person who might see us was the old man who lived across the road in an attic garret. He spent his days fussing over a goldfinch in a cage and his eyes were too misted to see what we were doing.

40

Nevertheless, leave the curtains . . . I lifted my eyes from the street to the second floor where my apartment was, as I always do. It was part of the training in Virginia. Always check your home base, the instructor commanded, because if you have enemies, your base is what they'll aim for. Survive was his order. And live to die another day, was our silent chorus.

So I lifted my eyes. The windows Michel and I had left bare were now covered by curtains.

I saw them and the night trembled. I stepped into a doorway. There could be an eye at a crack in those curtains watching for my approach. Not Michel. He wouldn't draw the curtains and wait in darkness. Not Madame Boyer, who'd already been in bed when I left. Someone else. Someone who had let himself in. The street door was locked but there was no problem about forcing that: an American Express card would do nicely. He, or they, had climbed the stairs and gone into my apartment and sat waiting with all the lights out. No chink of light showed. They had closed the curtains because it wasn't love that would be witnessed.

These men with the smell of oil money knew my name. PDS must have told them, screamed it, before he found death.

41

5

It's called Carthage Airport.

We wheeled round the bay, losing height all the time. The wing on the port side dipped down as we curved and I had an uninterrupted view of the coast. The beach looked to be of sand but there were no concrete hotels along it, hardly any buildings at all. Low hills came into view, misty blue with a heat haze. The sky was azure from rim to rim except above the city where smog gathered like a disease. We made our approach over scruffy yellow-flowered shrubs. After touchdown the reverse thrust roared like thunder and died away.

Carthage Airport makes you think that the Romans must have left it in ruins. There was rubble and the skeleton of buildings and rusting machinery. But it's just that they're tearing it down and putting it up like every other airport in the world.

'*Au revoir, mademoiselle, bonnes vacances.*'

I stepped through the door of the Air France 727 and thought at once: Borries, you're dead right, after a few months of this, Siberia must begin to seem a lovely dream. The sun struck my head and leapt up at me from the concrete. Yesterday had been a perfect day in Paris; this was Africa and the Sahara began somewhere over the horizon, not too far away.

You can tell a well-trained one. He'll look at your face first and then down to study your photo; because if he does it the other way round you start pulling faces to try and look like the terrible likeness. The immigration officer fingered through to the back of my passport and put his oblong stamp on the last page.

'Welcome to Tunisia.' His eyes flicked up again. 'Have a pleasant holiday, Mademoiselle Deschampsneufs.'

He spoke French. I hardly caught the words, his voice was so soft.

42

Downstairs in the main hall were the banks and the car rental desks. I changed money and got a car from Avis. It was a Renault 5, red as *Pravda*. Driving licence, credit card, signatures, all in the new name.

'Enjoy your holiday, Mademoiselle Deschampsneufs.'

Everybody wanted me to have a good time. Except I had the suspicion that someone might have the opposite idea entirely. People were coming out and milling round a coach marked Tourafric. Taxi drivers lounged and argued. A smart policeman blew his whistle at a car that parked on the painted lines. There were the usual men in ones and twos who dawdled for no good reason, tapping a cigarette out of a packet, taking time over lighting it. Every airport has them. They're waiting to greet a friend, they're seeing a relative off, they're airline staff, they're bank officials, they're plain clothes police, they're muscle for a local baron. Someone, I was half convinced, would be on the look-out for a lone woman of my age because word would have come from Paris. Of fifty pairs of eyes on the forecourt of the terminal, one pair would note me and the number of the car and the Avis uniform of the woman who'd fetched it for me. He'd go to the Avis desk and ask if he was too late to catch Mademoiselle Cody and the girl would look puzzled. She would check through documents and even show him, because he was so insistent, that no Cody had rented a car.

Cody was trapped in the apartment in rue St-André-des-Arts. I'd watched for half an hour last night and seen no flicker of a shadow behind those curtains. But I wasn't going up; I couldn't risk it. Passport, driving licence, credit cards, traveller's cheques – the whole of Cody was cut off from me. Instead I booked into the Hôtel Select and in the morning went for my first aid kit. Anyone whose life so much as touches the fringe of the security world needs a first aid kit. Some use a bank deposit box; others use a loose board in a suburban church. For me it was the Toilettes des Dames under the place de la Madeleine. You get a spacious cabin, art nouveau glass, floral tiles, an advertisement on the back of the door that promises: *Cobranama détache et ravive les tissus.* I kept a whole second existence in a waterproof pouch under the lid of the cistern. In my second life I was Suzanne

43

Deschampsneufs, aged 29, spinster, living in Chartres, teacher of English; and I had a French passport, *carte d'identité* and driving licence to prove it. The papers were genuine. They should be – they cost enough. But the toilet cost only one franc. It was the cheapest strongbox in the world.

So it was Deschampsneufs who passed through Tunis and headed down the main highway south.

It was the start of the evening rush hour when I reached Sfax and I realized a terrible truth: that the traffic was like Paris. The pedestrians placed their trust in God; the drivers believed they were God. If you were one-tenth of a second slow when the lights turned green you were treated to a fanfare of horns.

I came in through foul industrial suburbs and followed the signs to *Centre-Ville*. Suddenly I was back in France and in a provincial town in the south. It might be Perpignan or Clermont–l'Hérault, but hotter and gone to seed. Palm trees lined every street. Young men lounged outside cafés with glasses of mint tea or coffee. Cars were jammed against the kerbs and mopeds snarled everywhere.

Borries had stayed here. The people who hired him were paranoic about security, ruthless. But one night Borries had had a human need to talk to his wife and a telephone operator hadn't known of the need for secrecy. The Hôtel Something. All I could do was go the rounds and ask. And keep an eye on the dark corners of the lobbies because last night PDS had been killed and someone had shut the curtains of my apartment and whoever Borries's employers were they might just have come to Sfax to make certain I didn't trace him.

I turned into avenue Habib Bourguiba. In every town I'd driven through you knew you were in the main street when they used the President's name. This had banks and offices and municipal gardens and the French consulate looking very grand and the post office and the *Syndicat d'Initiative*. Yes, I told the girl behind the counter, I had just arrived from Tunis and was looking for a hotel. She wore a smart little uniform like an air hostess but her smile was shy like theirs never are. But we have several, she said, and produced me

44

a list and a sketch map of the town. Here and here and here, she pointed out. I thanked her and at the door I turned and asked, on the off chance:

'Do you have companies prospecting for oil round here?'

'Oh yes,' she said. 'Marathon is drilling on the seabed off the Kerkenna Islands.'

'Have they been drilling long?'

She made a monkey face, screwing up her forehead to remember.

'Eighteen months? Two years?' she guessed.

'They have an office in town?'

That she didn't know. Maybe in the town, maybe towards the airport, maybe down the coast in Gabès.

I thanked her again and went and sat in my red Renault and thought: Well, it's a possibility, a slim one. I put the likelihood at about one in a thousand that Borries was flying legit for Marathon Oil. First, he was a fixed-wing pilot but Marathon would need a helicopter to ferry the divers and roustabouts out to the rigs. Second, the men with the smell of oil money had wanted a pilot who could 'land on a goat track in the middle of a sandstorm'. Third, you didn't have to pay PDS's price to hire a pilot nor kill him afterwards to keep it secret. And last, there was the matter of Bert's clam-mouth with his wife. I revised the odds: one in ten thousand. Just about worth checking. Better to start with the hotels.

The nearest was the Hôtel Alexander. If Borries had stayed here, then the oil money had run dry. I banged a bell on the front desk and a figure in a *djellaba* shuffled from a back room. The *djellaba* stretched to his feet like an old-fashioned nightgown and with his gaping mouth and vacant eyes I might have roused him from deep slumber.

'Do you have a room?' I asked.

'A room?' he asked.

'This is the Hôtel Alexander?'

'Yes, this is the hotel.' He began pushing things round on the counter: an ashtray, a dirty tumbler, a seashell, a tattered school exercise book which served as a register.

I said: 'Tell me, what number is Monsieur Borries staying in?'

45

'Who?'

I repeated slowly.

'Are you Madame Borries?'

'Listen, Monsieur Borries *is* staying here? He is, isn't he?'

This proved too much for the desk clerk who stared over my shoulder out into the street. I turned the register round on the counter and scanned the page. It was a jumble, some entries in Arabic, others in Western script. I concentrated on the names I could read: Jones, Labiche, Gibez, Oudiné, Canizares, Hampson. There was no Borries registered during May nor during April nor even during March. I turned over pages that were dog-eared and stained and gave it up.

'Sorry to have troubled you. I think I've come to the wrong hotel.'

At the door he said something and I turned back to him.

'Is it a room you want?'

'It's all right,' I told him.

The Hôtel Mabrouk was in avenue Hedi Chaker and was altogether smoother. I was hoping to meet a friend who was passing through Sfax. When he did come to Sfax, I told the desk clerk, he always stayed at the Mabrouk. The name Borries drew blank with him and I became flustered and said it *must* mean something because he *always* stayed here. Together we checked the register and I became disconsolate. How could I have made such a mistake? How was I going to find my friend? Try the Triki, the clerk suggested, try the Hôtel du Centre, try the Oliviers.

The Triki was at the back of the Mabrouk, which says it all. Blank. The Hôtel du Centre stood on the other side of the *place*.

'Monsieur Borries? Of course,' the desk clerk said. Or maybe he was the proprietor. He wore a suit of the kind that is run up by backstreet tailors with foot-treadle Singer machines.

'Marvellous,' I said. 'What number is his room?'

'That is to say, Monsieur Borries stays here in principle.'

I looked more closely at the man. Yes, definitely the owner. His suit had shoulders that made him look lopsided and his shirt was nearing its weekly wash but his brain was alert enough. The French, when they ran Tunisia, would have had the schooling of him. *En principe* Bert Borries stayed here. But what is generously offered *en principe* is taken back *en effet*.

'*En effet* . . .' I suggested.

The owner dusted off a modest smile. 'In fact Monsieur Borries is not here at present. But he keeps his room. He pays for it by the month.'

It was almost the end of the month. What would happen to his room then? Could he be contacted?

'Alas no. If Monsieur Borries has not returned and his room is required, we shall be forced to remove his affairs.'

I brightened. I liked very much the idea that in this room Borries had left clothing, papers, possessions, whatever made up his affairs. There could be an address book, a receipt, a phone number, a map, any manner of things. Clues they used to be called.

'Was Monsieur Borries alone when he stayed here?'

There was only the smallest hesitation before the owner said Borries had been alone. The hesitation was perhaps because Borries had taken someone up to his room, as any man might do separated from his wife for so long. *En principe* he was alone.

'Did he make phone calls?'

'Yes.'

'From his room?'

Apparently the rooms had no telephones. The owner nodded to an open cubicle. 'He gave me a dinar to cover local calls. He was a generous man. Also, there was one to Paris a few weeks ago which I obtained for him. It was perhaps to you?'

But no, I was not Madame Borries asking questions about an erring husband. I was an old friend of the family, just passing through. I would take a room, if there was one free.

He didn't believe for one moment I was a family friend. He suggested without any prompting: 'Room number 15 is free. Monsieur Borries has room number 16, if he should unexpectedly return.'

'Good.'

It was dusk but my room was darker than that. In the square

47

outside were holm-oaks and the branches reached above my window. I liked the dark and shiny leaves. They blocked the view up from the café tables in the square. A breeze had got up, blowing from land out to sea. The Mediterranean was out there somewhere, a kilometre away. And in the tourist hotels up north in Sousse and Hammamet and down south in Djerba, people had come in from the beach and taken a shower and were going down to have white-jacketed waiters serve them dishes cooked without olive oil or garlic or spices, lest turmoil was caused in tender stomachs. Whereas I made do with a packet of biscuits from the airline lunch tray and a glass of water from the tap. Michel had said I was getting thin: love-making with him or the daily work-out at the place in rue Monge. A body needs fuel, so later I would go out for something more nourishing than biscuits. But first I'd have a peep at the room next door.

I went onto a balcony big enough to hang up a pair of socks to dry. It was protected by a waist-high wall. A half metre gap separated my balcony from the next. Dusk was deepening all the time and the streetlights had been switched on. The leaves rustled in the breeze and my shadow flickered on the wall. I checked before I hoisted my legs up and I double-checked when I stood on the next balcony and nobody in the square was watching. The french windows were old and the wooden frames had shrunk in the dry climate. I used my nail-file through the gap and lifted the latch and pushed them open. It was no more tricky than the door to my building in rue St-André-des-Arts.

And I was no better than those people who had stolen into my apartment last night. Except that I didn't have murder in my heart. That was a big *except* and I held on to it very tight indeed.

The curtains were unlined but I thought they would block most of the light. I switched on the bedside lamp and set to work.

I suppose that the Hôtel du Centre had been put up half a century ago, catering to *commerçants*, technicians on contract without their families, people like that. Like Borries in fact. The room had high ceilings and the walls that floral wallpaper which country hotels in France still favour. At

48

some stage a small *cabinet de toilette* had been partitioned off. The furniture could best be described as Flea Market style.

The room had been cleaned and there was nothing in the wastepaper basket. A bottle of Black & White whisky stood on the dressing table and Borries had bitten off about half of it. A copy of *Der Spiegel* lay next to the whisky; it was dated April 27th and the cover was torn. In the wardrobe was a raincoat, blue with shoulder straps and brass buckles so you'd think he was a Marshal in the Ruritanian Air Force. Shirts, socks, underpants that were in need of Cobranama. Strange they weren't washed; air crew should be self-sufficient because they spend nights away and can't come on duty next morning with grubby collars. There was a black Samsonite case. It had a tag with just his name, no home address. There were no airport destination bands round the handle.

The window rattled and I was quick behind the dressing table. My assumptions could be false. They could be checking on a woman called Deschampsneufs. The vibration in the panes of glass was dying and I heard a truck changing gears out there somewhere. Anyway, who would have followed me over the balcony? It was just nerves.

Inside the Samsonite bag was a camel, a wooden one like you see in souvenir shops. There was a package of Marlboro from the dutyfree shop at Charles-de-Gaulle Airport, three packets remaining. There was a sealed pack of envelopes and a pad of blue paper. That was all. So I took out the pad. If your luck's in and the pen has been pressed hard enough, you can make out the words on the sheet underneath. I opened the cover and found I was staring at the original letter. He'd written: *Mittwoch Abend, S---*. The letter began: *Liebchen*.

Assumption: a letter to Ella, never posted. But more than that: never written. German is a language beyond me so I wouldn't have been butting into their private world. But that single word *Liebchen* told me a lot. He'd sat at the dressing table with the pad in front of him. Another evening on his own. Perhaps not all the nights had been alone but this evening he'd downed a scotch and then another and begun to miss Ella. *Liebchen* he wrote and then ran dry. Perhaps he was a poor writer anyhow, someone who preferred to use the phone. He'd poured another whisky and words of love still wouldn't come. Security was tight so there was nothing about his job or the country that he could put down on paper. He'd been able to think of nothing to write.

Liebchen. He should have got further than one word. It seemed to sum Borries up. I had the overpowering impression that he had loved Ella but had now discovered a greater love: money, the promise of lots of money from his new and dubious job.

My bedroom had no telephone so I had to go down to reception and use the cubicle in the corner.

'Monsieur Miloud, I want to put a phone call through to Paris.' Miloud was the owner; his name was on the tariff card on the back of my bedroom door. Because it was an international call, he explained it must be timed by the operator so that I could pay the correct amount and he would speak to the exchange. This must be what happened when Ella Borries received her call. Miloud used the identical form of words.

'*Allo? Allo? Ici l'Hôtel du Centre à Sfax. Je vous donne Mademoiselle Deschampsneufs.*'

'Hello? Michel?' I was cautious. This was my own apartment I was ringing. Last night it had been a no-go area.

'Co? Is that you? Where the hell are you?'

'I'm not in Paris. I'm sorry I couldn't ring earlier. It's too complicated to explain.'

I'd thought of ringing him at home in the morning while I was still in Paris. Can't meet you tonight, I'd say. Why not? Because, well, just because. I'd funked that phone call. Then at Charles-de-Gaulle I'd had a surge of anxiety because Michel had a key and he might walk into a violent reception in my apartment. I tried his bookshop but he was out on a visit to the Sorbonne, finding out what was on the English literature syllabus for next year. So I'd rung Madame Boyer and asked her as a favour, a *great* favour, *chère madame*, if she would check whether I had left the gas on in my oven; I didn't like leaving the gas on in an empty apartment. She

50

snorted: We could all be blown up in our beds. Exactly, madame, you are right as usual. I stroked her ego and left her to go up. Murderers lurking behind the door? She'd soon sort them out.

'Not in Paris?' Michel asked. 'I've been two hours waiting in your apartment.'

'I'm sorry, Michel, I'm sorry.' I couldn't say any more. He was my *Liebchen* and I knew exactly how Borries had felt: one word and nothing else would come.

'Why did that operator call you Madame Deschampsneufs? Who is Monsieur Deschampsneufs? Was he the man who telephoned yesterday?'

'Not Madame, Mademoiselle. And there is no Monsieur.'

'Why have you changed your name?'

'I haven't.'

'But he said . . .'

'Michel, *listen*.' Listen to what? I could sense the whole of my personal life unravelling in these few moments. But what could I tell Michel? It wasn't just that Miloud was behind the reception desk, doing nothing because his ears were too busy. How could I explain what my trade was? That at one time I'd been recruited into the British Intelligence Service but got out because I couldn't stand the system? That my skills were still shiny bright and I put them to work for people who needed help? That I would make my own decision whether to help or not, and no command structure would issue me with orders to act or not. So I had once been hired by PDS because the kidnappers had insisted: no police. So I was now hired by Ella Borries because in her heart she knew Bertolt had strayed over the line onto the dark side of the law. How could I explain this to a lover when I had concealed it from him all these months? It was a part of my life that remained secret. Had to, always.

'I'm listening,' he said. 'I'm waiting for you to explain.'

'I love you,' I told him.

'Love me?' There was incredulity in his voice. Yesterday, if I'd said that, I would have received passion in return. My phone calls last night, my going away, my name change were too much.

'When this is over we'll . . .'

51

'When *what* is over?' he shouted. 'Co, what the hell are you doing? Where are you? The operator said Sfax, didn't he. That's somewhere in Tunisia. I'll come and join you for the week-end.'

'Your cousin,' I reminded him. 'The wedding.'

'Shit. You don't want me to come. You're with someone.'

'No. Honest I'm not.'

'Don't give me *honesty*. When did honesty ever have anything to do with a woman's behaviour?'

He didn't wait for an answer. He'd slammed the phone down in my apartment, 1800 kilometres away in another continent, another world. I put the receiver back in its cradle.

Monsieur Miloud looked at me. '*C'est fini?*'

'*Oui*,' I told him, '*c'est fini.*'

Ask anybody and they'll say all they want in life is to be happy. Money, health, family are only steps along the road and the goal is happiness. Then why is it everything we do drives it further and further away?

6

The breeze had dropped. The sun was up and aiming high. Tunis had been hot enough but Sfax was further south, closer to the Sahara.

'Hello.'

'Hello. Is that Ella speaking?'

'Yes.'

'Do you recognize my voice?'

'Oh, it's . . .'

'That's right.' I was always cutting her short before she spoke my name. 'Do you speak English?'

'Why is it necessary?'

'Because it's very public where the phone is.'

Miloud had a newspaper on the counter but I didn't think he'd turn any pages. So long as I spoke French he was all ears.

'I understand. You mean you have something to tell me?'

'I'm at the hotel where he's been staying. He's not here now but he's kept on a room with his clothes in it, so he must be thinking of returning.'

'Thank God. Was he staying . . .? I mean, was anyone else . . .?'

'There was no one with him.' And to hell with Miloud's little hesitation.

Ella had one or two more questions: Any idea what Bert had been doing? Where had he gone? But she was subdued. She had hired me and I was the one who could do the worrying now.

'I'll ring you,' I said, 'as soon as I have something definite. Goodbye.'

Miloud looked up. The *Hebdo de Sfax* hadn't been as gripping as my telephone conversation. '*C'est fini*?' Yes, my curious friend, it's finished.

*

I'd been more tired yesterday than I'd realized. I'd gone round the hotels asking for Borries. But if I was Cody and become Deschampsneufs, couldn't the same have happened with Borries?

'You haven't seen him?'

'No, mademoiselle.'

'You're certain?'

A narrowing of the eyes, a frown. But that was because I kept pressing.

'I'm showing you the photo because if he only came in for a meal, you wouldn't know his name. He's a friend. I was to meet him in Sfax but I don't know the name of the hotel.'

'I regret . . .'

I rechecked the Triki, the Mabrouk and the Alexander. I went on to the Oliviers and the Habib. Borries might have come back and be using a different hotel and a different name. He mightn't even be staying at a hotel; he might have taken an apartment. So I went to the Agence Immobilière down boulevard Ferhat Hached and tried there. I tried his name and showed the photo that Ella had given me.

'Handsome,' the man behind the desk suggested.

I allowed myself a demure smile.

'But I regret, mademoiselle . . .'

The approach road was dead straight. On the left was a plantation of almond trees. On the right was brown grass and a ribbon of runway. The carpark beside the terminal building had space for two dozen cars. It was that kind of airport.

I sat in the car a few minutes, using a comb and my eyes. I twisted the mirror, first to one side, then to the other. There were people about but they had no interest in a little Renault or the driver primping her hair. I was a woman, I was vain, so what else was new?

The terminal was of concrete and glass and could have been a small factory. The control box on top of the tower had tinted glass, inward sloping to prevent reflections, and I could see nobody staring out at the view. What was there to look at? It was flat in every direction. The sky was deep blue above, fading to white above a line of distant trees. To my left was the entrance to the service apron, the hangars and the runway. A red and white pole was lowered and beside it a man sat in a wheelbarrow watching the action. The action was a smallish aircraft coming from the south, a twin engine machine that sank out of the heat haze. The plane touched down and stopped without any of the roar the big jets make.

The aircraft was a couple of hundred metres away. A door opened and steps unfolded and half a dozen men climbed out. They started the walk towards the airport building, fanning out like a posse, or like men who wanted to stretch themselves because they'd been cooped up together too long in a small space. Such as an oil rig.

But you can't land an aircraft, even a twin-engine twenty-seater, on an oil rig.

There were voices whooping in greeting near me. Eight or nine men had passed the red and white pole and were going out towards the plane. They wore jeans and tee-shirts except for one giant with a black beard who wore red overalls and a cap that said: Marathon.

You can't land an aircraft on an oil rig.

But I was out of the car now and slipping through the wire and striding out across the parched grass towards the plane, swinging my shoulderbag as I went. Marathon had rigs out by the Kerkenna Islands, the Information girl had said. They might also have oil wells inland or an office a hundred and twenty kilometres away in Gabès and you could land an aircraft there. Borries could have been hired because he could put down on a goat track by a back-country well.

Someone was shouting behind me and I lengthened my stride. I was going to need a storyline and there was nothing in my shoulderbag except my identity documents. I dug out my credit card and half-turned to wave it at the Marathon giant.

'Press,' I yelled.

He kept shouting at me to stop and there was no access to the runway and I never slowed because it's hard to get going again if you ever stop. Anyway, what business was it of his if I skipped the wire? The airport didn't belong to Marathon.

'Press,' I yelled again, flourishing the Amex card. 'From the *Revue Mondiale des Pétroles*. Ask the damn police captain.'

Even at fifty metres I could see the pilot wasn't Borries, not unless the sun had turned him black.

'*Salut*,' I called out as I got close. The pilot had climbed out and was kicking at one of the tyres.

'Hi,' he said, 'how're you doin'?'

Well, it takes all sorts to make the oil world. He wore light blue slacks, a white vest and on top a khaki combat jacket, unbuttoned in the heat. He had patches sewn where medals would be: *Maryland – it's going to be Texas when it grows up; Vietnam – We won it, the politicians lost it*; and Cocaine done as a Coca-Cola logo. When my eyes reached his face I saw lines and weariness I'd missed from a distance. A lot of blacks had fought in Vietnam but not many had been pilots.

'I'm from the *World Oil Review* and I'm doing a story on exploration round the Med. You know, Small Countries with a Big Potential. What I'm really after now is some local colour.'

He took his time looking me over and then he said in his slow drawl: 'Hell, you want to go to the front office if you want a story. I don't know nothin' about drillin'. I just fly the boys in and the empty beer crates out.'

The boys were closing fast on us now. The giant in Marathon red was shouting and the pilot told him to stuff it where it kind of hurts while he was talkin' with the little lady.

Facts don't make a story, I told the pilot, you've only got to open a newspaper to know that. The further away from the facts, the better the story. He had a deep laugh and his eyes crinkled up. So I asked him about his job and how long he'd been flying with Marathon and was there a helicopter for the rigs and did he do aerial surveys or was there another pilot for that and where were the inland wells and how long was the tour of duty and what did he miss most about the States?

'What did you say you're with, honey? *World Oil Review*? That's a trade paper. They're not interested in whether I miss Big Macs and a six-pack of Coors. They print production statistics and did we strike oil yet.'

'Would you tell me if you had?'

He laughed again. His face was a map of everything that had happened to him in Vietnam and after. The lines round his eyes and mouth deepened. They were paths through a personal jungle.

The drillers had already clambered inside. Each window had a face. They were going back to a world without women and their eyes were fixed on me. The Marathon giant ducked under a wing. He had yelled heavy French at me; to the pilot he growled in international American to hoist his ass on board and fly those bastards out. The pilot responded with a one-two to the solar plexus in slow motion and warned him to have more respect for a star whose views on life were being sought by the world's press or he would personally break his ass for him.

'I'm going anyhow,' I said. 'Thanks for your help.' I had made the wingtip when a final question occurred to me. 'Oh, is Bert still flying with your outfit?'

'Bert? What Bert is this?'

'Bert Borries. You know,' and I even included the big man with the black beard. 'That German guy. Blond hair, well built.'

The pilot shook his head. 'Sorry, honey.' He began climbing the steps.

'You *must* know. Used to fly Lufthansa. Real good looker. I'd like to see him again. It's kind of personal. He got married and all but it'd still be great to meet him again.'

The pilot turned solemn eyes on me and then his face broke up with his slow laugh. 'Shit,' he said, making two syllables out of it. 'You're some lady. I'd like to help out but I don't know the guy. Listen though. I'm doin' nothin' tonight. If you're lonely why don't I fly up here? From Gabès it's only a hop and a skip.'

And a jump into bed. I gave him a grin and a flash of my eyes. 'I'll take a rain-check on that.' It was a couple of days since I'd handed out a rain-check.

I walked back towards the terminal building and my car. The man stirred himself from the wheelbarrow to lift the striped pole for me. Nobody asked what I'd been doing on the airfield. There were no police or army in sight. Even then it struck me how terrible the security was.

I bought a *casse-croûte* from a stall and sat at a table in place Hedi Chaker with a cup of coffee and took stock of the situation. I was in a strange town, without friends or contacts. I was looking for a man who'd moved on nearly three weeks ago. I'd no idea who his employers were or what kind of flying he was doing. The trail was old and cold and I needed help.

There was a kiosk in the centre of the square and the man said there were two local papers. I bought both and looked for the addresses of the editorial offices. If I chose *L'Hebdo de Sfax* it wasn't because Miloud had been reading it but because it was closer than the *Gazette du Sud*. It was down an arcade beside the Etoile cinema, up grubby stairs and on the first floor. A sign on the door said to knock and enter. I hesitated. The last time I had gone to an editorial office for information, it had been *Le Courrier* in Paris. I had spoken to one of their reporters and he had ended up on the wrong side of the Berlin Wall with his head bowed on the steering wheel. I had touched his cheek and felt the chill through to my heart. The bullet in his chest was none of my doing but still, I had been the last story he would work on.

I knocked and went in and the sound of typing stopped.

'Monsieur Nortier?'

'Yes,' he said.

There was nobody else in the room. Nortier, according to the masthead of his paper, was the editor. He had turned his head towards the door. He was a cat, a city cat, with that aura of alertness to danger. His hair was trimmed short over his skull, his face sharp-edged, chiselled almost to the bone. He was compact, probably no taller than me. He wore a cotton polo-neck shirt and tight slacks, both black. His face was utterly still.

That was unnerving. We are used to the tiny movements that breathe life into a face and his gave nothing away. It was the eyes that held me. You can meet a priest in a poor village and his eyes dismantle all the fancy ramparts you've erected to shelter behind. Or at a party a man says, 'A penny for them,' but you never bother because he's already seen your secret desires. Those kind of eyes.

'You're the editor,' I began, just to get the ball rolling.

'Editor, founder, leader writer, chief reporter and fifty per cent of the staff. The other fifty per cent is Taoufik.' Nortier's hand had been resting on the keyboard and he waved it to the other side of the room. 'The good Taoufik is out. He knows the right officials in the *gouvernorat*, covers the football, reviews the films, takes the photos and reads the proofs. *L'Hebdo* is a tight operation – any tighter and it would be squeezed to death.'

'Don't worry, I haven't come to sell you anything. I've come because I need your help.'

'Have a seat.' He'd remained at his desk while I stood like a beggar inside the door. 'You haven't told me your name.'

'Suzanne Deschampsneufs.' I had to bite back Cody. Cody was locked inside the Paris apartment. Deschampsneufs was what I had to believe in.

'And what sort of help do you think a journalist can give?'

'I'm trying to locate a man who's missing. He's a pilot who used to work for Lufthansa. He went freelance a few months ago. He came to Sfax. I know he was staying here at the beginning of the month. Then he disappeared. I need someone with local contacts to help me find him.'

I made simple statements because they always sound honest. He made simple statements back at me.

'He's a pilot. If he crashed into the desert four hundred kilometres away, I can't help. Nobody can help. He'll be dead.'

It was like tennis. The ball was over my side of the net and it was my turn to hit. I decided to smash it right out of the court.

'He may be dead. That's what I'm afraid of. You see, the man who got him the job is dead. I'd still like your help in trying to track his movements. In return you get the story.'

At this first mention of a story, he finally moved. He reached out for a paperweight, one of those big *rose des sables* crystals they find in the desert. His fingertips traced the sharp edges and then he put it down. For a journalist his desk was amazingly uncluttered: typewriter, telephone, cassette recorder, empty cup, a neat stack of typescript. All the mess of papers and files and boxes of old photos was by the desk of the good Taoufik.

'A story? Perhaps you should tell me something of this story. The man who's gone missing – does he have a name?'

'Borries.'

'He used to work for Lufthansa. Are you sure he's not Russian? That would be a story – Russian spies in Tunisia.'

Make allowance for French pronunciation and the name could be Boris. But Borries was German. And Soviet involvement was improbable. I shook my head.

'Well?' he persisted. 'Not Russian?'

'German. I'm sure of it.'

'Sure of it? People who are sure of something mean, in fact, that they don't know. So he's not your fiancé? Perhaps not even a friend?'

He turned his face full towards me. A nose, a mouth, two ears were ranged round the eyes. How old was he? Thirty-seven, thirty-eight? His eyes came from a different age. They stared at my face and penetrated behind my face where we distil the lies.

'Not a friend,' I said.

'In fact, you've probably never met him. So what is your connection? Who are you?'

'Someone who's looking for Borries. His wife is paying me.'

'Is that your profession? A tracer of missing persons?'

'Sometimes. I do odd jobs that people can't do themselves.'

'What sort of jobs? Illegal jobs? Dangerous? Political? Blackmail?'

I should have gone to the *Gazette du Sud*. I was annoyed with this crusading reporter act and those damn staring eyes.

'You see,' he said, sensing my growing anger, 'I'm trying to get a picture of what kind of person you are. If I'm to help you, that's important.'

'All right,' I said, 'okay.' I hadn't told Michel what I did, nor Dolbiac before him. The two halves of my life are separate. But Nortier I had to tell and I gave him a very French sort of answer. 'Society organizes itself and decides some things are taboo. Governments pass laws and policemen enforce them. Or there is a strong social disapproval that can force a person to conform or get out. Well, rigid legal systems and social pressures are not always right. There are things I approve of which are illegal and things I don't like which the law does nothing about. So if someone wants her husband traced and doesn't want the police involved, that's her business. And maybe it's mine. But I'll make my own judgement.'

Those were the articles of my faith. But Nortier wasn't

interested. The journalist in him was fully awake. 'You're saying – if I take your hint – that Borries is employed in something illegal, right here in Sfax. And it must be big because the person who fixed him his job has been killed. Yes, that sounds a ripe story. Squeeze it and the juice oozes out. Yes . . .'

Whatever else he was going to say was interrupted by the phone. *Ah, c'est toi*, he said, and *Où ça* and *C'est de la merde* and then something in Arabic that sounded rude, but then a lot of Arabic sounds that way. Nortier hung up and said to me: 'That was Taoufik. His car's broken down at El Djem and he can't get back for the Minister of Agriculture's press conference. So I must go, otherwise there'll only be Cefai from the *Gazette*. What time is it?'

I told him.

'Damn, damn, damn. I have to go now.' He groped on his desk for the cassette recorder. 'It's going to be tomorrow before you and I get down to it.' He stood up and moved round the desk with a cat's grace. He had the same fastidious way of putting each foot down, knowing that the earth is made of dirt. 'We'll get things moving in the morning. I guarantee some action. All right?'

For a moment I was too stunned to reply. Nortier had gone to the corner where a cane leant against the wall, a white cane. I had been so concerned with my problem, I had never noticed he was blind.

'All right?' he repeated. 'We'll start early.'

He walked quickly across the office without tap-tapping, as if he had radar in those eyes, those eyes that had stared at me and seen everything.

I telephoned Paris, the apartment in rue St-André-des-Arts. I wanted Michel to be there. I wanted it very much. I let the phone ring and ring.

'There's no reply.' I told Miloud. I gave him Michel's home number instead and took the receiver away when he had instructed the exchange. I didn't want Miloud to speak before I did. Michel answered.

'Hello,' I said. 'It's me.'

There was a long silence. Don't hang up, don't hang up.

I willed the message down the line. It's *not* the end between us, I said in silence. Then I thought: if he was going to hang up, he'd have done it at once. This was a lover's silence, hurt, wanting the hurt made better.

'Michel . . .' I broke the silence in the end though I had wanted him to. 'Don't let's quarrel, Michel.'

'I want you,' he said abruptly. 'Do you know that?'

'I know,' I said.

'I want to join you in Sfax. To hell with the wedding and the cousins.'

'There might be a pretty *cousine*.'

'They've all got warts and moustaches. I want to be with you.'

It was very difficult. I wanted him with me, in my bed. I sighed. There didn't seem enough air in my lungs. 'Michel, give me a few days on my own. I just need my own space for a little.'

Behind me was the deep silence of Miloud. He could hear my side of the conversation and was trying to make up the responses from the unknown man. Ella had reported that her Bert had said 'he wanted to kiss me and . . . you know.' I knew. But it was easy for Bert because he would speak German and Miloud wouldn't understand.

'Just a few days,' I said.

'I want you *now*,' Michel said, full of male urgency. 'My tongue wants to tell you how much I love you. Can you feel it? In your mouth, all over your body.'

'Go on,' I said. I could feel his tongue. I could hardly breathe at the memory of it.

'My hands want to feel you, all of you. I want to run my fingers over your nipples, like a blind man touching braille. Can you feel that?'

I opened my mouth. Why did Michel say that about a blind man touching braille? It was as if he knew I'd been with Nortier.

'Michel, go to that wedding. Don't sit in Paris and mope.'

Warts and moustaches and bad breath and fat legs. I wished a plague to descend on Alsace. I hoped to God there were no pretty *cousines*.

7

There's the *place* and the *avenue* and they're both called Hedi Chaker. The avenue was broad and aimed towards the medina. Down the central strip were evergreen trees and red and white flags. On each side of the avenue were arcades. 'By the Etoile cinema,' Nortier had said. 'What car do you drive?' He stepped out from behind an arch as I stopped. I leant across to open the door and we ran through the French ritual: *Bon jour, ça va*, handshake.

We turned left at the lights and I asked: 'How did you know it was me?'

'I didn't. I just knew it was a small Renault from the engine noise.'

We joined the morning rush. It was worse than the evening rush: the Sfaxiens were impatient to get on with the business of the day. We got caught behind a truck tipping out a load of builder's sand and the horns blared.

'What colour is the car?' he asked.

'Red.' How does a blind man see colours? I didn't know.

He said, as if he knew my thoughts: 'I haven't always been blind. I lost my sight on May 4th, 1970 at 14.22 hours.'

He stopped and I thought that was all I was going to get. His face was half-turned, feeling the morning sun. He'd been very precise about date and time. It's not an event you forget.

'It's a matter of record,' he said. 'Myself, I'm hazy about it. There are blank patches in my memory. I was a pilot in the French Air Force. I was stationed at Tours AFB when there was one of those freak accidents they swear can never happen. I'd come back from high altitude attack training, handed over my machine and was walking away from the engineering hangar when a Mirage III taxied close to me. A missile simply fell off like a ripe plum. *Boum!* The Mirage was okay but I lost my sight.'

The truck had finished unloading. We moved off and the

traffic at the roundabout took all my attention. I took the Agareb exit for the airport.

Nortier sighed and said: 'The chain of events was grotesque. The missile had been improperly secured but passed inspection. It shouldn't have been primed but it still exploded on impact with the concrete. Finally, it only carried a flash charge for training. It was the flash that blinded me. The doctor said in the report to the disability commission that I had suffered "total and irreversible scarring of the retina". In human language, my eyes were burnt out. Jesus, my head shrieked for about two weeks.'

He was gazing up at the sky. His dead eyes saw the past.

'I lived for flying. Can you understand that?'

'Yes, I can.' Some people live for football, others for their children or their politics. Nortier had been in love with the sky and the loneliness of it, ten kilometres above our sordid little world.

'I couldn't stand France after that. I tried drinking myself to death a bit in Spain. I moved on and ended up here. With the disability gratuity I started the *Hebdo*.'

'You'd no experience of journalism.'

'My wife had. She'd worked on *Le Matin*. So we got our little weekly paper going here. Me, Marie-Louise and a friend, another reporter.'

We took the turn-off to the airport, the straight road with the almond trees to the left and the runway to the right.

'Then after eighteen months she got tired of looking after a blind man and ran off with the other reporter. The *Hebdo* was reduced to one man who couldn't even check the proofs. It would have folded if Taoufik hadn't arrived.'

'I'm sorry,' I said. 'About your marriage.'

'Yes,' Nortier said.

I glanced at him. His face was angled towards the almond trees. It was a face of particular stillness. He'd lost his sight, lost his wife, almost lost his paper and now no emotion showed. I pulled into the carpark. Today it was half full. There were even taxis waiting, the drivers standing in a group smoking. Somewhere a radio was playing and an Arab singer was committing suicide, on and on and on.

'Still, it was best for both of us. I understand that now.

She had felt a martyr looking after me. I had to become much tougher. I had only myself to rely on. There were things she'd done that I learnt to do myself. I would go out and do an interview with the recorder and type up the article and let Taoufik correct the mistyping. She wasn't there to put a knot in my tie so I stopped wearing ties. Small problems, big problems. A struggle. What else is life?'

He didn't give me a chance to say anything. He didn't want sympathy and he'd grown beyond needing help. He had the door open and was out, waiting for me.

'My biggest problem,' Nortier said, 'since Marie-Louise left is that I don't smile enough.'

He did give me a smile then, his first. Then he was off towards the gate.

'*Ça va, Antoine*,' one of the drivers said.

'*Salut, Béchir. Ça va?*'

This is how you hijack an aircraft at Sfax Airport. You stroll up to the striped pole and say to the guard:

'Is Monsieur Jules here today?'

Be nonchalant about it. Don't look over your shoulder for army or police because there are none.

'Maybe,' the guard replies. 'He could have come while I was getting a coffee.'

At this point the guard comes out of his hut – the wheelbarrow is missing today – and leans on the counterweight at the end of the pole.

'Do you want to have a look?' he asks.

'Okay,' you reply.

Or in this case Nortier replied. We passed the pole and the guard grinned at me. He remembered me from yesterday. I was an old pal. Nortier turned his head to left and right as if aligning himself by radio beacons. In a sense he was. There was the chatter of the drivers on one side and hubbub from the terminal building on the other. He set off across the concrete and when we reached the grass he paused again to take his bearings. He'd left the white stick in the car and he walked with quick short steps. We went towards a corrugated iron hangar and, as we rounded the corner, we found the doors had been slid back. This was for ventilation. It was early but the sun on the span of the metal roof was already ferocious. Inside the hangar were two light aircraft, single engine machines. Two more were parked in the sun. This was the Aéro-Club de Sfax, all of it.

We stepped inside the hangar. It was like being inside a radiator. If they'd used heat-reflective paint on the roof it wasn't doing much of a job. There was nobody about, no Jules. I told Nortier and he nodded. He was standing by the nose of one of the planes, running his hand over the prop and engine cowling.

'This is a Beechcraft.'

'Is it? I know nothing about planes.'

'You've never flown a plane? This is a little beauty to handle.'

'Do you mean,' I said, 'that you have flown that plane?'

'Jules takes me up. Then he hands over the controls.'

'But you're blind.'

'You've heard of blind flying.'

'But not literally. The pilot can still see.'

'He reads the instruments to me, talks me through. I have the yoke and the throttle and the pedals. I can *feel* the aircraft, the wind passing across the flaps, the power in the engine. It responds to what I do. It is a living thing.'

Our voices brought a man in through a side door. He came in wiping his hands on the thighs of his overalls. He wore no shirt or vest under the overalls. It had a halter neck and the matted hair of his chest was grey and glistening with sweat. There was a cigarette stuck between his lips and to hell with the *Défense de fumer* notice. His eyes took me in and flicked over to Nortier and his face cracked with a grin.

'Antoine, ça va?'

'Ça va. Et toi?'

Nortier had his hand out and the other met it and they shook. Then it was my turn.

'Suzanne Deschampsneufs.'

'*Enchanté.*'

There was a chunky gold signet ring on the hand he gave me. Round his neck was a zodiacal pendant, a crab clawing its way out of the undergrowth of chest-hair. The pendant was also gold. His eyes were blue, brighter than the sky he

66

scanned when he was up in his little Beechcraft.

The men talked. There was a glider race at the week-end, a challenge between Essadi and Dabou. The goal was Gafsa, some hundred and seventy kilometres inland, and if the weather stayed hot and the thermals were good they might make it.

'How do they get back?'

'Huh?' Jules inspected me again. 'They'll get back.'

So that settled that. I went on to being the little woman on the outside while the grown-up men discussed their grown-up toys. Was the *Hebdo* going to cover both the start and the finish? The problem was getting to Gafsa, Nortier said. No problem, Jules would fly him. They would cover the preliminaries on the ground, the take-off, the climb to three thousand metres, the unhooking from the tow-aircraft. They would stay with the *planeurs* while they searched for the winds and 'the right angle of attack. Sometimes they must make a dog-leg.' That was Jules. I had another few moments of attention from him. He turned back to Nortier. They would leave the gliders and head over to Gafsa for lunch. Radio contact at Gafsa would inform them when the gliders were approaching. I gathered Essadi and Dabou were famous rivals and would keep each other in sight, snarling insults all the way like schoolkids.

At last we got round to Borries, as if it was a postscript to the real business of arrangements for the glider contest. Mademoiselle was searching for another pilot, a German called Bertolt Borries.

'Ah really?' Jules said.

There are ways and ways of saying that. We may have been in a town half way down the coast of Tunisia but Jules was French to the hunch of his shoulders and the lift of an eyebrow.

'He's married,' I said.

'Is he?' It was a detail, a nothing to Jules.

'His wife has asked me to find him.'

Jules had put another cigarette in his mouth and worked a flame on his lighter.

'I take it he's not reported to her for some time?'

'Quite a few weeks.'

He studied me. The cigarette was in the corner of his mouth and his head was tilted so the smoke drifted away from those bright blue eyes of his. One hand scratched among the matted hair on his chest. I think he was proud of that hair. I think he felt that women should be smooth and men rough. He nodded as if I had passed some sort of test and told me all he knew.

'He was here earlier in the year quite a lot. March? April? I didn't note it in my diary every time I saw him, you understand? To be honest – by the way, you're not a personal friend? Well, to be honest there was a quality about him I didn't find sympathetic. Right? He was at the airport a lot, made use of the facilities, the engineers, so on. Here we are *copains*, we are all pals. But Borries was withdrawn, aloof, didn't have a chat, never had time for a drink, didn't even shake hands and say hello. But – he was a superb pilot. I saw him land his plane with one engine cut out to test its stability. He was perfectly level when he touched down and that takes some flying. He was super-efficient. Imagine if there'd been more like him in the Luftwaffe in 1940. The bastards would have won the war, no doubt.'

'This plane he landed with one engine out,' Nortier said. 'What kind of plane?'

'Skyvan.'

'Skyvan!' Nortier gave a hoot of laughter. To me he said: 'A Skyvan looks like a shoebox with wings. It's the Renault 4 of the air. A workhorse.'

This was the plane for which PDS had found a pilot who could put down 'on a goat track in the middle of a sandstorm'.

'What's special about a Skyvan?'

'It's rugged,' Nortier said. 'It's simple to fly. It's got a short take-off and landing. There's nothing fancy inside. You can put in seats for passengers or stack it full of cargo.'

'It was secondhand,' Jules said. 'One of the phosphate mines was getting rid of it. Borries spent four days giving the engineers a hard time making sure that Skyvan worked to perfection. He painted out the mine's livery. And then one day he was no longer here.'

'He flew out?'

'Yes.'

'Where did he go?'

'I never asked.' He shrugged, dismissing Borries as no longer worth his attention.

Outside there was the growing din of a plane coming down the runway, slowing with reverse thrust. Jules moved to the open doors to look out. It was a 727 in Tunis Air livery.

'On time,' Nortier said. He had a wrist watch with a crystal that hinged back and the hours were marked by raised dots.

'Other airports have rush hours,' Jules said. 'Thursday is Sfax's rush day. That's the flight in from Tunis, continuing on to Tripoli. Then there's a lunchtime flight to Paris that returns in the evening. And an evening flight to Tunis.'

What he said struck a chord in my brain. 'Tripoli . . . Could the Skyvan have reached there?'

'No problem.'

'How can I find out if he did go there?'

'He'll have filed a flight plan with Air Traffic Control. Maybe it's lying in a file in Admin. You'll have to ask in the main building.'

I waited outside, feeling the sun burning a hole in my cheek. Inside Nortier made last minute arrangements with Jules for their Sunday jaunt. The Tunis Air jet had slowed and was turning off the runway onto a taxiway. There was a flicker, like a diamond necklace flashing, as the sun reflected off the windows. I could see the place on the parking apron it was headed for. There were mobile steps and a Total fuel tanker and a man with two bats beckoning. The plane came to rest and the whine of its engines died. A tractor was hauling a trailer out from the terminal building. It held a dozen suitcases of passengers joining the flight on to Tripoli.

Nortier came out of the hangar. 'Right, we've made a little progress. We know Borries took delivery of a Skyvan. We can try the phosphate mines to find out who bought the plane. But first let's see if we can trace the route he took when he flew out.'

'You have a friend in the administration?'

'Oh yes.'

We were walking back to the striped pole. A crowd had gathered beyond it: people who'd come to wave off relatives, taxi-drivers, the curious who imagine there's glamour at an airport with three departures on a busy day. The tractor had reached the 727 now and the hold doors had swung open. Baggage was being handed down and passengers were disembarking. A hostess stood at the top of the steps and bobbed her head at each: hope you enjoyed your flight, we look forward to feeding you filthy coffee again soon.

'Jules was asking about you,' Nortier said to me. 'How long you intend staying here. He thought perhaps you'd like to go to his house for dinner one night. He's boss of a fish cannery. He's got a villa on the coast to the north, very sumptuous.'

'What's his surname?'

'Gourdault.'

'And will Madame Gourdault be equally delighted to see me?'

'I understand from what Jules said that she is away on a visit to her sister in France.' We walked on in silence. 'Anyway, I said to Jules I would mention it to you.'

'Thank you.'

And did this great captain of industry speak to his wife each night like Michel spoke to me? Did he tell her his hands wanted to feel her, all of her, run over her nipples? Or was that all a bore? It got in the way of life's realities: getting his hands on the controls of a Beechcraft, and afterwards getting them on a woman who asked about a straying pilot.

I looked away towards the Tunis Air plane. Six passengers had disembarked. The plane was parked only a hundred metres from the terminal building but they stood like sheep. I could see what they were waiting for: the coach. In order to save making two journeys it was loading with the passengers for the onward flight.

'It makes me feel like a pimp,' Nortier muttered.

'Well, you shouldn't have agreed to speak to me. He's old enough to make his own running.'

'He's a friend.'

'Who happens to be flying you to Gafsa on Sunday. One good turn deserves another.'

We reached the striped pole and went through and turned towards the main building. There was a shout out from the parking apron. One of the disembarking passengers had tired of waiting for the coach and set off at a smart pace. It was the hostess who was calling out and then she went after him at a trot. High heels and a tight skirt are useless when it's a long-legged man you're after. He moved rapidly, an incongruous raincoat flapping at his knees. He must have been dripping inside all that clothing. I stared at that man, couldn't tear my eyes away. There was something familiar about him, his fawn raincoat, his thinness, the way he moved. He walked with his head thrust forward as if he was always poking his nose into other people's business.

'Let's forget I ever mentioned it,' Nortier said.

'Yes, let's.'

I felt angry: not because Jules was trying to take advantage of his wife's absence but because he took advantage of Nortier. Then the anger went. Everything went, every thought in my head. I was staring out at the apron with suspicions hardening about that hurrying passenger when it happened.

The initial flash wasn't large. I saw it distinctly on the luggage trailer under the belly of the aircraft. A microsecond later my eardrums felt the change in atmospheric pressure. Then came flames and thunder as the kerosene in the far wing went up. A cascade of fire erupted over the plane, the steps, the fuel tanker, the waiting passengers and ground crew. Screams from the crowd by the fence, answering screams from out by the aircraft.

Nortier reached for me, grabbing hold of my shirt, his fingers digging into my ribs.

'My God, what's happening? Tell me.'

Passengers were scrambling out of the open door of the plane. Fire drives people to panic, pushing, struggling, tumbling. A couple of dozen must have escaped when the Total tanker went up. It went like a tremendous bomb and kept going and kept going so that flames and black smoke boiled up into the sky. The blast sent passengers and crew flying along the concrete. The thin passenger in the fawn raincoat was sent sprawling. He was bowled over like a leaf in an autumn gale, his attaché case torn from his hand, his face white in a new flash as another of the plane's fuel tanks went up. There was a rictus on his face, like you see in a corpse that's met a violent death, a rictus without mirth.

Crevecoeur wasn't laughing.

8

There was chaos, overwhelming. Screams and cries came from out on the concrete apron, shouts and wails from close by. An explosion like a gunshot cracked out from the plane and I thought: tyre's blown out. A whistle blew and a man shouted an order in harsh Arabic. Above everything was the sound of the flames, like sea breaking on distant rocks, hungry.

'It's the Tunis plane?' Nortier shouted at me. 'It's gone up?'

'Yes, someone planted a bomb. I think in one of the suitcases being loaded here.'

'How do you know?'

'I was watching. I saw a flash. Everyone must have seen it.'

Except Nortier, the blind journalist.

'Are there many injured?'

'Yes. People are jumping out. There are flames everywhere. It's terrible confusion.'

I felt dumb. I didn't know what to say, how to put it into words for him.

'Jules? Is he all right? Has the fire reached the hangar?'

'No, it's . . .'

Nortier turned at a shout almost in his ear and then he was butted aside because he was in the way of a ferocious woman clutching a baby. People ran everywhere. I know what I should have told Nortier: it's like an ants' nest when you kick it over. Running in different directions, over to the fence, back to the building, round in circles. Do you remember what it was like when you stubbed your toe on an ants' nest? Remember when you had eyes?

'*Les salauds.*' It was a hiss, low and vicious. 'They were out to get me.'

I had moved into the lee of the terminal building. In the

open you could get knocked to the ground and trampled to death. Crevecoeur had come round the corner of the building and stopped. He stood with a hand in front of his face, fingers open a crack. It was because of the heat of the blaze, not as protection against the sights. And against the cries of terror and pain there was no protection. Light flickered on his forehead, gleaming on the sweat. The light wasn't from the sun, dirtied by billows of smoke, but from the inferno out there. The flames played on his features until finally he turned.

He'd known I was round the corner of this building. He must have seen me forcing my way through the turmoil. There was no shock on his face at seeing me. Nothing shocked Crevecoeur. A political assassination in Paris, a terrorist attack at a Summit meeting, a knife in his belly, a bullet parting his hair, he'd known it all. Meeting me in Sfax didn't surprise him one bit.

'Why are you staring?' Crevecoeur asked. 'What's wrong with my face?'

There had been some expression on it. It was important I understood that look. It was as if he was relieved or pleased or satisfied. Why the look of satisfaction? Not because a bomb had almost killed him. Finding me must be proof of something.

'They?' I asked. 'Who are they?'

'What?'

'You said *they* were out to get you.'

Somewhere a siren sobbed.

'Who was out to get you, Crevecoeur? Why?'

He looked away to see where the siren came from and when he turned back the shutters had closed behind his eyes. Jules had eyes bluer than the Mediterranean; Crevecoeur had eyes greyer than Notre Dame. Once I dreamt about him, that he was leaning too close and I spat in his face to force him away. I woke up trembling with the thought: that's what his eyes look like, as if someone has spat in them.

'Why are you here?' Crevecoeur asked. He always asked questions of me. He never gave answers. He let me work it all out.

'Go to hell,' I told him. 'I'm a private citizen and I'm not in France. And you're not in France either so you're a private citizen. You've got no powers here so go to hell.'

He stepped back, gave me more room. That's all I wanted, to get him to keep his distance. I hadn't been hiding round the corner of the building but maybe he thought I had. I had hoped never to meet Crevecoeur again. I would far rather take my chance on dinner *chez* Jules, chunky jewellery blinking in the candlelight, one hand searching among his chest-hair, the other searching under the table for my thigh. But looking at Crevecoeur now, I understood a very simple truth: we would always meet. Our worlds overlapped. We were like two powerful magnets: the like poles repelling, the unlike poles attracting. Our lives were once again touching.

Crevecoeur said: 'You're not working for them, are you?'

And I said: 'Who?'

'The people who tried to kill me. How else could you know I was arriving this morning? That's the reason I asked why you were here.'

It was four or five minutes since the explosion and the emergency services had got in gear. First out on the parking apron was a fire tender. They had asbestos heat shields and fire foam and they did their best, but twenty thousand litres of aviation fuel makes a brute of a bonfire. The main exit door was engulfed in flames, the wings were on fire, helpless faces and fists were at the windows. I don't know why they hadn't used the rear emergency exits, got jammed maybe. It took the firefighters to smash them open and figures tumbled out and sprinted clear. Finally no one jumped out.

'Crevecoeur,' I said, 'if I'm not working for them I'm working against them, whoever they are. Or I'm here for some unconnected reason.'

'Well, you're not on holiday.'

'How do you know?'

He looked at me and his tight lips stretched thinner. In someone else it would have been a mark of disgust. With Crevecoeur it was a smile. It was a year since I'd last seen him. It was as if we'd never been separated, not even for a minute. He was here by my side without so much as a *Ça va* or a handshake. He was prying and guessing, his specialities. Events last year at the Summit conference, events today in

Sfax, it was like one continuous disaster with Crevecoeur at the heart of it.

An ambulance approached the plane and then backed off: the heat, the danger. Survivors littered the concrete. Some couldn't move. Some crawled on hands and knees. One rolled over as if fire was trapped inside his *djellaba* and he could smother it. Police had appeared from the terminal building and were pulling the gawpers off the fence: Get back, get away, there could be another blast. There was a roman candle of sparks from the plane but still they stared.

'God help them,' Crevecoeur said.

'They're beyond help.'

'I don't mean the ones out there.' He leant a fist against the wall by my shoulder. 'God help the bastards who set this up, when I get my hands on them.'

There were white half-moons under his eyes where the fingers of death had touched him and moved on.

'Do you know who did it?'

He hesitated. Perhaps he was about to tell me when we heard a voice calling out: 'Mademoiselle Deschampsneufs.'

'Deschampsneufs?' Crevecoeur raised an eyebrow at me. 'Don't tell me you're actually using that passport?'

We stared at each other and I felt something stirring deep inside me. It was cold and sharp, like a hook twisting in a fish's guts.

'Oh yes, I know all about that passport,' he said. 'You got it off Bouguet. We pulled him in some months ago and he was like a bird. To begin with he was a crow, ugly squawks. He ended up a canary, singing sweetly. First it was about smuggling francs into Switzerland. He sang out the numbers of certain bank accounts. Then it was the identity of the woman who was compromising one of our illustrious politicians. Finally for good measure he gave us the names and numbers of three stolen Belgian passports, two Spanish and no less than eight French passports. Regular little one-man industry. Deschampsneufs is a well known name, believe me.'

'Then why didn't they stop me at Charles-de-Gaulle?'

'Ah,' he said. 'Perhaps I haven't told Immigration. You've no idea how busy I've been.' Nortier had pushed through

76

to us. Crevecoeur jerked his head at him. 'Who is this gentleman?' Only a French cop can make *ce monsieur* sound such an insult.

'Antoine Nortier, editor, *L'Hebdo de Sfax*. Crevecoeur, Chief Inspector, Sûreté Nationale.'

Oh so correct. So pleased you could come to the party. Dreadfully sorry about the heat and the noise and the crush.

'Journalist?' Crevecoeur was very sharp with that. 'You got your scoop, my friend. Feast your eyes on that.'

'Don't worry,' I told Nortier. 'You can be as rude as you like. He's French Sûreté not Tunisian.'

'There's been a terrorist bomb attack,' Nortier said. 'Why is that interesting to a French Sûreté officer?'

'Fantastic,' Crevecoeur said. 'An interview, right at the scene of the crime before they've even counted the bodies. Where's . . . where's your pen and notepad? Don't you want a quote?'

He'd faltered, even Crevecoeur. A mother had staggered past holding a young girl. They both wailed. The child had lost her socks and shoes and dark blotches covered her legs. Oil, blood, scorching. I had to block the thought out of my mind.

'Tell me', Nortier hung on in there, 'are you operating in Tunisia with official permission?'

'Jesus,' Crevecoeur muttered, 'some friend of yours, Cody.'

Two more ambulances were coming down the long approach road. They nosed through the crowd of sightseers, klaxons blaring. The red crescent on their sides was like the red cross, the exact shade of fresh-spilt blood, in case you should ever need reminding. The pole was raised but they didn't venture far out on the parking apron.

Nortier had spent perhaps half a minute thinking and he turned to me. 'If you are Suzanne Deschampsneufs, why did the Chief Inspector call you Cody?'

Hell, nothing slipped past him. You were ready to be sorry and help him out because he was blind but you might just as well try to help a crocodile. You'd reach out a hand and *snap* he went.

I might have passed it off as a nickname but Crevecoeur came straight out: 'She has two passports or two that I know.

of. The one I've seen is in the name of Cody. The one she entered Tunisia on is in the name of Deschampsneufs. You're a hot one with the questions – ask her why she finds it necessary to run two passports. Go on, ask her. What kind of person needs to do that?' To me he said: 'And note this. You're in Tunisia on false papers and the police could lock you in a cell for twenty-eight days while they make their enquiries. Might be longer. Sometimes a key gets lost for years. Who would ever ask why you'd disappeared?'

Always there were threats. It had been the same the first time we'd met. Winter had settled early on Paris that year. It was a cold afternoon. Crevecoeur had hammered his way into my apartment with three uniformed men and hinted at tax investigators and deportation and turning his back while men with heavy boots argued about how much my kidneys would stand before my urine turned red. He'd stood too close while he questioned me about an American agent's death, testing me, watching my eyes and my face. That had been our first encounter.

'You're wrong,' I told him. 'There'd be questions. I came with Nortier, don't forget.'

I'd dropped my voice. Crevecoeur had swung round to threaten me and he was so close the sleeve of his soiled raincoat brushed my arm. For a few instants we forgot the noise and the pain and the danger and the panic. We stared at each other. I saw a security cop with ice in his soul. I don't know what he saw in me. He sighed and reached out his cigarettes and his little Cricket gas lighter and inhaled deeply.

'Why did you have to come with a journalist of all people?'

Crevecoeur's voice was soft but Nortier picked up the question and answered for me: 'What business is it of yours? This isn't a French Protectorate any longer.'

'Do you hold a French passport?' Crevecoeur snapped. 'You don't want to lose it, do you?'

'*Fous le camp.*'

Nortier was frowning. He was puzzled by our relationship. Did Crevecoeur have a hold on me? Were we old lovers? How could I explain that, no, we weren't lovers, the idea repelled me. Nor was blackmail to do with it, not really, not any more. At one time I kept his pistol, which I was sure had killed that journalist near the Wall in East Berlin. And Crevecoeur could have revoked my *carte de séjour*. Perhaps that was at the root of it: we'd each had the capability to hurt the other, and had drawn back from using it. Crevecoeur was like a relation. Because he was from the Sûreté and because of my Intelligence background, there was kinship of a kind. It was like Michel and his cousins – you did nothing to create the relationship nor could you ever remove it. Crevecoeur would use me and abuse me, and I could damn him to hell. And he would watch my face and light another cigarette and find some use for my anger.

Nortier noticed it first and turned aside. Now Crevecoeur and I picked it up. There was something in the air. It was more a vibration than a sound. The vibrations got stronger and a wave of half a dozen helicopters swept across the northern perimeter from the direction of town. They split into two groups, a pincer movement round the burning wreckage. They touched down, their rotors beating at the flames, sending smoke swirling in every direction. Soldiers spilled out. They carried automatic weapons, like soldiers the world over, fighting fire with fire.

'Fourteen minutes,' Crevecoeur said, taking a peep at his watch. 'Not too bad.'

'Who are they?' Nortier asked.

'The cavalry,' Crevecoeur snapped at him again. 'How should I know what unit? They're too bloody late. They should have been here on security guard. It's no good playing soldiers now.'

'Why not?' Nortier said. 'If it's a terrorist attack they could still be around.'

I saw Crevecoeur stiffen. He dropped his cigarette and lifted his head to scan the skyline of the terminal building. He'd been a target once already today and there might be a new threat, a figure with a rifle. A sniper chooses a roof for preference because nothing obscures his aim and he can escape in any direction.

'Do you have a car here?'

'Yes.'

'Let's use it.'

I hesitated a moment too long for Crevecoeur's patience.

'Use your brains, Cody. There's been a bomb attack. Those soldiers there are going to seal the airport off and round up every suspicious character. Nobody arouses more suspicion than a foreigner. They're going to put the Deschampsneufs passport under a microscope. Then they'll get onto Paris to confirm it's authentic. And when the Authorities there tell them it's stolen, you're going to be slammed under the bright lights and squeezed until there's not a drop of sweat left in you.'

'You said French Immigration didn't know the passport was illegal.'

'One phone call would change that.'

He moved off towards the carpark, his narrow shoulders slicing through the crowd, his raincoat flapping at his knees.

9

'Not the journalist.'

Crevecoeur didn't give a damn that Nortier was within easy earshot. Nortier felt the same disdain for him.

'We'll have to come back tomorrow. We won't get sense out of anyone today. If you drop me at the *Hebdo* office, I'll tell Taoufik to come out with his camera.'

'*Croque-mort*,' Crevecoeur muttered.

It was a schoolboys' squabble. I unlocked the driver's door and got in. This was the two-door model Renault 5. Crevecoeur and Nortier both went round to the passenger's side and Crevecoeur rapped his knuckles on the glass. I was staring straight ahead through the windscreen. A helicopter had lifted off and was making a sweep on the far side of the terminal building. It curved away and sun glinted off the gun barrel poking through the open portal. A second helicopter rose and clattered over to the hangar Nortier and I had visited earlier. Someone was giving orders. Someone's brain had started to work. Crevecoeur banged on the roof of the car while I stared at a third helicopter making for the perimeter that was marked by eucalyptus trees. It swirled through black smoke and was swallowed up. Crevecoeur walked round to my side and made signs to wind down the window.

'What is it?'

'You've gone out of your stupid woman's mind. In about two minutes from now they're going to send soldiers over here to seal off the exit road. You're going to be scooped up. Let's get moving.'

'But you don't want to travel with Nortier.'

'No. He's a journalist. I want you to drive me somewhere, but not if he can see who I'm going to meet.'

'He won't. He's blind.'

'What?' Crevecoeur jerked upright to glare over the car

at the other man. He'd been made to look a fool and resented Nortier even more.

A fourth helicopter lifted off and turned towards us and drummed thirty metres above our heads over to the runway. It followed the runway, going slowly, as if someone might have dug a trench and be hiding in it. Crevecoeur turned to watch it. Suppose we were scooped up – what would his position be? A Chief Inspector of the French Sûreté, a terrorist bomb attack – someone would link the events. The Chief Inspector would be here on business and the Tunisians might turn very nasty if it had been hidden from them.

'I don't care if he is blind. He's not deaf and I'll be giving you instructions.'

'That's another thing I don't like about you,' I told him. 'You think you can order me about.'

A man in some sort of uniform with a peaked cap was watching us. Crevecoeur saw him and ducked down.

'Cody, that man in uniform . . .' Then he broke off.

'Antoine.'

We were joined by Jules who had changed into slacks and a sweatshirt. He nodded to me, ran his eyes over Crevecoeur who was bending down so intimately to speak to me, and went over to Nortier. So the matter was resolved: Nortier arranged to go back to town with Jules, Crevecoeur got in the front seat of the Renault. It wasn't so he could sit near me. He didn't want to fantasize about my profile. He wanted to hit the handle and bundle into the ditch if a motorbike swerved past with the pillion-passenger pointing a machine-pistol. That was natural: it was still only twenty minutes since the bomb that had nearly killed him.

'That man in the peaked cap,' Crevecoeur began on him again. 'Why is he waving you down?'

I took my foot off the accelerator and the car slowed. The man in the peaked cap blocked the exit to the car-park.

'Don't stop,' Crevecoeur said.

'I'm not running him down.'

'Go over the flower beds.'

There were scruffy geraniums, ox-eye daisies and irises. The flower beds were no problem but the kerbstone was high. The man obligingly stepped aside, holding out his hand.

'Keep going,' Crevecoeur said, but I had already stopped.

'One hundred and fifty millimes.'

I gave the attendant the coins and he passed a ticket through the window.

'You should pay before you park.'

There was a bombed plane out there, corpses, dying people, army, helicopters, raging fire, a pall of smoke. But he had his own priorities.

'Jesus,' Crevecoeur said, and stretched to try and get the kinks out of his nerves. He had his attaché case on his knees. He fiddled with a combination lock and took out a sheet of paper. It had what looked like typed directions but he turned the paper face down so I couldn't see. The whole of the man was in that gesture: I was to drive him somewhere but I would be told where bit by bit. He said: 'Do you know the highway to Gafsa?'

'The airport road joins it.'

'When we get to it turn left.' He hunched round to check the rear window and faced forward again.

'Where are we going?'

'To see a man. Don't let's waste any more time.'

We didn't waste any more words either. We drove five kilometres in silence. Crevecoeur turned up a corner of his piece of paper with the caution of a poker player inspecting his hole card. He studied the instructions and said: 'Take that road off past the wind-pump.' It was a dirt road that led through olive plantations. Olives look romantic on a hillside in Provence; here they were grown like corn, disciplined rows on flat land. They were wide spaced, with the earth between rough ploughed and bare. You could say much the same for the road. We bounced and lurched as far as a concrete bridge over a dry watercourse. A sign on the bridge read: Oued Kefiri. Montgomery's Desert Rats would have called it a Wadi. A track ran beside the *oued*.

Crevecoeur had been checking the distance from the instrument panel. He consulted his directions and said: 'Turn left before the bridge. Drive slowly, will you.'

There was no choice. The *oued* was dry now but in winter

it had flooded the track, abandoning small boulders. Eddies had scoured potholes. You could break an axle if you let your speed drift up. I kept the car in second gear. The pink-flowered tips of oleanders flicked at the windscreen. A wild fig had dropped a branch but a vehicle tougher than mine had driven over it, crushing the wood.

Crevecoeur took out a pistol, an old Browning like the one I'd lifted from him in Berlin two years ago. He wasn't getting me to a remote spot to put a bullet in my brain. You don't need typed instructions for that. On the other hand he had refused to have Nortier along, as if he didn't want a witness. I checked and the safety catch was on.

I slowed because I'd seen it.

'Stop.'

I braked. I kept the engine running because it might be necessary to leave fast.

Crevecoeur looked at his instructions again. 'It must be,' he said. 'This is the place for the rendezvous.'

On the right was the dried up *oued*. On the left, perhaps forty metres away, was a VW Passat. Its tyre tracks showed across the ploughed earth. There was nobody to be seen. Nothing moved. Crevecoeur got out his packet of Gitanes and lit up. Smoke drifted slowly out of the window in the still air.

'Switch off the engine.'

The silence was broken by the ticking of the engine as it cooled. Somewhere a bird called, not in alarm, not at human intruders. No sound out of place. Yet there was a weight pressing down on my shoulders: menace, I supposed. Crevecoeur reached out for the driving mirror and angled it so that he could see back along the track we'd driven. His eyes flicked round: the oleanders along the *oued*, a palm tree at the bend, the Passat, the olive trees as regimented as graves in a war cemetery, the mirror, the Passat again.

'Who was the meeting with?'

Crevecoeur frowned at the question and squeezed out an answer: 'Local contact man. Maalej.'

'Maalej a good man? Reliable?'

'He was a *contractant*.' In the French Security world a *contractant* is not a permanent officer working his way up the career structure. Instead he has a contract, renewable annu-ally, and can be used as the occasion demands. But Maalej would still have been given positive clearance. '*Is*, I should have said,' Crevecoeur corrected himself. He glanced at me and away to the car once more. 'Yes, a good man.'

We sat a full two minutes.

'You're going to have to take a look,' I said.

Crevecoeur put out his cigarette but still made no move to get out.

'You agreed Maalej was a good man,' I said. 'So he won't have gone for a stroll or fallen asleep. This is how I read the situation. That Passat is parked off the track under an olive tree. That's sensible. It's mid-morning, the sun already burn-ing hot. An olive gives broken shade, which is better than nothing. The thing that worries me is that the olive is shading to the rear of the Passat, not the car itself. The inference is that Maalej drove it under the branches some hours ago. Since then the sun has climbed and the area of shade has shifted. That car must be like an oven now but Maalej hasn't moved it. The question is *why*. Agreed? Has he gone? Is he tied up? What's happened?'

Crevecoeur nodded. He lit another cigarette. It was the last in the packet and he tossed it out of the window. Then he opened the door, retrieved the packet and flicked it back into the car. He seemed to notice the sun for the first time and wiped away sweat that came in a trickle down his cheek. He tore off his raincoat, which any normal person would have done an hour ago. The coat followed the empty packet, thrown onto the rear seat. He got back in the car.

'I arrived from France in an Air Force plane in the early hours of this morning. The Tunisian authorities wouldn't grant us permission to fly all the way down to Sfax, so I had to kick my heels at Tunis Airport. If I could have flown here direct I'd have made the rendezvous arranged for 6.15. I'm four and a half hours late. Maalej's car is here but, as you pointed out, it hasn't been moved to keep in the shade.'

'You didn't warn Maalej you would be late?'

'Not possible.'

'Well, his car is there and you'll have to find out why he hasn't moved it.'

Crevecoeur wasn't happy about that. He sighed and said: 'You'd better turn the car.'

I made a five-point turn in the narrow track and headed the car back the way we'd come. This time I left the engine running. Crevecoeur had the Browning in his lap and he eased the safety catch off. That journalist in East Berlin – Pasquier, that had been his name – must have been this close to Crevecoeur when he'd been killed. If Crevecoeur had shot him.

Crevecoeur took another deep breath and stubbed out his cigarette.

'Okay, let's get down to the nitty-gritty.' He said it, not in French, but in his American-accented English. I don't know why. Wanted some Hollywood toughness to rub off on him maybe.

He got out and closed the door gently. On second thoughts he opened it and left it ajar. I had never known him so nervous.

He bent to scrutinize the track. There were tyre patterns in the dirt where an earlier car had turned and driven away. Crevecoeur straightened up and looked at me. His eyes were bleak. He said nothing but walked away across the ploughed earth. He didn't bother to raise his pistol or use the trees for cover. When he got to the Passat he stood for a moment staring in through the open window. He put a hand through the window and when he drew it out there was something dark on it. He reached for a branch and wiped his fingers on the leaves. He rubbed and rubbed but couldn't seem to get clean.

Crevecoeur walked back, very stiff. He got in beside me and sat staring straight ahead. His mind was on something else. He rubbed his hands on his trousers and I don't think he was aware of doing it. Back and forth, back and forth, leaving streaks of brownish-red.

'Well?'

Creveoeur said simply: 'He's dead.'

'Dead? Is that all you're going to say?'

It seemed it was. He fished in his pockets, forgetting the cigarette packet was empty. He leant over to the back seat and shook the pack, just to make certain.

'*Merde*,' he said.

Maalej dead, no cigarettes in the packet, what a day.

'He was a good man and he's dead and you've got nothing to say, not even that you're sorry. But of course they're all good at the Sûreté Nationale, even the traitors and the double-crossers. Did one of your own kind betray Maalej?'

He was rough when he turned. I'd succeeded in making him very angry.

'Understand this, Cody. The security of France is my job. I'm in a war, a dirty little war. I'm up against the enemies of the state and, yes, some of them end up dead. Or sometimes one of our side. I don't lose any sleep over it. Not any more. It's them or it's me and I've got to be bloody fast to stay alive, faster than Maalej was. People spit at me. They've always got a label to hang round my neck: fascist, imperialist, class enemy. I'm the obstacle to the triumph of this year's fashionable cause. I'm anti-women or anti-black or anti-peace. The other side hates me too. I'm betraying the true patriots, I've gone soft on bearded revolutionaries. What difference does it make? In the end they're all anti-me. So I'm alive and Maalej is dead. What do you expect me to do? Grovel, sob, apologize?'

'Why are you shouting?' I said. 'Who are you trying to convince?'

We sat in silence. He'd crushed the Gitane packet and now he was trying to smooth it flat. At length he said: 'Maalej was shot from behind. I suppose someone sat in the front asking questions, someone else in the back with a gun against his neck. When they'd done, the trigger was pulled.'

PDS killed in Paris, a bomb blast at Sfax Airport, a bullet in the back of the neck of a man called Maalej. I had no doubt all three violent acts were linked because I believed Crevecoeur and I were travelling on parallel tracks.

I felt punchy, like an old boxer on the ropes. I was unable to grasp the power and ruthlessness of the people who had hired Borries. Crevecoeur was still smoothing out the Gitane packet when he looked sharply out of the window.

'Get the hell out of it,' he shouted.

He swung his door open and two black carrion crows hopped away from the Passat. He got out and strode over the ploughed land, waving his arms and shouting and the crows flew as far as the next tree. Crevecoeur opened the door of the Passat and wound up its window. He went round to the far side and wound up the window there too. He came stumbling back across the furrows and slammed the door of our car. I eased my foot off the clutch and we moved down the track, away from the Passat with its dead man.

'Odd they didn't wait for you to make the rendezvous.'

'There was no need. They were going to get me at the airport.'

'And by now they'll know they didn't.'

Crevecoeur put a hand to his mouth, as if it felt naked without a cigarette. 'Drive faster, will you.'

I took the coast road going back. I didn't want to pass the airport turn-off again. By now there'd be checkpoints and police with angry eyes and awkward questions. But you could tell where the airport was: coming in through the outskirts of Sfax a smudge of smoke darkened the sky to our left.

'Drive down to the railway station,' Crevecoeur said. I didn't for one moment believe he was going away. When we got there he directed me left for a block and left again for two more blocks. He said nothing else until: 'He wants you to stop.'

The rifle had been slung across his back but he shifted it as our car approached. He strode out of the candy-striped sentry hut waving his free hand. 'No entry, it is forbidden,' he shouted. The anger ran in furrows down his face because his petty authority was being challenged.

Crevecoeur got out of the car and pushed an identity document into the soldier's face. 'You can pass, *monsieur*, but not the car.'

My sentiments exactly.

The sign on the gate read: *Cercle des Officiers*. The fence was iron railings two metres high topped with revolving spikes. Through the railings I saw grass, unblemished green, the fairest lawn in all Sfax. There were palm trees like roman candles. The hibiscus had deep red blooms begging to be tucked behind a girl's ear. The officers' clubhouse was in French colonial style, white painted, a wide verandah outside where men in uniform lounged at tables. Children ran and shouted on the gravel among the parked Peugeots and Citroëns. Two boys played one of those football tables that small establishments in French villages install so they can call themselves the Café des Sports.

Crevecoeur ducked down to speak through my window. 'I must go and see their Security chief. Colonel Riahi is his name, if that's the way he gets his tongue round it. Imagine, if I was doing my job in this country I'd be a Colonel. Maybe a General. Riahi will have had a report that I arrived in Tunis on an Air Force plane and flew down here this morning so I'd better pay a courtesy visit.'

'What will you tell him? The bomb at the airport intended for you? Your agent shot in the back of the neck out by the *oued*?'

He shook his head. 'Some fairytale about hashish smuggling, drugs earning the big money for the crime syndicates in France, curse of our age, blah blah, have another glass of mint tea, my esteemed Colonel.'

When Crevecoeur smiled, the creases in his face deepened.

'I'm a regular little ambassador, oiling the machinery of international police relations.'

'Yes,' I said, watching his eyes. 'What's the classic definition of an ambassador? Do you remember? An honest man sent abroad to lie for his country?'

The smile never faded. The creases were like cracks in the ice where humanity had tripped and fallen out of sight.

'Where are you staying in Sfax?'

'Hôtel du Centre.'

He raised an eyebrow and was gone.

10

She was a prostitute, quite young. The poor kid couldn't
have been more than twenty. She carried the advertising
signs of her trade: twin circles of rouge on her cheeks, a thick
blanket of lipstick. Perhaps the layer of lipstick was to
discourage men from kissing her mouth. No one would want
to work his way through that goo, surely.

'*Voilà, une limonade bien fraîche.*'

'*Merci, monsieur.*'

'*Il ne fait pas trop chaud pour vous?*'

'*Pas du tout. Il y a un courant d'air maintenant.*'

'*Oui, mais au Sahara . . .*' The waiter puffed out his
cheeks and walked back into the café.

Maybe in the Sahara it was unbearably hot. But I sat in
the shade of palm trees. Seventy-two hours before I'd been
in Paris and there'd been potted palms outside the café on
the corner of rue de l'Eperon and boulevard St-Germain.
They'd whispered of lazing in the warm south and brought
back memories of kidnapping, violence and death and damn
Crevecoeur: he *knew* about me. He hadn't been surprised to
see me at the airport.

Mid-afternoon, the devil's time.

The prostitute sat at a table in the sun. Three men sat with
her. Pimps, friends, old clients? They stared at her, mouths
open like panting dogs. She was pouring out a tirade and the
compelling thing was that the girl was a deaf-mute. Her
hands flew in quick gestures; grunts came like punctuation
to the story. One of her companions interrupted with a
gesture that looked rude in any language and the girl cuffed
his ear and snatched his cigarette and began to smoke it. The
men at the table fell about laughing. She didn't.

It wasn't chance that had brought Crevecoeur to Sfax at
the same time as me. In our trade there's no such thing as
chance. If you believe there is, you won't last long. Survival

of the fittest sees to that. *They were out to get me*, Crevecoeur had said after the bomb blast. And they'd known where the rdv was arranged and had got to Maalej before Crevecoeur did. The Sûreté was the least secure organization of its kind in the world. Crevecoeur had complained of it, always worked alone, and even so his movements had been known. Only impatience at the airport had saved his life. There must be a moral there.

The prostitute decided it was time for a promenade. She wore tight jeans and high heeled boots and a frilly yellow blouse that made her olive skin look sallow. She did a round of the café tables. She grunted and spoke her sign language and patted a cheek here, shook hands there. There was a patch of municipal garden to one side. A gardener had given up weeding a bed of cannas and moved into the shade of the palms. He slumped on a chair borrowed from the café and a squabble of sparrows near his feet kept him awake. The girl shook his hand, had a puff of his cigarette and returned to her original table.

There was only one way Crevecoeur could have known I was going to be in Sfax. Damn him, damn his ears. I finished the lemonade and called the waiter so I could pay.

The sound of typing stopped when I opened the door. I hadn't knocked but Nortier had heard the hinges. His head was at an angle, like a thrush listening for a worm.

'Taoufik?'

'It's me,' I said.

'You?' He swivelled in the chair. His eyes couldn't see but he wanted to face me. 'And who are you? Cody or Deschampsneufs? I thought perhaps you were from Alsace but perhaps you're not even French. Who are you?'

Michel, I never realized. In eight months more than your skin rubbed off on me, your accent too.

'I'm Suzanne Deschampsneufs. It's in my passport and driving licence and *carte d'identité*. Are you going to put my name in your paper?'

He seemed surprised. 'Why should I include you in a story about a bombing at Sfax Airport? You were with me at the time; we had just been enquiring about Borries.' He thought

91

a moment. 'Is the Chief Inspector looking for Borries too?'

'Something like that. We're travelling down parallel tracks. I'm convinced of that.'

He gestured with a hand. 'You might as well read what I've written.'

He gave me two and a half sides of A4, double-spaced. There were typing errors but no more than I make. The story was straightforward: things I'd told him, stuff he'd found out elsewhere. There was a bomb in a suitcase being loaded into the aircraft, the fuel tanker going up, dead and dying, mothers and babies crying, quotes from airline people, police, government officials. No mention of me or Crevecoeur. He ended with a 'high official source' speculating that the bomb had gone off prematurely because 'the next stage of the flight was to Tripoli and bombs and bullets are the Libyan way of discussing politics.' There was no love lost between these two countries.

I said: 'If the bomb really was intended to explode en route to Tripoli, then Crevecoeur wasn't the target.'

'Precisely what I'm saying. He's so stuffed with his own importance he imagines it was for him. There's no proof of that.'

'Is there any evidence it was intended for someone else?'

'What sort of evidence?'

'There'll be a passenger list. Any troublesome Libyan army colonels? Opponents of Gadafy returning from exile?' When Nortier didn't answer, I said: 'The thing is, you just don't like Crevecoeur.'

'I don't trust him or any of his tribe. They are an abomination in a civilized society.'

I didn't like Crevecoeur either. But I found myself defending him. 'It's people like him who watch for the bogeyman while we sleep. They exist in every society, civilized or not. They're not well paid. They never get publicly thanked. They don't always draw their pension. They're not heroes, not even to themselves. They've got no morality – couldn't afford it. Their code is a simple one: stay alive and do the job. And if that means the opposing party doesn't always stay alive, so be it.'

'Well, God help us all.'

'And you're wrong about that bomb blast. It was meant for Crevecoeur.'

'That's a guess. He's brainwashed you into believing in his importance.'

'I'm not in his fan club,' I said. 'But I drove him to a rendezvous ten or twelve kilometres from the airport and when we got there we found his contact in a car. He'd been murdered, shot in the back of the neck.'

'I've heard no reports of this.'

'Crevecoeur hasn't told the police or he'd have a lot of explaining to do.'

'So you leave a dead man to rot in a car. You do a lot for Crevecoeur.' Nortier got up and wandered round the office. He touched things, the corner of a desk, a telephone, a filing cabinet. 'But I imagine with the life you lead, you have to keep things sweet with the Chief Inspector.'   .

'Don't speak to me like that. Don't you dare.' I stopped Nortier in his tracks, confronted him. 'The first time I met Crevecoeur it was because I was a witness to a hit-and-run accident. I visited the victim in hospital and he died half an hour after I left him. I didn't murder him. But that didn't stop Crevecoeur coming round with his heavy squad.' Nortier didn't like my talking at him. He tried to turn aside and I stopped him with a hand. 'You get this straight. The jobs I do may be legal or illegal but they're moral. No one orders me to do something dirty. I'm being paid to find Borries. It's my belief that the people who employed Borries planted the bomb and shot that man. But there's nothing wrong in Ella Borries employing me to find her husband. Crevecoeur knows about me. He pressures me to do things like drive him to his rendezvous. But in the Sûreté they're all like that. They are vampires.' I had a sudden image of Crevecoeur's teeth when he smiled. 'They believe your life belongs to them and they suck your blood dry and toss away the husk when you've nothing more to give.'

I suppose my voice must have risen. Nortier's sneer had made me angry and my relationship with Crevecoeur always raised my blood pressure. I let go of Nortier's sleeve. There was silence between us, just the distant sounds of the afternoon traffic.

'That was well said.' Nortier's voice was soft. Curiously, he held out a hand for me to shake. 'Then we still have a deal?'

'I haven't broken it. You got a lift with Jules and I drove Crevecoeur ten kilometres out of my way. I brought him back to Sfax and dropped him. Then I came to see you. Our deal still stands.'

It was mutual self-interest: he had the local contacts, while I knew the background and provided the eyes.

'Tomorrow morning we'll go back to the airport and find where the Skyvan flew to. Right now I've got to put the paper to bed.'

I had dropped Crevecoeur but he hadn't dropped me.

I asked for my key at the reception desk and Miloud handed me an envelope. It was addressed to Mademoiselle Deschampsneufs. Inside was a note that said in its entirety: *Cody, meet me at the Restaurant Baghdad at 8 . . .* It wasn't signed. There's security for you. I'd never seen Crevecoeur's handwriting before but this was how I imagined it would look: tiny, even crabbed, sloping backwards. And those three dots at the end: a suggestion of unfinished business, a promise of something, I couldn't tell. Of course there was the faintest of possibilities someone else had left it.

'The man who gave you this note,' I said, 'was he tall and with a cramped face?'

Miloud gazed at me. He raised a hand and with a crooked finger beckoned me close. 'Room 23.'

'He's staying here?'

'Ssh.'

I wasn't close enough and he drew me in with that clawed hand.

'He gave no name, nothing is filled in the register, so he is not officially staying here. He paid a week in advance and gave me something extra so I would tell nobody. A *pourboire* he called it. I don't drink. I am a good Moslem. But I accepted because he is a gentleman. He meant no offence. He said I must let him know if anyone enquires about him.'

'But he didn't give you his name.'

'He said if any person asked about a Frenchman staying

94

here, or about a man with a thin face and narrow shoulders, then I was to deny it but warn him afterwards. He said if someone did ask and I warned him, he would be most generous. A gentleman, you see. I tell you because you are already acquainted with this monsieur and also because he leaves you a note.'

Miloud laid his hand on my wrist. He stared in my face. He lacked the final courage to leer because of my phone calls to Michel or to wink because of Crevecoeur's pursuit of me.

'And has anybody asked for him?'

'No.' There was a note of regret in his voice.

He brightened when I slipped two five-dinar notes across the countertop. 'If anybody does ask for him, be so kind as to tell me too.'

'But certainly,' he said, 'at once.' He sat back in the chair and prepared to wait for the coming riches.

Never mind its name, the Baghdad was very French. The menu by the entrance was written in the same purple ink as old-fashioned Paris restaurants. I stood by the menu, staring at the plate glass of the window. The wall of the medina opposite was reflected: battlements, small turrets, old stonework bleeding with bougainvillea. Taxis, buses and trucks battled it out in the dusk. Other reflections were like ghosts: figures in spooky robes, student spirits, fleeting shapes riding bicycles or hawking into the gutter or peddling buckets of eggs. Under the wall of the medina an ice cream stall served half a dozen shadows.

I walked into the restaurant and saw Crevecoeur across the room. He had his back to the door. You wouldn't think he was in danger of his life or that his local contact had been murdered that morning. But a back can be anonymous, a face never. In any case there was a mirror on the wall and his eyes had been watching me from the moment I entered.

'I've ordered this,' Crevecoeur said when I sat down. This was a bottle of wine in an ice bucket. 'It is a *muscat sec* from Kelibia, all the fragrance of the grape but with the sugar completely fermented out. It's not bad. Not as good as a *muscat* from Alsace, of course.'

'Of course.' And had my Michel left early for his week-end

in Alsace? I would ring when I got back to the hotel in case he couldn't face the *cousines*. The girls in Paris don't have warts and moustaches. Why did I call him *my* Michel? We none of us own others. Tell that to Crevecoeur who always assumes rights of ownership.

'They're making a big effort with their wines here. It's not like Algeria where the French farmers grew nothing but *gros rouge* to ship to France. Now what was the name of that French scientist who tried to help the Algerians find other uses for their vineyards?'

'Ladouceur,' I told him. He hadn't forgotten. He was simply reminding me of my past. Ladouceur had ended his life on a platform at an election rally in the Rond-Point. A sniper's bullet hit his chest. I hadn't been able to save him. Crevecoeur hadn't even tried.

'I don't think much came of his ideas. The Algerians still have a lot of vineyards. They find it simplest to export their hangovers to the Soviet Union.'

The lecture was interrupted by the waiter with the menu. It was French from *artichaut vinaigrette* to *mousse au chocolat chantilly*.

'If you take my advice you'll stay with the fish. They have the best in the Mediterranean here.'

'You've been in Sfax before?'

'The *crevettes royales*.' Crevecoeur turned to the waiter. 'Are they this morning's catch?'

'This afternoon's, monsieur.'

'There,' Crevecoeur turned back to me. 'You see?'

Maybe he'd been in Sfax before, maybe he hadn't. He'd evaded the question. If I pressed he'd say: oh yes, I passed through on vacation once. And if I pressed again, about this business, he'd top up his glass and ask how it was that I found myself here while these terrorist attacks took place. I'd end up feeling responsible for the killings.

We ate this afternoon's prawns. They were huge and grilled on skewers. He asked me about Nortier and I repeated the story that would lead tomorrow's *Hebdo*. He raised an eyebrow. 'So it's a Libyan political squabble. Fancy that. I can sleep more easily tonight.'

We ate red mullet and little fritters of courgette. It was

typical of Crevecoeur to find the best restaurant in town on his first evening.

'Why did you invite me to dinner?' I asked.

'Strange town, lonely man, attractive woman.'

'Another reason.'

'I had hoped we might save it for the coffee stage.' He shrugged. 'Let me test you on your ABC.' *Abécédaire* was the little French nursery mode he used.

'A is for Antoine Nortier, B is for Bohme, C is for Crevecoeur.'

'Bohme? Who is Bohme?'

'You don't know? You surprise me.' Bohme is my Alsatian, my Michel.

'Let's skip on a bit. MNOP,' he prompted. 'What comes after P?'

'Q. Why are we playing games?'

Crevecoeur laid down his fork and stared at me. He simply watched my face. Q was the letter after P, wasn't it? What had I got wrong? He was waiting. Then I understood: it wasn't the alphabet we were running through, he wanted initials. In his *abécédaire* it went PDS. You bastard, I thought.

'How long have you been tapping my phone?'

Deep down I'd known it. I'd worked it all out while I sipped lemonade and a young prostitute had tried to drum up custom. Crevecoeur hadn't been surprised to see me at Sfax Airport because he knew I was looking for Borries. He'd known that because he'd tapped my line and heard the call where Ella Borries gave her name and mentioned the initials PDS. I'd headed her off but it had been too late. I felt anger flood through me all over again.

Crevecoeur seemed to be holding his breath. 'Don't worry. I shan't tell your mother your little secrets.'

'How many months?' I asked. 'Or is it years? Do you think I'm a danger to the state?'

His lips thinned in a smile. I thought of all the phone calls with Michel and Crevecoeur rewinding the tapes and playing them again to listen. Crevecoeur wasn't a peeping tom, he was a listening tom. What's the word for that? A bugger? Did it send a little shiver through him? Perhaps all he *could* do was listen and imagine.

'Cody, listen to what I say. I'm saving your life. Do you understand? Get out of this, go back to Paris. Better still, go and lie on a beach somewhere and cultivate a tan. Anything, just get out. You're in deep water way out of your depth.'

I said: 'I can swim.'

'That wife – the German woman with the American first name . . .'

'You haven't forgotten her name.'

'She hired you. How much?'

'Haven't you had her under the bright lights?'

'How much?'

'Ten thousand francs.'

'Is that all her husband's worth to her?'

Not a question, just an insult. I had watched Ella count out the money. She'd insisted, right there at the top of the Montparnasse Tower. She had it in her bag and couldn't wait to give it to me. It was as if it would bring Bert back quicker.

'You've become cheap.'

I felt it with his eyes on me.

'You used to be classy,' he went on.

The hell with Crevecoeur. He made me want to spew. He made me want to put great red weals down his cheeks with my nails. He was a manipulator, a self-centred bastard who tricked and cheated and lied. He was the king; the rest of us were pawns.

'Why did you invite me to dinner?' I asked again. 'Just to be rude?'

'I've already said. You've got to get away. It's a friendly warning I'm giving you. You're messing with things that are right out of your league. Ten thousand francs buys you now. You've become small time.'

I should have dumped the prawn shells in his lap. I should have flung my wine in his face and stormed out. Instead I swallowed my bile because there were things he could tell me.

Ten thousand was all Ella had had. It was as if she had broken open her piggy bank. She was a woman, heavily pregnant, husband missing. She was worried to death and she'd hired me. 'Is it enough?' she'd said. 'It's all I've got.'

Plane tickets, hotels, car hire – I wasn't cheap, I was doing it for nothing. She was desperate and I wanted to help.

Crevecoeur took out a packet of cigarettes. 'The trouble with flying courtesy of the Air Force is there's no stewardess to bring you dutyfree cigarettes.' He lit up and turned the pack over on the tablecloth. It had a picture of a smiling Arab woman swirling her robes as she walked through an archway. The name on the pack was Supérieure. He coughed. '*Vachement inférieure.*'

'Who hired Borries?' I asked. 'You know.'

'Your fixer didn't tell you?'

'He was dead by the time I got to his place on Monday night. But he'd already had a visit from the police.'

'Yes,' Crevecoeur said and studied the writing on his cigarette. 'He was alive when I saw him but none too happy. He talked a little, just enough to keep me from taking him into custody. Wish I had now. He can't tell me any more. And he kept no papers, do you know that? No contracts, no accounts.'

I thought back to our only meeting. 'He had a card index. He kept it in the safe. I know that because he took out the card with my name on it.'

'Not any more. Gone.'

'You mean stolen?'

'No. He'd become computerized. There's a terminal on his desk. It's connected into the telephone system. You have to know what number to dial before the terminal functions. That number died with him. As for the tapes or floppy disks, they could be anywhere. He'd bought the best protection money could buy – politicians, police, mafia. But I impressed on him this was too big to be hushed up. So he talked a little. One of the things he confirmed was that he'd given your name to Ella Borries. So I went to see you, to warn you not to get involved. You were out.'

'You waited in my apartment?'

'Yes.'

'Last Monday night?'

He blew a smoke ring.

'How did you get in? Did Madame Boyer unlock my door or did you break in?'

He blew another smoke ring and stuck his finger through it. I'd thought it was the people who'd killed PDS who were waiting for me. I'd seen those curtains drawn and I'd never gone up.

'So tell me: who hired Borries?'

He shook his head. 'This one's not for you, Cody. It's too critical and too terrifying. I can't tell you what's involved.'

'It's to do with the security of France, or you wouldn't be interested. And to do with Tunisia, or you wouldn't be here. Did you tell the Tunisian Security Colonel?'

'I couldn't trust him with this.'

'If it's so big, why are you on your own?'

'I have been picked by the very highest authority. He knows I can be trusted. There is not one other Frenchman he knows that about. A single leak or mistake at this moment would be a catastrophe.'

'The people who hired Borries,' I hammered on. 'They're political? A revolutionary group? What's the name of the group? Every group has a name – it's part of the magic of revolution.'

'God, you're stubborn,' he said, jabbing out his cigarette. 'Why do I bother to try and save your life? I just don't want to be the one who's called to the mortuary to recognize the body on the slab. Maybe there wouldn't be enough to recognize.'

His eyes dropped down. I was wearing a black and gold shirt, a present from Michel. *My tiger* he'd called me when I'd put it on. I'd brought it with me as a link to him. I'll never be able to wear it again. The top two buttons were undone. Crevecoeur's eyes made it three buttons, four buttons, five. I don't know whether he pictured my body underneath or simply smashed bloody flesh. I don't understand the dark currents that flow through him. But I felt like that girl at the café this afternoon, the men staring with their mouths open. For me the shirt was irredeemably soiled. I would have to throw it away.

'Where are you going?' Crevecoeur asked.

'I'm taking a walk. The medina maybe.'

'I can't come with you. I've got to go back to the hotel and make out a report.'

'I didn't expect you to come.'

'You're a woman.'

'What's that supposed to mean? Alone in the medina at night? Is that it?'

He shrugged. We were standing on the corner of the street just past the restaurant. It was a warm night and the door to the Bar des Amis stood open. They opened the door to the Café Charlot on summer evenings too, to get a breath of air and entice in passers-by. I wouldn't be enticed into the Bar des Amis: men stood in groups gulping rough red wine straight from the bottle.

Crevecoeur said: 'You can take care of yourself, I suppose.'

'Then what do you mean? That I'm a woman and you're a man?'

'Women are either boring or hell. You're not boring, Cody.'

That is how he left me, striding along the pavement towards the Hôtel du Centre. A tall man, thin, an academic you might guess, until you saw his eyes. I watched him out of sight and turned and walked the other way.

There was a stall at the gateway doing no trade at all. Night had come down and the medina was deserted. The pedlar had wicker baskets of roast chick peas and seeds and nuts and a pair of old brass scales for weighing them. He turned his face as I passed and it glinted. I went back and bought a twist of watermelon seeds, not because I was hungry but because the glint intrigued me. He had one glass eye and it caught the light from a lamp on the wall and winked, icy and dead. That is the detail that stays in my mind. I can recall the glitter of that glass eye vividly because at that instant I heard it. There was a crump from the centre of town, then a second and a third. It sounded like blasting in a distant quarry.

There are no quarries in the centre of Sfax.

11

A vulture soared into the night sky.

Low cloud had rolled in from the sea and giant wings beat against it. Black and midnight grey, full of menace and death, the vulture grew by the second.

The pedlar had clambered out from behind the stall to look. He spoke and I couldn't understand what he said. But I understood the meaning of that vulture swirling above the city. I dropped the paper twist of seeds and began to run.

I was sprinting across avenue Belhaouane when there was a flash so vivid it seared my brain. The vulture changed to yellow and orange, patches of colour that flickered and consumed themselves and boiled up again. That vulture was made of smoke but it looked heavy, solid.

People stared at the sky. Some ran in panic. Others were drawn by the vulture, for vultures hover over bloodshed, and death is a dark attraction.

The bank of low clouds was lit now as the flames danced higher. Shouts, footsteps, the clamour of emergency vehicles were in my ears. At the corner of place Hedi Chaker I hit someone's shoulder and we both went sprawling. I was up and running hard through overturned café tables and chairs and then I was brought up short at the edge of the crowd. The Hôtel du Centre was an inferno. I had no idea a building could burn so fast.

A siren approached from the far side. An army jeep bumped on the pavement and slewed round to a halt. A soldier had a two-way radio to his face, talking into it.

The army was quick but the fire had been quicker. The old timbers crackled and I could feel the heat on my face, even across the square. The fire seemed to have started upstairs in one of the bedrooms. That's the easiest: you just hide the explosives and petrol in your luggage, tip the porter who complained of the weight, and after the door is closed you rig your bang at leisure.

I began pushing through the crowd.

An ambulance arrived and two uniformed men got out. They went to consult with the army. A soldier got on the nose of his jeep and waved an arm in the air. I think he was shouting at the crowd to get back. Words were lost among the roar of the flames, the cries and the high-pitched wailing of women. Glass shattered as a window went out. Against a background of smoke and flames I saw a man scramble on to the ledge of the window and teeter for a moment. Courage or panic triumphed. He jumped. Screams from the crowd went out to him.

The ambulance klaxon had been left on and sobbed for the victims.

The fire engine arrived last. It got stuck at the corner where parked cars blocked the street. Soldiers lifted the cars bodily onto the pavement to clear a passage. The fire engine nosed through and then I lost interest in the firefighters.

I edged through to the front of the crowd. I had a grandstand view. Flames licked as high as the gutters at the front of the hotel. At the side there was only smoke caught by the wind. Billows of it poured out of a broken window but I could see the whole length of the second floor. Six little balconies, six pairs of french windows, six rooms on this side. The shutters of the second room were closed. The slats slanted upwards but there was light on them reflected from inside. That was room number 15, my room. Before going out I had switched the lights off.

Crevecoeur: the thought jumped into my brain.

The wind gusted from the sea, catching the dark-stained smoke, spiralling it down into the crowd.

'Did they all get out?'

'What?'

There was a policeman in front of me. He swung round at my question.

'The guests – did they all escape?'

'God has taken some.'

He meant Allah. The policeman had spoken French to me. He jerked away and yelled Arabic at a teenager running

103

with something tucked under his arm, screaming abuse at the kid above the crackle of the flames. Allah kicked the old building and sparks showered up, angry as wasps.

Crevecoeur hadn't come back to the hotel to do paper-work. He'd asked where I was going and when I said for a walk, he'd come back and let himself into my room to nose among my things. That was the kind of man he was. He could never leave me alone.

Salaud, I hissed to myself, bastard.

As I stared up, the lights went out. My room went dark, the whole hotel was blacked out as the circuit was destroyed by flames.

Bastard, I thought again, as I stared and stared. The poor bastard. He'd gone to search my room and been trapped in the blaze. Oh God, that's the worst end, choking on fumes, breathing in flames, helpless as your skin blackens, burning to death. It shouldn't happen to a dog, not even a Security cop.

That building held me in a fierce grip. Crevecoeur. He was inside and I hated him and damned him to hell but not to flames scorching his lungs and turning his hair to a torch. Crevecoeur. I felt the pull of the man inside. I couldn't simply stand and stare. He was inside and screaming and beating at the flames as the sparks fell on his clothes and face and hands. There were hundreds of people gawping at the spectacle like a Roman mob watching the lions tear the Christians apart in the Colosseum. But they didn't know the man inside that building. I did.

'Crevecoeur.'

'What?' The cop wheeled round at my voice and I ducked the other way past him. Firemen were everywhere, a couple with an extension ladder, another pair hauling a hose. I dodged between them, a voice sharp behind me, a glow on faces turning, a downdraught bringing furnace heat from a gaping window above. Palm trees lined the pavement and a dry frond danced as it took fire.

I stumbled into the jaws of hell, sparks stinging my skin. I dragged the black and gold shirt over my head to stop my hair catching alight.

'Crevecoeur.'

He was a bastard. Why had he gone to my room? Did he

think I had information about Borries there? Perhaps he just wanted to bury his face among my clothes. There was a twist in his nature I didn't understand. I hated him. I didn't want him to die.

A stretcher came out, two bearers coughing, soot on their cheeks, tears streaking it. One of the bearers shouted as I bent to the shape on the canvas. The head jerked away from me and back. Blood streamed from the gash above one eye and had stained the shoulders of his suit. Miloud, not Crevecoeur.

A hand clutched at my shoulder and dragged me back into the street. I swung round to see an army lieutenant, his uniform turned the colour of vomit by the flames.

'Keep out of there.' He bawled it in my face.

But there's a man trapped inside. He's a ruthless scheming bastard who'd make use of you and drop you without a moment's hesitation. I've got to save his life.

I jabbed a finger high in the air where a window spewed flame. As the officer glanced up I kicked at a kneecap and twisted away from his grip. I went through the gaping hotel entrance again and was almost blinded by smoke. It was a thick November fog eddying down the stairs, graveyard grey, lights all fused, just pulsing illumination from the emergency vehicles outside, blue chasing orange, blue, orange, blue, orange. Crazy rhythm.

Coughing came from above. It was the sound of someone convulsing, forcing out the smoke, dragging it back in when he had to breathe, coughing it out again. I was retching too. My eyes were streaming. I spat on my hands and slapped at sparks. I moved towards the sound of coughing. It was on the left, where the staircase was. Smoke poured down with the stench of scorching paint and dusty floorboards and the acrid fumes of linoleum and the sweetish smell of roasting don't think about it.

I'm saving your life, he'd said, *get out of this, go back to Paris.*

He'd warned me but it was him they were after, the employers of Borries, the murderers of PDS. They'd tried with the bomb at the airport; they were succeeding with this. There were only moments left to get Crevecoeur out.

On the third or fourth step I raised my head, saw a figure on the landing. He was stumbling away from the stairs, confused and blinded.

'Crevecoeur, it's this way.'

He turned at my shout, hands over his face, protecting his eyes and nose from the smoke.

I was choking, giddy with fumes, spasms shaking my body as I began to vomit. Smoke is least dense low down and I crouched on all fours. But smoke was everywhere and there was no escape. I made another two steps, crawling. Water trickled past my knees from ruptured plumbing.

'This way.'

He swayed at the sound of my voice. I knew what was going to happen, rehearsed it in my mind, saw it in slow motion. I rose to my feet to catch him as he fell. It was as if someone had put a rifle bullet in his back. He threw up his arms, crumpled at the knees and came tumbling down the stairs. He was far heavier than I expected and he caught me off balance, sweeping me backwards with him. We went down in an avalanche and landed in a jolt against the reception desk. His body was on top of mine, his face turned towards me.

Then it all went. The noise, the smoke, the furnace glow span into oblivion. My last thought as I blacked out: So I've failed. It wasn't Crevecoeur at all.

I opened my eyes and found the face bending over me.

'What is your name?'

'Cody.'

'What?'

'Deschampsneufs.'

The cop glared at me. His face was out of a nightmare of the future, flashing blue and orange. Or was that inside my head? I was concussed, rambling. The world didn't hold together or make sense.

'You could have been killed.'

'That man who fell down the stairs on top of me . . .' I brought the face back: pockmarked and swarthy. I had failed. I hadn't saved Crevecoeur.

'He's in the ambulance. Is he your husband?'

106

I shook my head. Nothing stayed steady. The noise and the crush and the flashing lights were like a wild wild party.

'You were a fool.'

Amen to that. Why had I tried to save Crevecoeur? What did I care?

He must have dragged me out, this toughie. He looked angry, his eyes threatening to explode. I'd forced him to be a hero and he didn't like me. He turned away. Inside the hotel the staircase collapsed in a vesuvius of sparks. I got to my feet. My head was wet. I touched it and looked at my fingers but it was only water. Hoses snaked across the square, hissing with leaks.

The crowd had grown to over a thousand, filling the little square and spilling back across avenue Hedi Chaker. There's nothing like a good fire as a tourist attraction. I looked at faces. They were drunk on fire. Police and army pushed the sightseers away but they came back, ducking under arms, breaking through where the soldiers themselves had turned to watch the spectacle. Men stood on café tables to see better. Boys were in the branches of trees. I thought of Miloud, sitting back in his chair, waiting to grow rich. I thought of Miloud, bleeding, head twisting as he was carried out on a stretcher. Someone had known Crevecoeur was staying at the Hôtel du Centre.

I was part of the crowd now. There was a flash beside me and I turned. A man held a camera up and beside him, a hand on his shoulder, stood Nortier. I touched his arm and he turned his head when I gave my name.

'Thank God you're safe. I was told the top floors were cut off by the fire.'

'I wasn't in bed. I hadn't gone back to the hotel. I don't know about Crevecoeur. He may have been trapped.'

'No. Taoufik says he's behind one of those pillars. This is Taoufik, by the way.'

We shook hands, a brief French handshake. Taoufik wasn't French but he wasn't Arab either. There's a bit of everything in Tunisians, because every hundred years or so somebody invades them. In Taoufik there looked a Sicilian nose, Berber skin, negroid hair and a Turkish plumpness. Taoufik muttered. 'Mademoiselle', and found the fire more interesting.

107

'It was a bomb, wasn't it?'

'Three,' Nortier said. 'That's what the army told me.'

'That's twice they've missed Crevecoeur. Unless you still believe what you wrote in the *Hebdo*.'

I left Nortier and went and found Crevecoeur. He was standing in the shelter of one of the big pillars behind the Hôtel Mabrouk, as Nortier had said. Myself, I would have said he was hiding. For the second time that day life had been given back to him.

'You were lucky.'

'I was an idiot,' Crevecoeur said. 'I told Colonel Riahi where he could find me. At my age I did a thing like that. Trust *nobody*. Why did I forget that? Naturally he told his assistant and his wife and his mistress and they confided in their ten best friends and somewhere along the line was a member of Skorpion.'

'Scorpion? With a poisonous sting?'

'With a "k".'

Crevecoeur wasn't looking at me. He was scanning the crowd, checking. He stood in the shadows but his face caught the flickers from the flames. I saw him in parts – a mouth gaping like a dead clam, an ear sharp as a leaf, brows pinched together.

'Skorpion is what they call themselves?' I asked. 'They're the people who plant the bombs?'

'Forget them. Forget I spoke.'

He was on edge. Sometimes holding secrets is too much, even for a person like Crevecoeur. You have to share the burden even though you regret it a moment later. This little confession had slipped out because death had brushed so close.

'Why were you in my room?'

'I wasn't in your room?' His denial was flat. I didn't know whether to believe him.

'The light was on.'

'So someone unlocked the doors of all the rooms and yelled "Fire". Nothing to do with me. I was getting cigarettes at the kiosk when the blast came. Look, they have French cigarettes.' He dug a packet out of his pocket. They were Gitanes, not Supérieures.

'This thing about Skorpion,' I said. 'They're not just run of the mill terrorists. If they've got agents in France and informers in Tunisian Security and they plant bombs and hired Borries as a pilot, they're a big organization. What's their purpose?'

He stopped checking faces in the crowd and checked mine instead.

'You look terrible. Your cheeks are black with soot. Your hair is soaking wet. What happened to the buttons on your shirt?'

I began walking away. He wasn't going to tell me about Skorpion. When he starts the insults, it's instead of giving answers.

'Cody, for your sake I hope they haven't seen you talking to me.'

Was he trying to frighten me off? Rouse my pride to hook me in?

'I've just talked to someone in Security,' Nortier said. 'He's playing down the idea those were bomb blasts. He said it was most likely Butagaz cylinders in the kitchen.'

The kitchen was on the ground floor at the back. The flames had been upstairs at the front.

'Do you believe him?' I asked.

'The kitchen was closed. The cook had gone home. He might have left a gas tap open. It's possible.'

'Find the cook. Ask him how many gas cylinders there were. Three explosions were heard. That cook doesn't prepare meals. He does nothing more than heat coffee for breakfast. One gas cylinder is enough, maybe one as a spare. Never three.'

Taoufik came through the crowd holding the camera high above his head. 'The man who jumped from the window was called Jamil Iddir. He was a Government Schools Inspector from Tunis.'

'Was?' Nortier asked.

'Was. Three other bodies have been recovered so far. There are more. The police don't know how many were trapped inside.'

Nortier said to me: 'Taoufik and I have work to do. We

must get the front page back from the printer. Where are you going to sleep now?'

'I don't know. Another hotel.'

'Don't choose the same one as Crevecoeur.'

'You're coming round to the idea that he is the target?'

Nortier thought about that. He took a keyring out of his pocket and selected a key. 'Perhaps you should stay in my apartment.'

Four dead and more bodies to come. I didn't know how many killed at the airport. Maalej murdered in the olive plantation. Perhaps I should stay in Nortier's apartment. I took the key he held out and asked the address.

The hinge needed oil.

There was a coffin with its lid yawning and . . .

Suddenly I was fully awake. The dream evaporated. The hinge was real. It was on the door to the corridor and it seemed the door had been stilled at the instant it began to squeak.

There was no light and I could see nothing. I had pulled Nortier's curtains tight and now I stared into the dark. I could have been followed here. Someone from Skorpion might have reported seeing me talk to Crevecoeur and been ordered: Follow her, find where she spends the night, while she's asleep go in and kill her. She has been hired to track down Borries and she is an unacceptable risk to our enterprise. Damn Crevecoeur. Why wouldn't he tell me what Skorpion were involved in? What manner of people were they? Highly trained professionals or mere thugs?

I hadn't heard the key turn in the lock. Nortier had given me his own key and when I had used it there had been the dull sound of metal rubbing on metal. I had come into the sitting room and closed the door to his entrance hall behind me. That was why the sound of the lock was muffled. It was the higher register of the hinge that penetrated through the shut door and sank into my brain while I slept and roused me.

The hinge again. The front door of the apartment was now closed. I slipped off the settee where I had stretched out. The cushions were upholstered in corduroy and made no

12

Never park outside your own hotel. Always choose another hotel. If the other side know your car, they'll be watching the wrong entrance. If, on the other hand, they know your hotel, you at least keep your car secure.

Who were the other side? A group calling itself Skorpion. Crevecoeur knew more about Skorpion and hugged the knowledge to himself. It was a state secret, that's what his cold eyes divulged. I had talked to him while the plane burned and again while the hotel burned. I had dined with him. I'd driven him to a rendezvous. I'd had a room at the same hotel. A dozen times we could have been seen together. The connection would be made and someone in the hierarchy of Skorpion would issue the order: Neutralize Crevecoeur's associate.

So beware of Skorpion.

How can you beware of something you can't recognize? They were shadows, without substance, vanishing in the air like Borries.

My Renault was parked in a sidestreet by the Hôtel Triki.

I spent a long time checking it. I went in a shop that sold lamps and asked prices but let my eyes wander outside. Doorways, windows, roofs: I was particular about the roof-tops. They were flat, providing perfect cover and giving wide angles of view. They had put telephone poles on top of the buildings and slung the lines from roof to roof. Crevecoeur would appreciate that; make the bugger's job easier.

Thank you, I told the little man who was enthusing about a chandelier, if ever I buy Versailles I'll come back.

No one with a gun had shown himself above the roofline but how could I tell if I was being watched? A man had a ladder against the trunk of a palm tree and attacked a dead frond with a hatchet. A trader had set up a stall at one end of the street to sell apricots. Someone else stared in the window of a travel agency, admiring the poster of skiing in the Alps. A man shouted in Arabic through an open window. There was a kiosk that sold papers. I could see the headline on the *Hebdo*: SEPT MORTS EN VILLE, NEUF A L'AEROPORT. Nortier had used the largest type-size the printer had; in the trade they call it the Second Coming size.

I walked to the Renault. Everybody was staring at me. Nobody paid any attention. Nerves. I got in and drove off.

I put the car in a parking slot on avenue Belhaouane and visited the boutique on the corner. They played scratched disco records and had flashing lights. There was a Ted Lapidus sticker on the door but none of his fashions inside. I bought a striped matelot shirt, and tan slacks with a safari jacket to match. The boutique was called Tout Joli. It had never heard of grenades inside fishnet tee-shirts. Then I went to pick up Nortier.

'*Papiers.*'

The Garde Nationale were at the airport and they were a whole lot tougher than the police I'd seen. This one had a square face and a thumb of a nose. Lines ran out from his eyes like spokes on a wheel. The lines hadn't come from smiling but from squinting at the sun. He couldn't smile, this one; it hadn't been part of his training. He turned the pages of my passport slowly.

'And what does a French teacher want here today? The airport is closed. There are no planes.'

'I'm driving Monsieur Nortier. He has come to check developments for his newspaper.'

I could see the charred wreckage out on the parking apron. Soldiers stood guard in a clump. There was nobody working on the burnt out plane. Perhaps they were waiting for orders from Tunis. I stared at Skorpion's work while the Garde questioned Nortier. Ella Borries was in my thoughts. Her husband was connected with this. If I found him, would she be grateful? *I want you to find Bert, I don't care about the rest.* Did she still have her head in the clouds?

The carpark was deserted. The official cars and the hefty motorbikes were jammed in the no-parking zone outside the terminal entrance. I thought of joining them. But the little red Renault would look just as conspicuous there as on its own in the carpark. Next time I'll rent a big black Peugeot.

'Where's your white cane?' I asked Nortier. 'People don't turn a blind man back.'

A pair of Gardes Nationales stood sentry outside the double doors. Their long leather boots had taken root there. Crash helmets hid their brains.

'Give me your arm,' I said. We walked in unchallenged.

The hall had check-in counters for Tunis Air and Tunisavia on the right. On the left was a bar with Ricard and Johnnie Walker, coffee and doughnuts. A rack held packets of old biscuits – the ones with the dust flavour. Behind the counter was a boy who polished glasses that didn't need polishing. Near the windows a man stopped stirring the dust and leant on his broom.

'I don't like it,' I said. 'People are staring.'

'You're a woman. You must be used to it.'

This hall was all there was to the public part of the terminal building. One 747 would have filled it twice over. Nortier struck out across it at a blind man's pace.

'Crevecoeur let something slip last night.' I spoke softly, for no one's ears but his. 'The group he is interested in is called Skorpion. I don't know what Skorpion's aim is but they don't appreciate a Chief Inspector of the Sûreté arriving in Tunisia. A bomb here, a hotel up in flames. Crevecoeur says the local Security police have been penetrated by Skorpion. There's no doubt they will have a member here at the airport. That's why I don't like these men watching.'

We walked towards a door marked Cinema, which seemed unlikely. The door was partly open and inside was a switchboard. The operator was a soldier who looked up as we passed the gap. Perhaps the army had taken over communications because of the attack. Or perhaps the soldier reported to Skorpion.

'In which case,' Nortier said, 'we shall have to be careful.'

He was so calm it was maddening. Having been blinded, nothing worse could happen to him. A corridor led off to the left with a sign pointing to the Airport Administration. There were office doors, the sound of a typewriter, a couple of soldiers who looked too big indoors. Nortier never faltered, touching his stick against the wall, finding the gap where the corridor ran off, the wall again, doors to the toilets.

'Who are we seeing?'

'An old pal.' *Copain* was his word, Jules's word too. They were all *copains* here, apart from the members of Skorpion.

We passed a deserted bank counter. Next to it a door was wedged open to encourage a breeze. A policeman had taken off his jacket and sat with his feet on the desk, a telephone to his ear, a matchstick exploring his teeth.

'The door ahead,' Nortier said.

A sign warned No Entry in French but not in Arabic. We climbed stairs, up and up, raw concrete scuffed by shoes. There were no windows and it was lit by neon tubes. Finally we emerged into the daylight of the control tower. All round lay the airport, given a faint tan by the tinted glass.

A man looked up to inspect the intruders. 'Antoine,' he said, his face breaking into a smile.

'Ahmed, *salut*.'

The two men shook hands. The Controller was a small man in a blue uniform with a shine to it, like the plumage of a tropical bird. He tipped his head on one side to look at me. His eyes were dark and round and didn't blink.

'And this is . . .?'

I was introduced. Ahmed was explained to me as the only indispensable man at the airport, at which he modestly ducked his head. Also a valued friend of the Aéro-Club.

'Will the airport by reopened by Sunday for the Essadi-Dabou race?'

'*Mon vieux*, it would be open now if it wasn't for the men with big cars and smart uniforms.'

'A terrible business.'

Terrible, Ahmed agreed. He had been watching and felt helpless, trapped in his box above the buildings. He had witnessed the explosions and the people running and the huge fire and smoke that blotted out the sky like a thunderstorm. While he talked a small fan on a table twisted its head back and forth. Terrible, terrible, Ahmed kept saying. He had actually been talking to the captain of the airliner about weather conditions onward to Tripoli when – *boum*! Terrible, terrible.

116

'We were here,' Nortier said.

It was a planewreck. If you can have shipwrecks, why not a planewreck? I stared down at it while Nortier explained about my search for Borries. The planewreck was set in a greater sea of disaster. From this height I could make out the gutted hulk of the tanker; it was a whale, stranded. The concrete was waved with grey and black and littered with unrecognizable pieces of the plane. A jeep was curving out with officers in dark glasses. The soldiers dropped cigarettes and rubbed them out under heels.

'Borries,' Ahmed was saying. 'Certainly I remember him.' The blue of his jacket shimmered as he shrugged a shoulder. 'I had him up and down, up and down for a couple of days. I would give him instructions and he would repeat them. "On final visual approach. Cleared for landing. Surface wind one-twenty, speed eight. Out." He said it as if he was correcting my accent. We always spoke English, he insisted on that.'

'He had completely overhauled the Skyvan.'

'So they told me.'

'When did he go finally? It was about the beginning of the month. He must have filed a flight plan. Can you get it for us out of Records?'

'*Mon vieux*, there is no need to trouble Records. It's not so busy here that I cannot remember a flight like that. He reported that he was flying to Gabès and took off in the early afternoon. I had given him the weather pattern, winds, so forth across the gulf. One hundred and twenty kilometres. In the Skyvan, thirty minutes or less. I warned Gabès Control of his ETA. But he didn't land there. He swung east without making radio contact. He could have been making for Houmt Souk on Djerba but he vanished off the radar screen. Gabès kept quiet for half an hour and then informed the naval and air force authorities. A search was made and nothing found. The next morning a patrol vessel made two or three sweeps and gave up. Nobody enquired why Borries changed his mind. He had deliberately turned away from Gabès and presumably had his own reasons. The matter was simply forgotten.'

'Did he go down in the sea?' I asked.

117

'I thought about that quite a lot. Borries was a superb pilot, no doubt, so he wouldn't have forgotten to fill up with fuel. The Skyvan is a reliable machine and it had just been serviced. I don't think he ended up on the seabed. Gabès Control is much the same as here. The radar is limited. We don't need anything sophisticated. I never have more than one movement on the screen at once so I don't mark its transponder code or height data. I know, you see. I had cleared Borries to fifteen hundred metres. Suppose when he turned east from Gabès he had dropped to thirty metres above the waves. He would have been lost from the screen at Gabès Control and nobody would ever know where he'd gone.'

Ahmed had coffee sent up. The girl who brought it had a special smile for Ahmed. When she noticed me she became languid in her movements. Her skirt rustled and Ahmed's eyes followed her until she disappeared down the steps, her eyes catching his and dropping. Sweat studded Ahmed's temples. The windows were hinged at the top to let through a breeze but it was air that had baked over concrete which drifted in. The fan turned one way and another, stirring the hot air.

'Ahmed,' Nortier said, 'it's possible Borries dipped down so no one would know he'd gone to Tripoli. He could have continued out to sea until he was beyond radar range and then gained height again and headed towards Libya. On the other hand his intention could simply have been to get round Gabès unseen and continue to the south of Tunisia.'

'Why should he have done that?' Ahmed asked.

'I don't know.'

'There's nothing down there.'

'That's not wholly true.'

There was silence for a spell. The fan went back and forth as if watching a slow motion tennis match.

'What is down there?' I asked.

Ahmed fetched a map that covered the lower half of Tunisia. He unfolded it on the table and I saw at once why he said there was nothing down south and why Nortier had contradicted him. The northern two-thirds of the country had towns and roads marked. The southern third jutted down like an appendix and had a single road and only half a dozen place names. To the east was Libya, to the west Algeria. Across the region was written: SAHARA. The desert respected no frontiers.

Ahmed said: 'The deep south is a military zone. There are army camps at Remada, Borj el Khadra, Borj Mechaab and Mechiguig. Drilling for oil and gas here and here. Pipeline from Algeria to the coast runs like this. Nothing else. A few nomads, a few goats and camels, a lot of sand.'

'Could Borries have flown down there?' I asked.

'He could have landed in the desert. It's not all shifting sand dunes. A lot of it is hardpan.'

'The army camps all have landing strips,' Nortier said.

'He would need permission,' Ahmed said.

'He would need permission,' Nortier agreed.

'That is not easy for a private plane.'

'It would be impossible for a Libyan-registered plane. But Borries went to some trouble to get a plane with Tunisian registration.'

Ahmed frowned. He drew breath to ask again why Borries should do something like that and then shrugged.

A military aircraft came in. Ahmed gave it his attention for five minutes. It appeared first as a blip on the radar screen and then out to the northwest on its glide path to touchdown. The language of the skies is English but, to the military, Ahmed spoke Arabic. The plane was a personnel carrier. It was painted in drab desert colours with no shiny metal surfaces to catch the sun. It closed down its engines and the doors opened and steps unfolded to let down a couple of dapper men in Ministry suits. Nortier had been waiting for the whine of the jets to die away.

'I want to speak to Borj Mechaab. Can we do that, Ahmed?'

'You can telephone.'

'On your radio. I prefer that.'

Ahmed swung round to the transceiver, put down a switch and twiddled with a knob to change frequency.

'The man in charge is Mahrez, Colonel Dhaou Mahrez. He's the one I want to speak to.' To me Nortier said: 'He

119

came on a course to Tours AFB when I was still flying. He wasn't a colonel yet but you could tell he was going to the top. In one of those countries south of the Sahara he'd be President by now. We got on well. He understood the illusion of France: "It's a middling-sized country strutting on a stage that's only big enough for two bullies. Stay in the Air Force. Enjoy the flying. But don't imagine you frighten the Russians. At least my country doesn't have an enemy a hundred times more powerful." Then he'd clap me on the back. "Come and have a glass. Stop worrying about France's mission in the world. Leave that to the politicians and the madmen." He developed a taste for Vouvray. We shared a lot of similar tastes: gliding, pinball machines, Georges Brassens. Also Brigitte Bardot.'

Nortier gave one of his rare smiles.

Ahmed had been speaking into a throat-mike and listening on his headphones. He covered the microphone and said over his shoulder: 'You'd better try.'

For Nortier there was a hand-held microphone and a loudspeaker high on the wall in a corner. Ahmed had spoken Arabic; Nortier spoke French.

'Is that Borj Mechaab camp?'

'Speak more slowly please.'

'Are you Borj Mechaab?'

'Yes.'

'I want to speak to the commandant.'

'Who do you want?'

'I want your commandant, Colonel Mahrez.'

'That is not possible.'

'Not possible? In what way is it not possible?'

'He is not available.'

Anger takes people in different ways. I watched Nortier stiffen. 'You cannot say he is not available. Either he is there or he is not there. Colonel Mahrez is not a society lady deciding not to be at home to callers. Is he away on exercises? Is he in a conference?'

'Who is asking for him?'

'It's none of your business who wants him.'

'If it's necessary to return your call, I must know who you are.'

'My name is Nortier. I am editor of the *Hebdo de Sfax*.'

'One moment.'

The power of the press. One blind editor, one podgy assistant. Sixteen pages, tabloid size. Half the pages were little display ads for clothes and farm equipment and cinemas and furniture stores. *One moment*, Nortier was told. Can't offend the gentlemen of the press.

He put his hand over the microphone. 'Borj Mechaab would be like exile to anyone else. But Dhaou seems happy enough. He's constructed irrigation canals and . . .' He broke off.

If that was a happy man who came through on the speaker, then St Anthony was a bundle of joy. Dhaou Mahrez hardly sounded an acquaintance of Nortier's let alone an old drinking mate.

'Hello, Dhaou, how are you?'

'I'm well, thanks. And you.'

'I'm well.'

Such banal phrases for Nortier's face to set so hard. The social chat went on to cover Mahrez's family, who also blossomed with health.

'And your wife?' Mahrez asked. 'How is she?'

Nortier considered this question. 'She's on a visit to France,' he replied. By now he had hunched round so I could see the frown on his face. For one thing, Nortier had begun by using *tu* and only slipped into the formal *vous* because Mahrez used it. For another, Nortier had had no wife for years.

'And what can I do for the editor of one of our leading provincial papers?'

'I remember your interest in gliding. The Aéro-Club in Sfax has a glider challenge on Sunday which would greatly interest you.'

There was the slightest of pauses. 'I regret,' Mahrez said, 'I shall not be able to attend.'

'That's too bad. I remember the visit we made to the gliding championships in Epernay. Do you recall?'

Again the pause. 'Yes.'

'Afterwards we made the rounds of the champagne houses – Taittinger, Lanson, Roederer . . .'

'So we did.'

'Memorable times.'

'You're right.'

More expressions of mutual goodwill. End of conversation.

In the main hall the man with the broom was still sweeping. He stopped to stare at us a second time. At the bar two cops drank orangeade. They were very macho about it, swigging straight from the bottle. Out in the open the sun crashed on our heads and the glare hurt my eyes. Did it hurt Nortier's eyes?

He said: 'The point about that is that Mahrez and I have never visited Epernay. Anyway those champagne houses are all in Reims. The whole conversation was bizarre. There were no jokes, he was stiff and formal. He spoke as if he had a pistol jammed down his throat.'

There had been pauses, awkward silences as if neither had known what words to use. Is something wrong? That is what Nortier had been asking with his bogus memories of champagne guzzling. Yes but I can't tell you. That had been the Colonel's reply.

We headed for the carpark. The sun silvered the tarmac. My car shimmered in the heat so that I had to look twice to be certain. Someone sat in the front seat.

'Now do you believe in the existence of Skorpion?' I asked and didn't wait for an answer. 'The bombings, the Sûreté man from France, the disappearing aircraft, the Colonel who can't speak.'

'So what are we going to do?'

'We?' I stopped and Nortier had to pull up.

'We have a bargain. I've helped you but I don't have the story yet. I don't know what's behind it all. Do we go to the police, the Security Colonel, the army?'

'What good will that do? They think the bombing of the plane was a Libyan squabble. They think the burning of the hotel was a leaking gas cylinder. When Crevecoeur went to the *Cercle des Officiers*, the Security Colonel was enjoying lunch, he wasn't at the airport leading the investigation. They're hopeless.'

'Perhaps that's why I like the country.'

I was staring at the car. The man was lighting a cigarette. The sun was too bright for me to pick up the flame but smoke drifted out of the window. He raised his head and saw us and got out of the car.

Crevecoeur was in disguise. I recognized him at once. A panama hat and a cravat knotted under his chin did nothing to bulk out his narrow chest. He still wore his jacket buttoned up. A shoulder holster is a damn nuisance in a hot climate.

'Right now,' I said, 'we have other company.'

Crevecoeur was staring over my shoulder. Before I could turn, his eyes swept away on a tour of the buildings and the parking apron where figures crowded beneath the wreck, and, on to the hangar which the Aéro-Club used and along the length of the runway. There was no breeze today and the heat was fierce. It made distances deceptive, piling eucalyptus trees on top of a line of pylons on top of the field of almonds. The pylons swayed and rippled to unheard music. Crevecoeur turned back to us. His face had the hazed look of the sleepless.

'I want to speak to her alone,' Crevecoeur told Nortier. He made us sound like guilty lovers. 'We'll take a little stroll.'

He walked away from the buildings and the activity on the apron. I caught up with him at the fence where he was staring across a patch of brown grass. He took a breath that went on and on. You wouldn't have thought those narrow lungs could suck so much air in.

'I'm tired, Cody, I'm tired.'

'Didn't you get any sleep?'

'I went down to the harbour and climbed the fence and lay up in one of the sheds. I couldn't risk another hotel. And you?'

'I slept in Nortier's apartment.'

'Oh yes?' He peered sideways at me.

I was furious at him and furious at myself. Why waste sympathy on him? What did I care if he'd slept or not?

'Why did you want to speak to me?'

He sent his cigarette spinning. He did it so he could spread his hands in front of me, empty.

123

'I'm asking you again to get out. I'm very concerned about you.'

'I can look after myself.'

'I'm not talking about your life now. That's your business. I'm worried you'll mess things up for me.'

'With Skorpion?'

Crevecoeur screwed his eyes tight. You do that when you're exhausted. Also you do it when you regret having said or done something. It's as if the world ceased to exist when you closed your eyes.

'Cody, there is a certain company in France that manufactures *matériel de guerre*. Now it has been the policy of successive French governments to maximize the sale of arms abroad. The more we sell, the more jobs are created. It is regrettable that one of the by-products of armaments is dead people but at least they aren't French. This company I'm talking about attracted the interest of the Sûreté some time ago. At first it was just one of the directors dining with the representative of a foreign state. Then one of our Inspectors took a closer look at their affairs and there turned out to be certain shortcomings between their output and their certificated sales. We watched. We asked some quiet questions. We listened to one or two telephones – that fixer PDS was one. No doubt of it: they were exporting without a licence.'

The illegal exporting must have been going on some time while Crevecoeur tiptoed round in his socks making enquiries. 'Until you came along there must have been official blind eye approval about those sales. I mean someone has to tell the customs people to go for a cup of coffee while the stuff is loaded on planes.'

Crevecoeur chose that moment to check his own safety. No one had tried to kill him since last night. Skorpion could have a man behind the venetian blinds in one of the offices, or lounging against the wall by the official cars, or on his stomach among the almond trees on the other side of the road. He came back to me.

'Early this week a Skyvan with Tunisian registration flew from a small airport near this nameless factory. It carried a load of crates. As for the question of the customs officers being told to go for coffee, that didn't arise. The flight plan filed with Air Traffic Control was to Nice. ATC at Athis-Mons confirms the departure. Nice denies the plane landed. However in the afternoon a Skyvan did put down at Luqa Airport in Malta for a refuelling stop. It had no proper cargo manifest, nor international air clearance. However it was going on to Tripoli. In Malta they don't ask too many questions about Libyan deals. So the police went off and looked instead at the English girls in the departure lounge and the Skyvan was refuelled. Paid cash, dollars. It took off and I know nothing more. But perhaps my agent here did. It needs something vital for a man to be murdered.'

'The Skyvan was registered here?'

'Yes.'

'Borries was flying it?'

'Yes,' he said again.

A man had come out of the terminal building. He lounged against the wall, just by the doorway. In his hand was a cup of coffee. It seemed too hot to drink for he took it in sips.

'Cody, this is very, very serious. That's why I'm telling you. It involves the governments of three countries. A hundred thousand lives are at risk. It's much bigger than you can handle. Don't you see that?'

A hundred thousand lives? Such a round number, a convenient figure. How could he know so many deaths were threatened? A hundred thousand was the population of Sfax. It would take weeks of killing to finish off a city this size.

'You were hired to find Borries,' he said. 'That's what I'm trying to do – find Borries and recover the crates from the Skyvan. We want the same thing. We'll achieve it quicker if we pool our resources. So is there anything you can tell me?'

He had the habit of very tall people of standing too close and talking down to you. Moving away from him would be a retreat. A hundred thousand? He was trying to bludgeon me with the weight of numbers. The last time I had been involved with him, Crevecoeur had called up not a hundred thousand but one little girl to help trap me. I wouldn't let him work on my conscience again. I wouldn't do his bidding.

'You know all the facts,' I said.

Colonel Mahrez at Borj Mechaab? That was a conjecture not a fact. I chose my words with care. Just as Crevecoeur hadn't talked of 'guns' or 'bombs' but had chosen to use the phrase 'matériel de guerre'.

13

The land was pressed flat by the sun.

It was 345 kilometres to Borj Mechaab. Given a straight highway and no snarl-ups and the Renault running sweetly, I estimated the driving time as four and a half hours. Add on time spent in getting lunch and filling up the tank before we entered the empty south. Add on more time because of the state of the roads. We should arrive in mid to late afternoon.

We passed through a straggle of houses with the smell of oil from olive presses. The taint lingered inside the car long after we were clear of the village. Live in that place and you would never be free of the smell. In the end you'd not notice it.

I've helped you, Nortier had said, *but I don't have the story yet. Do we go to the police, the Security Colonel, the army?* The Security branch in Sfax was penetrated by Skorpion. Most likely the regular police too. Which left the army.

Nortier had been facing forward. Now he hunched away as if he was looking out of the window. 'What did he want with you?'

'He wanted me to get away. Skorpion is dangerous he warned. As if we didn't know.'

'And he's worried for your safety?'

'No.' In front was an old *louage*, a shared taxi, with luggage strapped on the roof rack. A crate held live chickens. They cowered in one corner, white feathers being plucked away by the wind. When we were past I added: 'Crevecoeur is never worried about other people. He is concerned about himself and the security of France. In his view those are not two separate things but one and indivisible.'

'He has an inflated ego?'

'Maybe.'

'Do you think so?'

'He has his job to do.'

'He's doing it now? The bombs and killings aren't a Tunisian tragedy but to do with the security of France?'

'That's how he sees it.'

'Then he should get the hell back to France and let everybody here live in peace.'

'If Skorpion go to these lengths to stop Crevecoeur, do you imagine their aims are peaceful?'

Nortier thought about that.

The road ran beside a railway. Beyond the track was a sea of olives. The terrain here was already more arid and the trees were spaced further apart, the land in between bare and dusty.

Which left the army. I thought about that. Trouble in Borj Mechaab? Then it would have to be army units from up north that dealt with it.

Gabès, where Borries had turned left and disappeared from the radar screen, was first a foul chemical plant, then lines of pottery stalls, then a vast oasis-by-the-sea with a zillion palm trees, then a chaos of buses and *louage* taxis. I stopped to buy a *casse-croûte*. It was too hot to feel hungry. We ate and shared a bottle of mineral water.

'Why are we doing this?' Nortier asked.

There were tiny black olives in the sandwich. I spat a stone the size of a rice grain out of the window.

'You mean going to Borj Mechaab?'

'Yes.'

'To see why your old friend Colonel Mahrez wouldn't talk freely to you.'

'You agree there's something wrong in Borj Mechaab?'

'It seems so.'

'Then let me repeat the question: Why are we going? What can we do?'

'That's two questions.'

He shrugged his eyebrows. He wouldn't be put off.

'All right, why are we going?' I hesitated a moment. Shouts and whistles and bells and horns and the clash of gears filled the car's silence. We're going because a wife in Paris is worried sick and is paying me. We're going because you scent a story, not a local rag story but a world exclusive story.

I could have said that. It wouldn't have been true. I started the engine and turned onto the highway to Medenine. 'We're going because there's nothing else we can do. There's no one we can trust: not the police, not Security, not even the army. That is why we're driving south.'

That wasn't the reason. Or there was another reason behind it, my reason. I was going to see what was happening because that was my life. There was mystery, danger, excitement. Those were things others experienced from television. I was going because this was real. I was seduced by its whisper: come and find out the truth. It was a siren call I could never resist. Ella Borries's money meant nothing. I wanted to hunt down Skorpion, take it apart, discover its secret. That was what I thrilled to.

'But what will we do?' Nortier prompted.

'I'm still thinking about that.'

At Medenine a road branched left towards Djerba. We continued south. Palm and olive trees vanished. This was semi-desert. Nothing grew. Nothing moved. Nothing gave shade.

We were silent most of the time. When we talked, we'd graduated to the familiar *tu*. Nortier started calling me Suzanne.

At Tataouine I filled the tank and we drank warm Coca-Cola at a café. I was the only woman. Nortier was the only man not wearing a *djellaba*.

'How much further?'

'A hundred kilometres. An hour and a quarter, say.'

'The road gets much worse.'

The highway dwindled to a single strip of tarmac. When we met an army truck, its headlights stared me out. I was forced onto the grit shoulder. It was a Magirus, with wheels as high as the Renault 5's roof. We passed the black leather tents of nomads. They were low-pitched, hugging the ground. Small boys jumped up and waved. The highway took a bend and dipped into a *oued*. A sign warned: *Eau stagnante*. Dust stirred. Purple and yellow flowers peeped up between rocks. The road ran straight to a rise on the horizon. Dunes appeared and sand slipped over the tarmac so that the tyres suddenly lost their grip. Looking in the mirror I saw the sand skittering in our wake like smoke. On our left were tiny patches of barley no more than a hand high and dead under the sun. In quarter of an hour the country had grown arid, as if we had crossed a continental divide. On our right were hills. They formed a ridge, sharp like the tail of a dinosaur laid across the plain. Beyond the hills was the Sahara.

The road took another curve and I said to Nortier: 'There's a checkpoint ahead.'

The man wore the uniform of the Garde Nationale and had slow careful eyes. He began with the car: certificate of ownership, rental agreement, *fiche de visite technique*. He moved on to my passport, checking my face against the photo, checking my face again when he came to the date of birth, turning to the back to see the Immigration stamp. Nortier also had a French passport but with a resident's visa stamped in. Seeing this the Garde tried him in Arabic. Nortier answered. His Arabic was like my Spanish – fair enough until he had to fish in his memory for a word.

I got out of the car to unlock the boot. The sun was three hours past its zenith but it still shrivelled the skin of my cheek. Sweat ran in a single rivulet from the corner of the Garde's eye as if he was crying. There was a hut for him to sit in but a chair was tipped against the wall outside the door. The hut would be an oven, the iron roof an infra-red grill. There was no breeze here and the flag hung limp from its pole beside the radio aerial.

He closed the boot, handed me all the documents and said: '*Bon voyage*.'

There was no smile. It was too hot for that.

The checkpoint was by the turn-off to Borj Bourguiba. We continued straight on to Remada.

'This is where I told him we were coming,' Nortier said. 'From here on south it is a military zone and we would need special permits to travel in it.'

'Borj Mechaab is forty kilometres inside the military zone.'

'I know.'

'Why didn't you tell me?'

'I'm telling you now.'

'So do I crash the next checkpoint?'

It was hot in the car. Sweat stuck my shirt to the back of the seat. My eyes burned from tiredness. My calf muscles ached from pressure on the pedals. We said nothing more. Words were enemies.

I took Remada slowly. French *colons* had once lived here. Their villas housed army officers now. Soldiers loafed at street corners. The main square had a hopeless open air market, stalls with plastic bowls and cheap mirrors, strings of red peppers spread on the dirt. Sentries guarded the gates to a barracks. A pair of veteran field guns threatened a café across the street. Conscript boys in sombre fatigues played cards, one bottle of lemonade per table as rent. A Land-Rover came out of a side street and cut across my bows. The driver ignored my squeal of brakes. He wore a neckerchief in a camouflage design that would have looked chic down Boul' Mich'.

'Bloody army everywhere.'

'It's been a garrison town ever since the Romans marched in.'

Road junction. A sign pointed left to the Libyan border. Straight ahead was Borj Mechaab. We left the town behind. A couple of kilometres away was a gentle rise and I braked the car half way up it.

'Why are you stopping?'

'I have this theory about checkpoints on both sides of a town.'

It was nothing so grand as a hill but sweat was in my eyes by the time I reached the top. The view was drab, the plain flat and treeless. Tufts of withered weed waited for the next rain to set them growing. The Romans must have engineered the road. It ran straight to an upthrust of rocks a kilometre or so away and disappeared from sight. I studied the upthrust. An army division could hide behind it. I scoured the plain and there was nowhere else. I looked back at the upthrust. Yes, at the extreme right, that wasn't a bleached rock. It was a patriotic patch of red and white, hanging limp.

The checkpoint before Remada was matched by one after it. The first was needed because of the turn-off to Borj Bourguiba, which was in the military zone. Remada, however, wasn't. If you had a mind to, you could travel there freely. But only with the military's permission could you go further. So a second checkpoint was necessary. After that there was no need for further checks. In logic the system was foolproof.

The logic therefore had to be bypassed.

I wrenched the wheel over.

We missed the boulder but lurched into the hole it had left behind when the *oued* had flooded. Whenever that had been. Last year, last decade. This was not like the *oued* where Crevecoeur discovered his agent murdered. There was no underground water to keep oleanders alive. The riverbed was a shallow depression but it was enough to bounce the noise of the engine back. We laboured in second gear and the sound was redoubled. You'd think it would wake them up at the checkpoint.

The *oued* began just over the crest of the ridge. It looked no more than erosion to begin with. It deepened and widened where the storm waters had gathered strength. As we reached the plain, it ended in what was once a lake. The water had dried to mud. The mud had dried with the hoofprints of goats clearly visible. There was no water or mud now, just fissures which the sun had cracked open. You see Florida widows with faces like that.

The car began to run better. We must have been half a kilometre to the west of the checkpoint. From this lower viewpoint the scrap of flag was out of sight. Once we turned south the checkpoint would become visible to me. And, of course, vice versa. Not a damn thing I could do about that. I had to hope the Garde was watching the road. Why should he be staring out to the west? No point in that. Let him stare north towards Remada or south towards Borj Mechaab. There was nothing to look at in this direction, only the blinding sun.

I turned south.

'How far off the road are we?'

'About three-quarters of a kilometre.'

'Shouldn't you have gone further?'

I wished the car wasn't bright red. It should have been a

dun colour to match the plain. Also there should have been anti-flare sprayed on the metal surfaces.

'We're beyond earshot. We could go five kilometres and still be in sight if anybody turned this way.'

Nortier shifted to face the checkpoint and then back again to stare ahead. He sat bolt upright with no expression on his face. You'd think there was radar in those eyes. There should have been, to warn me. We hit something – sharp stone, broken glass left behind by General Leclerc's Free French, I don't know what – and the off-side front tyre went.

'Great timing,' I muttered to Nortier. I was too frustrated to say more.

We sat and listened to the engine clicking as it cooled. There was no other sound. I was looking to the left, checking the checkpoint. We were deal level with it, as if someone had drawn a boundary line which it was forbidden to cross. The white walls of the hut ached in the sun. There were touches of colour: red of the flag, blue of the Garde's shirt. The shirt wasn't on the man. It drooped from a nail in the wall.

'Is anyone watching?'

'If there was, you'd have heard the shouts.' Or the shots. We were lucky. 'The Garde will be round the other side of the hut, sitting in the shade. There's no call for him to come round and glare into the sun.' He won't come, the Garde has not heard us, believe that, convince yourself it's worth making an effort. 'Come on.'

In the race track pits they change all four wheels in eight seconds. They don't use blind mechanics. I fetched the tools; Nortier did the strong arm stuff with the jack and the wrench. He wanted to very badly. He hated being helpless.

I stared at the hut. The Garde could come round the corner for a piss at any second and I started working out my move. I gave it up. There wasn't one.

'One of the nuts won't shift.'

'Hammer it with this.'

I gave him a stone the size of a grapefruit. The blows rang out while I stared at the checkpoint. Nothing moved, not the shirt, not the flag, not a curious Garde drawn by the noise. The last nut came free. I lifted the spare into place and let Nortier tighten up the nuts while I stowed the punctured wheel in place under the bonnet. A piece of tyre the size of my hand had torn away and the inner tube had split. The thing was beyond repair. I'd have to be careful. I'd been careful before. All right, I'd have to be extra careful. Also extra quick. Our luck couldn't hold for ever.

'The nuts are as tight as I can make them without using the stone.'

'Makes too much noise.'

'Then let's go.'

Careful now, extra careful, there's no spare if another tyre goes.

Tufts of grey-blond grass, clumps of dead weed, a plastic yoghurt pot, scraps of paper, powdery earth, patches of sand. I liked the sand. The wheels slipped but the sand didn't rise into the air behind us as the dusty earth did. I looked back and nobody was watching. Our luck held and held.

I made for a knoll and in the lee of that turned back to join the highway. Some highway. The tarmac strip had vanished. It was now dirt. A grader had smoothed the worst of it but wind and traffic had corrugated the surface so that the whole car vibrated. Nortier sat very straight. There was no way of stopping the juddering going up your spine. I gave up looking in the mirror. It shook so much the view behind was a jumble. I concentrated on the road ahead and what to do when we reached Borj Mechaab.

'Why Borj?'

Nortier turned his head. His eyebrows were raised.

'Borj Mechaab, Borj Bourguiba, Borj el Khadra.'

'It means Fortress. Turkish, Arab, French, whatever army conquered would dig a well, build a fort round it and sit and wait to be attacked.'

'Who built Borj Mechaab?'

'French Foreign Legion.'

'How big is the place?'

'Smaller than Remada.'

Ahead was a road sign, a big S in the centre of a triangle. In smaller letters underneath: *Sable*. I looked hard but the surface appeared the same. If sand drifted here, the grader must have cleared it. By my reckoning we were now seven or eight kilometres from Borj Mechaab.

I said to Nortier: 'At the airport this morning you said we had three choices: tell Tunisian Security, the police or the army. There was a fourth choice you didn't mention.' In peripheral vision I could see his face was angled towards me. 'Tell Crevecoeur.'

His face turned aside.

I'd thought about it. A long drive and long silences make for reconsidering. Crevecoeur had said it was too big for me to handle and I'd ignored the warning. Pride, what else. Don't be ashamed of pride. It forces you to achieve things you couldn't do otherwise. But there was a limit to what I could achieve, and reaching Borj Mechaab was that limit.

There was silence from Nortier. He didn't trust Crevecoeur. He didn't like the idea of telling him.

'The mechanics of it are like this,' I said. 'We stop a little short of Borj Mechaab. You stay put with the car. I walk into town with the can from the boot. The gauge is faulty and we've run out of fuel. I'll walk round searching for the petrol station.'

'There won't be one. There's very little traffic.'

'That's what I'm banking on. It gives me the excuse to wander round looking. In the end I'll beg a canful from the military.'

He took a deep breath. Perhaps it was tiredness. Perhaps it was despair over me.

'There are two things we want to know: Is Ella Borries's husband here? And is this the Skorpion base? So I'll make certain I get within sight of the airstrip. If the Skyvan is in sight, that answers both questions. I can't go pleading with Borries to go home to his wife. But I can use my eyes to tell you what the situation is. Then we get out, go back to Sfax. I'll tell Crevecoeur where to come. He'll love me for that. Let him and the big boys take over.'

'Suppose the Skyvan isn't in sight? Suppose it's in a hangar?'

'If . . .'

I'd been going to say: If Skorpion is a revolutionary group, there are always signs to look for. Increased patrols in the streets, slogans on walls, President Bourguiba's name painted out of the name plaques, new insignia on uniforms. I'd been

135

going to say that. My head was full of it.

The fortress town was still out of sight. I had nothing but the foray into it on my mind. Confirm Skorpion had its headquarters there. Then get out and let Crevecoeur loose. If my luck held I would be back in Paris by tomorrow evening.

The thrum of the tyres over the corrugations hid the noise. The first I knew was when the helicopter appeared from above and behind the car, swept a hundred metres ahead and swung round like a horse with its reins jerked.

'Watch out!'

I yelled as I stood on the brakes and it was the new tyre that saved us. The unused tread dug into the grit and swung the car off the road while ahead of us a soldier in a dark khaki uniform wedged himself into the open portal of the helicopter. He gripped a submachine gun. I fought the wheel while the car swerved into the shallow ditch. A line of bullets danced up the road. They made no noise. Everything outside the car was silent. In my ears was the sound of the wheels throwing up stones, the loose jack and petrol can crashing in the boot, Nortier's shout.

I banged open Nortier's door, released his seat belt and pushed him out. I followed him and lay on the ground with an arm across his shoulders to keep him flat. I twisted my head to see beneath the chassis. The helicopter hovered and settled. Soldiers, ten or a dozen, climbed down and fanned out to encircle the car.

14

The ground was the colour of bones bleached by the sun. It lay hard against my cheek.

I heard men's voices.

What were they arguing about? What to do with us? If the car hadn't swerved off the road they wouldn't have this problem. I couldn't understand what the voices were saying.

There was one language I understood. It was in the stance of the boots, slightly apart, close to my body. Brown boots, scratched and scuffed, dull with dust. One lace had broken and been tied in a knot. Above were rough socks. Khaki leggings were tucked inside the socks. Above was a webbing belt. Then the beginning of a khaki shirt with pale buttons. The material had faded with wear. There was a small stain where the appendix was, as if it had leaked.

Details. Keep the brain occupied. It's important.

I couldn't see the man's face. It was beyond my range of vision. I couldn't raise my head to gauge his expression because the muzzle of his rifle bit into my temple.

He threw a tiny shadow. It was the shadow of a dwarf. That was the evidence of my eyes. My brain told me that was nonsense. The shadow was merely foreshortened because I was at ground level.

Keep alert. Don't brood.

There was a fresh sound: the slam of the car's boot. They were searching and finding nothing more than a petrol can and a jack. Voices were raised again. Perhaps they were arguing about what to do with the Renault. People fuss over the damnedest things.

'What are they planning to do?'

'The captain is saying . . .'

Nortier's voice ended in a grunt. There was the thud of a boot somewhere in his body. I couldn't see him. He was lying on the ground at my back, a soldier with a rifle and downcast eyes standing guard.

'Don't move. Don't talk. Don't try and escape.'

The captain had walked into my field of vision. He had a toothbrush moustache and poker player's eyes.

'Do you . . .'

I got no further. The rifle was raised from my skull, a single shot was fired into the ground so close I was spattered with dirt, the muzzle returned to my temple. Its heat scorched me. The captain walked off to the helicopter. My head was angled in that direction and I could watch him all the way. He had a vigorous stride, as if he was full of purpose and had a lot to achieve. He used the helicopter's radio, turning to stare at us. Then he stood with his hands on his hips and shouted orders to the soldiers. To us he added in French:

'Stand up. Get over here. You will be shot if you attempt to escape.'

The sun burned in through the open portal of the helicopter. It was an Alouette, a French model. It is the destiny of France to civilize lesser peoples and in what better way than selling them arms? Or *matériel de guerre*, in Crevecoeur's phrase. The pilot swung the helicopter round until it was on course with the sun shining directly in his eyes. The glare was tremendous and the pilot didn't spot the isolated palm until the last moment. The Alouette lurched over it like a drunk surprised by the kerb.

An *alouette* is a lark. The body of this lark was hot from the sun. The eyes of the soldier were cold. His rifle was aimed at my stomach. Simple thoughts are easiest.

We were flying so low because it was only a hop over the next rise to Borj Mechaab. There was nothing much to the place: cement cubes that had been whitewashed, a sprinkling of bigger houses, single storey, with interior courtyards and the outer walls blind; a patch of greenery round an artesian well; a minaret topping a group of palm trees. The army camp was to the west of the village. We passed over the perimeter wire and a pair of sentries by the gate turned their faces up. Barrack huts with semi-circular roofs were in two parallel lines. Beyond was an encampment of tents that must have been hell under the sun. There was a substantial stone building but we turned away from that, passed over a cabin with radio aerial and radar dish and hovered above the airstrip.

There was no sign of the Skyvan.

Dust swirled in through the portal as we settled. The engine was shut down and my ears ached with relief. The army captain turned in his seat.

'Get out.'

Nortier and I stood close together. The soldiers carried their weapons across their chests and never moved their eyes from us.

The captain said: 'Move forward, prisoners.'

'Where are they taking us?' Nortier murmured.

'To the fort.'

It was built of stone with look-out towers at each corner. The windows were slits lower down, small squares higher up. On top was a parapet, a dragon's spine to protect defenders. Close-to I could make out the grooves and pockmarks of bullets. A working fort but absurd and theatrical. There was even some ceremony about the approach road, with double ranks of eucalyptus trees. A Land-Rover loaded with soldiers was drawn up by the entrance.

Nortier stumbled and I took his hand to steady him.

'What a Godforsaken posting,' I said.

'There was a French general who addressed his men: "You Legionnaires became soldiers in order to die; therefore I am sending you where you will find death." '

Here, in this place.

The captain had a word with an officer in the Land-Rover and said: 'Prisoners, advance through the gate.'

Inside the fort was an area too big for a courtyard, too small for a paradeground. It was of beaten earth. In one corner was a stand of three or four eucalyptus, their trunks whitewashed to shoulder height. There was a straggle of geraniums in a raised bed. A path across the square was marked by old shell cases. Nortier tripped again and the indignity of it made him draw up.

'Where are you taking us?'

'For interrogation,' the captain said.

139

'I insist you take me to see Colonel Mahrez.'

The captain stiffened. He took a couple of brisk paces to confront Nortier.

'He is no longer the commandant here. He is a traitor. Furthermore you are in no position to make demands of any kind. You are now in the Islamic People's Republic of Tunisia.'

Every revolution starts in a small way: Castro and Guevara and a ragged band in the hills. The movement codenamed Skorpion had its beginning in Borj Mechaab in this wedge of land between Algeria and Libya. Crevecoeur had known it was a revolutionary group and how fanatical it was; he simply hadn't found its base.

'The garrison?' I asked. 'What happened to them?'

'When we took power in Borj Mechaab, they were given a choice. Most chose to support the revolution.'

'And the others?'

'They chose to die.'

There is a smell to such places. A slum smells of the poverty of imagination. A cheap hotel room smells of an illusion of love. This place smelled of despair. It was a cell.

Physically it was contained in the former Foreign Legion fortress, but its smell was of a prison. We were escorted through a low doorway, down half a dozen steps, along a short corridor, into a room that had the feel of being only partly above ground. That was important too, for we feel terror at the thought of being buried alive. Nortier was put in the cell round the corner.

The door swung shut and that was when I understood it was a prison cell, a punishment block where bloody-minded Legionnaires had been left to rot. The door echoed when it was closed and locked: it was of metal. It had a small spyhole.

The light had been left on. Let the prisoner's actions be known. Let the prisoner's face be observed.

Footsteps died away. That, too, would be part of the routine. The prisoner is abandoned, forgotten, as good as dead. The purpose is to break down all mental resistance.

A bunk, a pillow, a blanket. A jug of water and a basin.

A bucket with a lid under the table. A rush-seated chair. A high narrow window that rationed the sun.

I could get out of this cell. I knew that. Whether Nortier and I could get clean away from Borj Mechaab was a different matter. There was only one road. To go across country in this waterless region was to look for death.

I could get out because that was what I had been trained to do. The place in Virginia is very good at that. It isn't a question of using a pencil and a piece of string to pick the lock. Or a fretsaw blade in the heel of your shoe. Or an explosive button. They had toys like that but, as with children, your toys can always be taken from you.

The Virginia training is harder: they teach you to think. There is no corner so tight your brain can't find the way out. They teach you that until you believe it because self-confidence is supreme. Stop believing in yourself and you're already dying.

I lay on the bunk. Hundreds of prisoners before me must have lain like this and stared up. The walls of the cell were of stone and the ceiling was plastered and whitewashed. It was vaulted, like a chapel, with a damp patch where the whitewash had flaked away. For most prisoners their prayers would have risen but never reached heaven.

The day was dying.

I waited for the interrogation the captain had talked of. I waited and waited while it grew dark. I had discounted something: I was a woman. In Moslem thinking that diminished my importance. In any thinking. It was Nortier they interrogated first.

Nortier was a journalist and would carry a Press card. Skorpion was a revolutionary group and they like to make use of the media. They are politicians after all, violent politicians. But they expect to manipulate the flow of information. They issue demands and manifestos. They react badly to being investigated. Perhaps Nortier had been noted by one of their agents in Sfax. What had Crevecoeur told him? Was he a spy for the French? Why had he contacted Colonel Mahrez this morning? Why had he come to Borj Mechaab?

I didn't know what answers Nortier would give. Since he

was a journalist, perhaps he would ask questions himself: How long had Skorpion been in charge in Borj Mechaab? Who was financing them? What did they need the Skyvan for? What was their next move? How soon? He wouldn't get answers. It wasn't a press conference.

Finally they'd come round to it. Who is the woman? What is her function? Why does she know the Chief Inspector from the Sûreté?

Footsteps grew louder. Army boots marching raggedly. Three pairs I thought. They halted. The key turned in the lock of my cell.

The man stood with one hand on his hip, above the holster, and the other hand outstretched. In this hand was my passport, taken from the safari jacket I'd tossed onto the back seat of the car.

'Your name?'

'You know that.'

'Tell me your name.'

'Deschampsneufs.'

He was standing in front of me, the naked bulb directly over his head. He was well aware of the sharp contrasts it caused: the shine on his forehead, the dark pools of his eyes.

'First names?'

'Suzanne.'

'Is that all?'

'Yes.'

He knew my name. I didn't know his. To me he appeared a stubble-hopper, a military tough. There was no subtlety in him, no variation in his voice because he saw no need for it. He had begun by barking his questions in a loud abrupt tone and he knew no other way. He had both hands on his hips now and he glared at me. From the other side of the door came the scrape of a guard's boot. Inside the room, from the corner on my left, came a cough.

'Where do you live?'

'Chartres.'

'Occupation?'

'It's all in the passport.'

There had been a smell to my cell. There was a smell to

142

this place too: the arrogance of a uniform. He was dressed as an officer. I couldn't tell what rank. There was something odd about his shoulderboards. He was bending towards me and I could see them distinctly. They showed the Tunisian emblem – a crescent embracing a star – but instead of red and white they were green and gold.

'A teacher?'

'Yes.'

'Teacher of what?'

'Of English.'

There was a cough again from the corner. I couldn't see who watched from the shadows.

'You're not a journalist like the man but a schoolteacher? Is that what you're saying?'

Like any person, from graduate of Dzerzhinsky Square to freelance minnow wriggling in the shallows of Intelligence, I had my story prepared. I was holidaying in Sfax, made the acquaintance of Nortier, agreed to drive him south to look up an old friend. Those were the bones of it. I would add flesh as it was needed: why I'd chosen Sfax, in what circumstances I'd met Nortier, perhaps even invent a blind brother he reminded me of. I would tell that story and insist on it up to a certain point. With a bully such as this officer, there was bound to be a certain point. I would trip over a detail, contradict myself, and finally break. I had prepared the position I would withdraw to: a friend in Paris, Ella Borries, had asked me if I could find any trace of her husband while I was in Tunisia. True enough. What I must not divulge was any connection with PDS, or previous acquaintance with Crevecoeur, or knowledge of Skorpion. If this man once tasted blood he would never let go. The point was to make him work for my second story because something which is freely offered is not valued. A hint, a confusion he could pounce on, a reluctant confession: Ella Borries is worried her husband might have crashed, I just want to take her back good news.

'A teacher on holiday. I've been ill and . . .'

'Lies.' The interrogator shouted in my face. 'You're a spy and a counter-revolutionary.'

I was totally unprepared for his hand. Even the most

physical interrogator salves his conscience by giving the suspect a chance first. It wasn't his hand that stung but the ring with the glitter of a stone. My cheek felt warm. I couldn't tell if it was from bruising or if the flesh had been laid open across the bone and I was feeling the warmth of blood. I didn't touch my cheek. He would take it as a sign of weakness and his type are encouraged by that.

Again there was a stirring in the corner. I couldn't make him out, just a shadow among shadows, a shadow with a cough.

'You've driven several hundred kilometres south when there's nothing to see, no beach to lie on and no hotel to stay in. You took great care to evade the checkpoint outside Remada. What's more you have no luggage with you. Is that how a schoolteacher behaves?'

I said nothing. He fished a cigarette out and lit it, blowing the smoke into my face. I don't think it was deliberate, in the way that the back of his hand had been. He simply didn't consider me of any value.

'You're a fool,' he said. 'Your mistake is to imagine we know nothing. You arrived in Sfax four days ago. You stayed in the Hôtel du Centre. We even know the room number. You see, you came very early to the notice of our Intelligence Directorate.'

I watched him closely. Twice I'd been mistaken about my visitors: I'd thought it was PDS's murderers in Paris, I thought it was Crevecoeur in Sfax. Instead it was his snoopers, by whatever inflated title he cared to call them.

'What was your purpose in going to Sfax?'

'I thought you knew all about me.'

Couldn't stand his manners, that's all. I never did take to men who thought they were the centre of the universe.

He dropped the cigarette and used the heel of his shoe on it. Even that simple action carried a message: that he had it in his power to extinguish any spark of life.

'Not everything about you. About the journalist Nortier we know a good deal. We know of his job in Sfax, though that may not be his only work. But you do not live in Tunisia and we need to know more about you. Why did you come to Sfax? It is not a holiday resort.'

'I told you . . .'

I stopped when he grasped my hair in one hand, the left hand that had hit me, a Moslem's dirty hand.

'You have been observed in the company of a Chief Inspector of the French Sûreté. You were seen driving him in a car. You were seen together in the evening. You are his assistant, isn't that true? We shall check on that. Why did he send you to Borj Mechaab? What did he imagine you could achieve here? Why didn't he come himself? Why hasn't he informed the organs of the corrupt Tunisian regime?'

His eyes slipped round my features, as quick as a snake. I felt the roots of my hair pull as he tightened his grip.

I was not important. I understood that. He was important and I was nothing, an irritant like a pebble in his shoe. He gave me no time for answers. I had been called into this room to be abused. I had poked my nose into the Skorpion's nest and must be punished.

'Western whore.'

He breathed it for my ears only. In his eyes I could see his private greed: that I was in his power. He hit me with the back of his free hand and hit me again, and it was then I made my move. There is a terrible lust in his kind which feeds on itself and grows more powerful until it bursts through all constraint. I have heard of interrogators who woke in confusion to find a corpse on their hands. Their lust had blotted out everything. The blood had gone racing through their veins, a red fog that deadened them even to the confession they were supposed to be extracting.

It wasn't an immaculate *seoinage*.

I was hampered. I began from a sitting position against an opponent who towered over me. My choice of move was limited because he stood to one side and I couldn't use a simple knee to his groin. The *seoinage* has none of that brutality and I'd seen Shikohishi demonstrate it on the mat against opponents one-third his age and twice his weight. In the end it was always Shikohishi who was bowing and giving his apologetic smile. His favourite opponent was a US Marines Sergeant called Fernau who could lift him with one hand and shake him like maracas. 'Thank you, Fernau-san, you have demonstrated superior strength. I shall now demonstrate superior skill. Please be so kind as to hit me in the face.' The fist Fernau aimed at the old man's chin was blocked. He had no time for a second fist. A flurry of limbs ended with the sergeant on the mat, back down, arm gripped with optimum tension in a straight lock between Shikohishi's thighs. 'I am obliged, Fernau-san. Of course, lady and gentlemen, in an alley in Yokohama you would finish with a strangle lock and your opponent would be unconscious and already dying.' Shikohishi was a legend. Like all legends he declined to talk about himself. He was rumoured to have fathered children in every NATO country and all of them boys, as if he possessed some special technique.

I had to loosen the officer's grip on my hair so I used the heel of my shoe on his instep. It was enough to distract him. The pressure on my scalp eased and at the same moment he jerked his left foot back. I stood straight up, not attempting to back away, because with a *seoinage* it is essential to have body-contact or the throw won't be successful. It is a question of breaking the opponent's balance and doing it quickly before he can counter.

I doubt this officer intended to counter even if he had possessed the skills. His brain was too blocked by blood-thirst to think. I stepped in close with my right foot, turning it as far as I could, bowing my body in towards him because I was going to need maximum leverage to lift his bulk. An army jacket is not as loose as the judo outfit but I was able to get a grip on a pocket flap in my right hand and a shouldertab in my left and I was well into the action where training takes over and the moves become automatic. I eased my left hip away from him and swung the right foot round, bending both knees, letting go with my right hand, still pulling him forward with the left, and scooping my free hand under his arm and winding it over his elbow. I think he began to shout but it was hard to distinguish because at this point in the *seoinage* the balance of the body is transferred to the left leg and a hip is thrust back into the opponent's pelvis and it could have been the sharp expelling of breath I heard. His balance broke when I leaned forward and I was still turning to the left as his body came off the ground and swept over my hip and I let him go because there was no future in the move, not here.

He ended up against the wall, knocking over the table and sending glasses on a brass tray smashing into the stone.

The classical *seoinage* takes three seconds.

I could feel the sweat spring in the palms of my hands and on my temples. That was something I had never observed with Shikohishi. But Shikohishi wasn't faced by an army officer with a frustrated blood-lust and a guard breaking in through the door with a rifle searching for a target.

There was nowhere I could hide and no way I could escape. I was convinced I had done the only possible thing even if I now faced a rifle because that officer would have gone on using his hands on me until my vertebrae snapped. The Agency had the training of me and they teach you to use your head to get out of a tight corner. But it's no good if the head has been broken, no damn good at all.

The officer had scrambled back on his feet. His hand went at once to his holster because if I could put him down like that on his back among the broken glassware I could have taken his pistol. They always need to check their power-source is still there. But I was wrong. He wasn't just checking.

'I'm going to kill you for that. I'm going to kill you, whore.'

The pistol jerked up level with my chest.

———◆———

15

There was a dry cough.

I closed my eyes against the light. It had no shade. It shone on my eyelids, pulsing red to my heartbeat. Somewhere far away I could hear a dog howling against the darkness. A soldier gave a shout, muffled by the barrack hut, and was quiet. The night was still. This was Skorpion's base and I expected activity. It was as if they were holding their breath: the night before D-Day, the night before an execution, that kind of feeling.

I opened my eyes and said: 'He might have shot you dead.'

'It would have been only a little premature.'

He coughed again.

He'd saved my life. I should have been more grateful. He had simply appeared out of the shadows and stood between me and the pistol. There'd been an explosion but it had been of anger. There'd been a lot of shouting from the officer. It's what you would expect. He'd been humiliated by a woman and he wanted revenge. One bull of a voice, one soft voice. I hadn't understood the words but the meaning was plain: *Get out of my way, I'm going to kill the whore.* And against that: *No, we need to question her further.* I'd been marched out, a soldier to each arm, a rifle muzzle between my shoulderblades. Back in the cell I was shoved onto the bunk.

This man who had saved my life stood where the doctor in a hospital stands, at the end of the bed, studying the patient's face and movements. But it was he who needed medication. He stood stiffly because the juice had gone out of his joints. His body had dried up. He looked no more than bones connected with string, bent inwards, without substance. His chest was thin: he'd coughed everything out of it.

He said: 'You didn't tell Major Fellah much.'

'He didn't give me much of a chance.' Personally I didn't think that toughie who used the back of his hand on me before I could talk was interested. In his view he was the only important person in the whole world. If he had had to listen to my answers, that would have meant I had some value too. I asked: 'Who is Major Fellah?'

'The leader.'

'Is he in the Tunisian army?'

'He was in Military Intelligence.'

'And you?'

'I am Rachid Jaafar.'

'Also Military Intelligence?'

He wore a *djellaba*, not a uniform. But with Intelligence officers you can never tell. Jaafar shook his head.

'I was in the Foreign Ministry in Tunis. Then I served in the embassies in Paris and Washington. Without pleasure, I may say. It was in America the pains began. The doctors told me I was dying.'

'Doctors can be wrong.'

'Possibly. It's been a year and a half.'

He coughed. Something like a cloud passed across his face. Not a smile. Not scepticism. Perhaps resignation.

'No, the doctors were right. My life has simply been preserved a little longer than expected. Among much wrong with my body I have cancer. They operated. But the growth is malignant. In here.'

He'd spoken the whole time with his hands gripped in front of his belly, and he moved them up as if they were shackled together. That cloud which had passed across his face had been pain. It was the shadow of death easing its way into his body. Jaafar wasn't an old man but had aged, wasted away. His eyes had aged: there was a moistness about them. The pupils were sharp enough and I wondered about morphine to ease his pain.

'Allah willing I shall last to see final victory. What happens to me then matters nothing.'

'The establishment of the Islamic People's Republic?'

No, no morphine. His brain was sharp enough. 'Crevecoeur told you that.'

'No, the officer who brought us here.'

He gave a slight nod. 'All right, we have talked enough of me. Now we shall discover about you.'

149

'You already know . . .'

'Please.' He moved his hands. I had seen priests stand with their hands clasped like Jaafar. Admit you are a sinner, my child. Repent all evil and God will forgive you. 'We have already talked to the blind one, Nortier. You know that. But I confess you are something of a mystery.'

Jaafar's voice was gentle and reasonable. It was a classic of interrogation: first the bully, then the kind one who offers sympathy. Fellah hadn't seriously tried to learn anything. He was simply softening me up. His way was the way you soften an octopus, beating it against a rock. Jaafar seemed to be waiting and I looked back at him.

'Nortier maintains that he first met you three days ago. Incredible to think that three days' acquaintanceship could land a man in a place such as this. You are not friends, not colleagues, not lovers. What are you? You pretend you are a teacher of English. Perhaps if you said you were a teacher of unarmed combat I would believe you.'

'A woman must know how to defend herself.'

'Oh please, that was professional.'

'I belong to a club. We take it seriously. I train three evenings a week.'

'As an agent of the French Sûreté you would be expected to keep your skills sharp.'

'I'm not an agent. I've told you.'

'But you know Crevecoeur. You were seen driving him from the airport.'

'We met by chance after the explosion. I was French and he asked if I could help him.'

'Yes?'

'So I helped him. That's all.'

He had been standing rock still. At last he made a gesture, moving his hands up to cushion his chin.

'Please.' He was very polite as an interrogator. I couldn't tell what he believed. 'You drove him to the *Cercle des Officiers* in Sfax.'

'I said I helped. He asked me to drop him there.'

'At the *Cercle des Officiers* he met a Security Colonel. Later he went to your hotel. Half a dozen others to choose from but he picked yours.'

150

'I'd told him I was staying there. I was just making conversation.'

'In the evening you were seen having dinner with him at the Restaurant Baghdad.'

'You've lived in Paris, Monsieur Jaafar. It is not uncommon for a man to invite a woman to dinner.'

'When that woman has been asking questions about a certain Captain Borries and the man is interested in the same person, I suggest that the dinner conversation was not about the latest play or political scandal in Paris.'

I'd been wearing Michel's black and gold shirt and Crevecoeur's eyes had dropped down. His eyes had fingered my body. *I'm saving your life*, he'd said, *get out, you're in deep water way out of your depth*. Now I was in a cell while a revolutionary coup was set in motion in south Tunisia. Who'd been Skorpion's agent at the Baghdad? The waiter? They probably knew the name of the wine we'd drunk.

Jaafar was staring as if he couldn't quite add me up. 'But we don't think you actually work *at* the Sûreté.'

'You mean you've penetrated the French Sûreté as well as your own? And your man there denies I'm on the staff?' That was the only sense I could make of what he said. Well, Crevecoeur had once confided that the Sûreté was no better than a sieve: it leaked on Moscow, Langley and London alike. A few more holes had been punched in it and it even leaked on Sfax and Borj Mechaab. 'Monsieur Jaafar,' I said, 'if you know I was asking about Borries, you'll also know that was *all* I was asking about. His wife Ella is very worried about him. She hasn't heard from her husband for weeks. She said would I please see if I could trace him.'

'Why did you think Borries was in Borj Mechaab? Who gave you that idea? Crevecoeur?'

'Borries filed a flight plan at Sfax. He was heading south. Perhaps someone down here had news of him. That was what Nortier was going to ask Colonel Mahrez.'

He coughed. When he closed his eyes his face became a death mask. He opened his eyes again and they were watering. It was just the coughing fit. He wasn't crying.

'You were asking everywhere for Captain Borries. You are well acquainted with the Chief Inspector from the Sûreté.

You drive down to our base camp, avoiding a roadblock. You are highly trained at unarmed combat. I think . . .' He broke off to study me.

In the wardrobe, back among the long-ago fashions, was the secret I had to keep from him: that years ago I had been recruited by a department of British Intelligence. You can say: 'I was a prostitute once, and stopped.' Or: 'I used to shoot heroin, and am cured.' You can never say: 'I was a spy, but no more.' Because spies cannot be believed. Spies always lie. Scratch a reformed spy and you find the spots are still underneath. That pure white paint was nothing but cover. If Jaafar knew of my past, he would be convinced I worked for Crevecoeur.

'You see,' Jaafar said almost apologetically, 'there are things we need to know urgently: how you pinpointed our base, what action you planned, where Crevecoeur has vanished to, how you make contact with him. You could be a freelance. That is Major Fellah's opinion. It is why he called you a whore, hiring yourself out for money. Or you could be on the Sûreté's payroll but we don't know your real name. The Deschampsneufs papers could be false. We have asked our organization in France to check on them.'

He was still gauging my reactions. I hope nothing showed in my face. If they found out the Deschampsneufs papers were not mine, Major Fellah would get out the thumbscrews.

Jaafar crossed the cell and knocked on the door. The soldier who unlocked it had a submachine gun cradled in his arm.

'I will leave you alone a little,' Jaafar said, 'to reflect.'

He was standing at the end of the bed.

How had he got there?

In normal conditions it takes nothing to wake me. A floorboard relaxing, Michel turning over, a moth beating against a windowpane – any tiny change in the aural pattern penetrates into my subconscious and I'm awake in the instant, my breathing unchanged. Tonight I'd been physically and mentally drained and I'd gone to a deep level of sleep and never heard the key turn in the lock. Jaafar hadn't slept. His face had turned the colour of raw pastry.

'Your passport is stolen,' Jaafar said. 'We have heard from

our contact in France. You're not a teacher of English at Chartres. You must be a freelance used by the Sûreté.'

There was a hiss to his breath. It made his voice more urgent.

I shook my head. 'Ella Borries hired me. She was worried about her husband.'

'That is just your cover story,' Jaafar said. 'In reality you have been hired by Crevecoeur. He doesn't trust his colleagues. That is why he came to Tunisia alone.'

'I've told you . . .'

Jaafar was glancing away. There were voices outside, footsteps echoing. His eyes went to the high narrow window. There was a patch of sky visible. It was turning grey as the night sky paled.

'You *must* tell me about your connection with Crevecoeur. There's so little time.'

I shook my head. I had no connection with him.

He tried a new tack. 'What is your real name?'

I shook my head to that too.

A very loud voice was approaching down the corridor. The door was unlocked and Major Fellah bustled in. He had changed his uniform: when I had gripped him at the start of the *seoinage* I had torn the shoulder tab loose. Now he wore an immaculate jacket. He was the leader and had appearances to keep up. He spoke in Arabic to Jaafar who turned slowly to reply. Major Fellah, loud, angry, full of his power; Jaafar, quiet, exhausted, drying out until he would be dust. There was a disagreement, that was obvious. But Major Fellah was not to be denied. From his face it was apparent a decision had been made and his mind was no longer open.

Major Fellah crossed to the bunk and hit me across the cheek. I felt the sting of his ring again. There was no explanation needed. He hadn't enjoyed that *seoinage*, particularly from a woman.

'It's your last chance,' Jaafar said.

'I don't work for the Sûreté. I don't know what action Crevecoeur is taking. I don't know where he is or how to contact him.'

'She's wasted enough of my time,' Fellah said. He turned on his heel and walked out, shouting orders in Arabic. Two soldiers entered at the double and my arms were twisted behind my back and handcuffs locked on.

'I did warn you,' Jaafar said. The urgency had died out of his voice.

There was no colour in the world yet. Jaafar stood with his face down and his eyes opaque, like someone thinking of love or trying not to think of death. His *djellaba* looked drab and wrinkled in the dawn light. Under it he wore a shirt unbuttoned at the neck; the weight of a tie would be too much for him. He coughed in the cold air.

'Suzanne?'

Nortier's voice was desperate. I moved so our bodies were touching. His hands were manacled behind his back like mine. He twisted his head to each new sound.

'What's happening?' he asked.

'They think we're spies.'

'But we're not. I'm a journalist. They know that.'

'They think Crevecoeur employs me.'

'I told them all I know about Crevecoeur. Major Fellah came in the night and I told him you were hired by Ella Borries to find her husband. I said you'd clashed with Crevecoeur in the past. Crevecoeur was a bastard and you would never work for him.'

So they knew I'd met Crevecoeur before. Was that a reason for doing this?

Two or three little clouds high in the sky caught the rays of the coming sun. There is an innocence about early morning clouds before day imposes its reality. The reality was this: that Nortier and I were in the square inside the fortress, by the eucalyptus trees, armed soldiers standing guard over us. Behind the trees was something I had missed before – five heaps of sand, about the length of a man. Five had chosen to die rather than become soldiers of the Islamic People's Republic.

A door banged open in the building opposite and a dozen soldiers filed out, Major Fellah at their head. They marched in a ragged line across the square to this quiet corner where the French had planted trees and the revolution had already claimed its first lives. Major Fellah barked an order and the soldiers halted.

'Fellah,' Nortier called out. 'What's going on? I don't understand.'

'You came here to spy on us. You know the punishment for spies.'

'Suzanne?' Nortier twisted his head towards me, his eyes wide. There was a new scar on one cheek. It looked like the burn a cigarette makes in human flesh. I could imagine who did it. Major Fellah wouldn't believe a spy could be blind. He would push the glowing tip of the cigarette towards an eye as a test. At the last moment Nortier would feel its heat and jerk his head.

'She's a whore,' Fellah said. 'Do you expect her to feel sorry for you? She hired herself to the French. She has a mission here and the means of reporting to her employers. If she speaks it might be worth saving you both.'

'I have not been hired by the French. I don't know where Crevecoeur is. I have no means of communicating with him.' I denied everything and Fellah simply shrugged.

This was no normal place of execution. There were no stakes, no sand-filled bags, no bullet scars in the wall. This was special. Fellah gave his order and soldiers grabbed us. They tied us to the trunks of the eucalyptus, its peeling bark rustling to the rub of ropes.

'For God's sake, Suzanne, do something.'

'Ask Ella Borries. She'll tell you she hired me. It's a purely personal matter – she's worried about her husband. Go on, you've got people in Paris, ask her. Why don't you do that?'

'I'll tell you why,' Fellah said. 'There's a police guard outside her front door. The French are worried we might question one of their own.'

Was that Crevecoeur's doing? Protecting Ella, condemning me.

The clouds had pink edges that were fading as the sun grew in power. Its rays were catching the tops of the towers at the corners of the fort. I looked along the length of the building and the windows were blocked by impassive faces.

Think about the Foreign Legion building this place. Think about them swilling their litres of *gros rouge*. Think about Edith Piaf singing their battle-hymn: *Non, je ne regrette rien*.

Think about Michel. Think about the feel of him inside you. Think about anything. Don't brood.

But the sun was creeping down the walls. This was the Islamic People's Republic and strictest Islamic custom dictates that the condemned to death shall not see the sun rise.

I believe in myself, I believe I can always win. That is the credo the Agency drives into you. But as the rifles were raised and aimed at our chests I faced the final truth: I was not invincible. I stared into the faces of the soldiers and the black holes of the rifles. Nortier was struggling with his knots. I'd tried and given up. Even suppose the ropes came undone, what good would it be? There was no hiding place from a dozen rifles.

Jaafar had turned and was shuffling away, his sandals scuffing sand. The sun was flashing off windows now, reaching down to me.

'You can't do this,' Nortier cried out. 'You're murdering us.'

The tradition is to offer a blindfold. It's so you don't look in the eyes of the man who will kill you. A blindfold provides no magic armour against the bullets. But then, we raise our arm as the car heads for the brick wall. The soft machine struggles to protect itself. Why hadn't I been given a blindfold? I closed my eyes.

Footsteps approached. I felt a coldness at the side of my neck under my ear.

'Open your eyes.'

Major Fellah had his pistol against me. What kind of threat was that? I faced a line of rifles. Why should five seconds more or less matter?

He took a fistful of hair and jerked it and my eyes flew open. I glanced sideways at his face. He was mad. I could see that in the eyes that stared at me and through me and into a private vision of his own. One of his eyelids had gone berserk, a wild dance.

Somewhere far off I heard Jaafar cough, dry as a desert breeze.

This is not happening to me. I don't believe it.

I felt the suck of Major Fellah's breath before he shouted his final order.

The world exploded.

16

So this was death. Silence, dome of a chapel, pale religious light.

I'd never thought of it before, never tried to imagine an after-life. Who could believe in choirs of angels or eternal flames? I couldn't. Yet here I was, drifting through a haze.

There was pain in my heart. No one ever warned that you go on feeling the pain you die with. There wasn't pain all over my chest so perhaps only one rifle had a live round. The bullet had entered my chest and penetrated the left ventricle. Major Fellah had delivered the *coup de grâce*. I still had the memory-trace of the savage brilliance that exploded in my consciousness as I died.

It had been a Walther PP that Fellah had jabbed below my ear. I had glanced sideways and recognized the profile with that same squat businesslike look of the Browning. He had filled his lungs to bellow his order and I was helpless. I had learnt about the pistol along with a hundred thousand other things they force-fed you with during the four years' training. Knowledge is survival, Cody, remember that. Knowing it was a Walther hadn't saved me from dying, but it's no good snivelling like that. Knowledge had helped me survive East Germany and Istanbul and Holland. I had been immortal.

Until the Walther ended my life. There are two models: 7.65 or 9 mm. Muzzle velocity, Cody? I can't remember. You got to remember, Cody, because one lousy day in Tashkent or Managua it could be important. 280, 300, maybe 320 metres per second. Be precise, Cody, don't just sit there flashing your tits at me. Sergeant Moesser, don't speak to me like that, don't do it ever again or I'll take you apart one dark night. Shit, I think the little lady means it. Damn right, sergeant.

Okay, muzzle velocity 290 m/s. Not significant. You can't jump far when the muzzle is digging into your neck. And the proof: I was now as cold as a tombstone, so cold I was shivering.

Shivering?

Which soldier had been issued with the live round? No matter. They all shared the guilt. The bullet had split the skin and passed between my fifth and sixth ribs. It made a bloody mess of my heart. It had continued on through my left lung, leaving the destructive evidence of its passage. Medics who specialize in bullet wounds call that the permanent track. If no solid bone obstructed it, the bullet would have passed out just below the shoulderblade and exited through my skin. Otherwise its final resting place would be somewhere in my chest cavity. The brutal disfigurement it inflicted on my body would be matched by the damage my body had done to it: the bullet would now be distorted.

I moved a hand and felt my back and there was no exit hole. I had died with the bullet inside me still. That would explain the particular pain.

But when I felt there was no entrance hole in my breast either, no stickiness, no bullet inside. The pain in my chest was the power of imagination, no more, quite enough. The pain began fading at once. I wasn't dead. My hand could feel the pumping of my heart. It is a lover's heart you feel strongest, with your head resting on his chest. My heartbeat sent a faint message of life.

And I was shivering because that's the way the body reacts to unconsciousness. The ache in my head was real enough: the butt of Major Fellah's pistol? When I felt, there was a bump. I winced at shooting stars of pain.

I got off the bunk and dizzied for a moment, a foot stumbling against the bucket. The door was unlocked at the noise and a submachine gun poked in, followed by the soldier on guard. He was nervous. It was something to beware of or something I could use. But take note of his nerves because I had to plan *now* for escape.

They were applying the abortive execution technique. They only try that once. Next time it wouldn't be abortive.

'My head hurts.'

Jaafar gave a shrug as if to say: had I considered the

alternative? 'One of the guards was acting under my orders. It was the only way to stop the execution going ahead. Major Fellah is a great leader. He has much to achieve. Naturally he is an impatient man.'

Jaafar went for a little walk. It was four of his shuffling paces to the wall and he peered up where the window was set into the stonework. There was a patch of blue up there, no sun visible. The window faced east and the sun was already high overhead. He came back to the end of the bunk. For him it was a lot of activity.

'You are alive,' he said. 'That is something to be grateful for. I wake up half a dozen times in the night. For normal people this would be intolerable. But each time the pain wakes me I feel glad: pain means life. Now, there are certain things we really do need to know.'

Life having been granted to me again, I was supposed to feel gratitude, a desire to make a gift in return. It is one of the classics of interrogation: a sympathetic listener is meant to produce an irresistible urge to unburden yourself. In their quieter moments even the Gestapo appreciated that, as a thousand cellars could testify.

'Shall we start with the timing? The day before yesterday you met Chief Inspector Crevecoeur at the airport. You left Nortier and drove Crevecoeur away. It takes twenty minutes at most to drive into the centre of Sfax. But it was two and a half hours later that you arrived at the *Cercle des Officiers*. That would allow the Chief Inspector plenty of time to brief you.'

Jaafar was watching me. I said: 'He had a rendezvous arranged. You know that. He asked me to drive him there. The meeting never took place because his agent had been killed.'

'Did you inform the authorities about this dead man?'

'No.'

'Why not?' When I didn't answer he said: 'You knew you would both be questioned very closely by the police, perhaps taken into custody. You didn't want that. You had work to do.'

'I never saw the body. I'm only taking Crevecoeur's word for it. Don't ask me why he didn't report it.'

159

Jaafar didn't move. He was like a piece of cinnamon bark – brown and thin and curled in on himself.

'Suppose,' he said, 'the police had questioned you. They would have looked at your passport. It is routine in such matters to check its authenticity with the issuing authority. The French would have informed the Tunisian police that the Deschampsneufs passport was stolen last year. Then your troubles would really have started. Why did you have a stolen passport? That's what they would want to know. Well, we can hazard a guess at the answer: you were a freelance fitted up by Crevecoeur. That explanation squares with the facts, doesn't it?'

You can hide a lot under a *djellaba*. A knife or a pistol, for instance. But even if Jaafar had come armed it would be the easiest thing in the world to take him. He was ill, weak and inexperienced. But he came alone and unarmed because he was unafraid. I couldn't use him as a shield or a bargaining counter because he placed no value on his life. He would sacrifice it for the revolution.

He was staring at me. The gentle eyes hardened. I was not cooperating.

'You left France,' he said, 'using a stolen passport. The official at Charles-de-Gaulle Airport inspected the passport. They know the numbers of stolen documents but they let you through. Why?'

Because Crevecoeur had kept that piece of information inside the building in rue des Saussaies. Skorpion had a contact there and had found out about it. The passport department hadn't.

'Once again we can supply the answer that fits the facts: you were let through the departure gate because you work for the Sûreté. Now can . . .'

He stopped. His face changed. It was like those big banners in parades that are caught by a gust of wind. Pain rippled across his features. He turned slowly and knocked on the door. He held onto the wall before it was opened and he left without another word.

It moved.

I felt it, though I longed not to. I tried to block it from my mind, not to brood and let my imagination twist and turn because that was what Major Fellah wanted. But the nerves in my skin would not be denied and they screamed their message to the brain: it is moving.

I had heard boots approaching and had got up at once to stand against the wall. I didn't want to be lying on the bunk when Major Fellah entered. 'A great leader' is what Jaafar had called him. He hadn't showed his charisma to me. Even the greatest of leaders has a side that is in the shadows and Fellah's darkness was all that I had experienced.

He had spoken at once, as if he had no time to waste: 'Turn round. Face the wall.'

There had been commands I did not understand, urgent shouts in Arabic, and I was totally unprepared for the hand that wrenched my shirt over my head. I turned, ready to kick, to dislocate a shoulder, to strike with the blade of my hands, but Major Fellah had his pistol out and aimed at my belly. It is one of the worst places to be shot and I believed he would. He wanted to. His mouth was open and there was an invitation in his eyes. In another man it would have a different meaning. Perhaps for him it was the same, the only release he ever got.

He had spoken and the soldiers stood back against the wall. And then to me in French: 'They will leave me a clear line of fire. Finish undressing yourself.'

The two soldiers were looking at my body but Major Fellah had eyes only for my face, wanting to see the humiliation there. The *seoinage* had hurt him and he nourished his bruised pride.

The pistol dropped abruptly until it pointed at a kneecap. 'If I shoot you there you will never walk straight again and I'll make you wait for a doctor until you do as I say.'

The knuckles of the hand that held the gun were white. I moved slowly, not wanting him to misunderstand any gesture. And while I moved I calculated the odds: even if I flung my clothes in his face and avoided his bullet, I faced the two soldiers; even if I disabled them, I faced the guard outside; even if I outwitted him, I faced the whole of the barracks who would be alerted by the disturbance and then the perimeter fence and finally the trek to Remada. The odds were

161

disappointing. The zip of my jeans tore the silence and Major Fellah swallowed.

'The rest.'

There is no way to undress without noise. The rustle of cloth on skin is a powerful aphrodisiac but his eyes wavered only once and were quickly back on my face, as if to be caught looking was a confession of weakness. The skin that was bared to him wasn't the means of gratification. He had lusts that lay too deep for that.

'You will lie on the bed. Face down.'

Whatever I had been mentally preparing myself for, it wasn't this. They had come in with a jar, an ordinary jam jar with a screw lid, and it had been placed on the table against the wall. I had paid it no attention. Major Fellah snapped his fingers and the jar was brought to him. He stood above the bed and barked out: 'Look.' When I wasn't quick enough he grabbed my hair and forced my head round so I should see. He held the jar towards me, a precious offering in the palm of his hand.

'We took this as the symbol of the revolution,' Fellah said. 'Skorpion we called ourselves. We too come from the desert. Our home is sand and rocks and sun. Our strength is our sting. A scorpion can kill something two thousand times its size. That is what our revolution will do – sting and sting and sting until we kill the corrupt regime.'

He tilted the jar and sent the scorpion slithering. It was longer than my middle finger. Its front legs were like the pincers of a crayfish, alert for prey. The tail was arched, holding the sting high. The cephalothorax was squat and broad and coloured greyish rose. As Major Fellah tipped the jar the light caught the scorpion and the abdomen appeared smudged with dirt as if it had been casually gathered in the desert by some bedouin.

'You are terrified,' he said. 'That is what Skorpion will do – provoke terror. We shall strike and strike again. Our cells are poised to act and are waiting for my word of command. Skorpion will strike and the people will see the regime is powerless. Out of chaos comes creation: the new Islamic People's Republic.'

Major Fellah's left eyelid was flickering. There was turmoil inside him, as there had been at the abortive execution, and this was how it showed.

'The regime cannot stop us. Crevecoeur can't stop us. Nor can you – you are nothing.'

But that didn't prevent him doing what he did. It was a private lust he had and it demanded gratification. He dropped my head on the bed.

'Now we begin.'

Arabic looks sensuous when written. It was harsh in Major Fellah's shout. He hurled his orders and the soldiers grabbed my wrists and held me tight. There was the sound of the lid unscrewing and I waited and waited. Fellah's face loomed beside mine.

'I am a soldier and my way with the enemy is to have them shot. But you are different. You are a spy. You will tell me where Crevecoeur has gone and how you make contact with him. You will tell me what you were instructed to do here. Those are the most urgent questions.'

There are people you reason with and people you don't even bother to try. *I don't work for Crevecoeur. I don't know his movements.* What was the point in telling him again? His eyelid trembled and I knew he had a mind that was closed. He didn't want information – that wasn't why he had come.

Fellah's head withdrew from sight and the scorpion was on me. It fell like a trickle of sand in the small of my back. It made a little run and there was a shout from Fellah and the movement stopped. I couldn't see the scorpion. In front of my eyes was the stone of the wall and to each side of me was a figure in khaki.

It was burning a hole in my skin.

I mustn't move. I mustn't provoke an attack.

I mustn't think about it.

Impossible. The scorpion was part of me now. What was it doing? Tail high? And the eyes – were they inspecting the body it rested on or were they watching the watchers?

In an alley off boulevard St-Germain there's a shop window with such things: tarantulas, stuffed snakes, the teeth of crocodiles, and scorpions in formaldehyde, a row of jars. A square of curling cardboard rests against one of the jars. It gives the Latin name and states: The killer from North Africa.

The soldier to my left gave a grunt that was half laughter. By twisting my head I could see his face. There was a shine to his skin, the excitement breaking out in sweat. He said something and the soldier on the other side answered and the two of them smacked their hands together. There was bitterness in my throat and a cold band constricting my forehead. They were betting on the scorpion. Would it sting? Would it sidle away? At the moment it did nothing. It was enjoying the warmth of my body.

And Michel, there's warmth in your body and softness in your skin, not the skin of your cheeks with the morning rasp, but the skin of your belly and who was it who said love was nothing more than the touching of two pieces of epidermis? Who? Must be a man, must be a Frenchman with that skidding sideways glance at the ways of the world or it could be a German with that sudden clinical word *epidermis* dropped in where anyone with a touch of romance in his soul would think of skin or maybe he was a bastard child of both nations, from that region where the first names are French and the surnames are German, just like you Michel Bohme my dark-eyed and smooth-bellied Alsatian and oh God it's moving.

'*Allez! Allez!*' I remembered a taxi-driver shouting that. It was a hundred years ago in an eerie street in the Sixteenth *arrondissement* in Paris. Did Fellah imagine it was some bloody football match too and his team had just made a break? His face jutted next to mine. His voice was hoarse and low. He could have been passing on some urgent secret of love. 'Spy, whore, this will be the last day of your life.' His eyes searched my face for terror and guilt. 'Tell me before it's too late.'

It wasn't the hope of a confession that had brought Fellah. The tide of his desires had washed him in. His weakness showed in the drumming of his eyelid and the hunger of his voice and the sweat on his upper lip and the greed of his dark eyes and Michel also has brown eyes but the whites are not stained with yellow and the left eyebrow rises not like this erupting lid but in irony which Michel argues is the true French virtue along with logic of course and bold inventiveness and a sort of creative heat of the imagination and I cannot stand the French when they start preening themselves so I put on my quizzical look and told him his countrymen surpassed all people in their tolerance and honesty and generosity and humour and sense of fairplay not to mention modesty and in the end Michel came over to shut me up and the only way to close my mouth was with his mouth and it was in November with an exhausted sun touching the slates on the roof across rue St-André-des-Arts and those city noises that sound so forlorn in the afternoon because that is the time of betrayal and we had fallen on the blue carpet in the living room and he said that too was ironic because to the French the colour blue had a touch of innocence and I said it was appropriate then because a man was never so innocently occupied as when he was making love to a woman and our eyes were locked together and I'm sure mine had opened wider as he entered me because I saw the twitch of a smile at the corners of his lips and it's no bloody good because the thing's on the move again and the nerves in my skin are screaming with it.

'It's not quick,' Major Fellah whispered. 'If it stings it will be an hour at best, maybe half a day before you die.'

It had moved onto my buttocks and stopped again. There was a quiver in my flesh and perhaps the scorpion was alarmed by it. Or perhaps it had just paused to luxuriate in the warmth, like the warmth of the sun yesterday afternoon when Nortier and I had lain on the sand with rifles jabbed into our temples and I'd felt that secret dampness which others never see but a polygraph machine can detect and judge you a liar as if the machine was God and knew every fear and love and hate and why did M in Washington say before I ran out on him that I cannot handle emotion so instead I acquire expertise and that I need to go on proving myself better because I am frightened of standing still and undressing my soul in front of another human being and isn't that plain stupid and oh no please no it's on the move again.

The others in the room were still, absorbed in watching. There was a bastard form of ecstasy in Fellah's face. He was questioning, asking for a telephone number, an address, something. His voice was soft, half crooning, whispering his form of love in my ear.

And then I nearly lost control because I understood what they were waiting for. A scorpion enjoys the sun but it likes to take shelter in crevices and cracks. It was poised at the divide of my buttocks.

If I writhed my legs, and they had been left free deliberately, it would sting me. But if it scuttled down into the depths of my body no power could prevent my violent convulsion. My nerves would be beyond the control of my will.

Michel help me. Paul, M, Nortier . . . No use. My mind would no longer cruise on automatic pilot. I could occupy myself with none of them. There was only the scorpion.

'I'll tell you what happens,' Major Fellah breathed in my ear. 'The sting works like snake venom. You feel nausea and aches in your muscles. The poison attacks the nervous system. It affects your heartbeat and finally there are convulsions and unconsciousness. I have watched a man's toes and fingers turn blue before he died. It is the first time with a woman. How will it affect . . .'

Gone.

It ran without warning over my hip and the tickle of its feet left my skin as it scuttled away across the bunk. One of the soldiers was quick because it came towards him and he jumped aside and stamped once, twice, with his boot and grunted.

Major Fellah swallowed. His face had set and his eyes showed shock. He had achieved no release. He stretched to his full height and left the cell without speaking. I didn't watch him leave. I was shaking as if every nerve in my body was wired up in a giant circuit and the switch had been thrown.

It was so quiet.

When you're in a cell and the door is locked and there's a guard with a submachine gun, you listen for noises. You create the world outside.

There was the dog. I'd heard it before. It wasn't a big dog. The bark was yappy. Somewhere in Borj Mechaab there was this cur that gave voice at passers-by. Not many passed by. Why weren't there more sounds from the village? Because

166

there were no flocks of animals, no machines, no factories, no building rising higher than the palm trees. It was an isolated community, with no farms out in the desert, no passing traffic. That's what the absence of sounds meant to me. Did the villagers know the army camp had been taken over by Skorpion? If the soldiers were confined to barracks, possibly not. There was the occasional noise from within the camp. A shouted command, marching feet, a jeep, whistling. Nothing out of the ordinary.

They were waiting. Some final preparation had to be made and Major Fellah would give the command that would create chaos. When the time came to give that order I would lose all value. Fellah would bark out a few words. Soldiers would come and do it in the cell. Why waste time on a theatrical performance out in the central yard? No prisoners would be taken on the road to glory. Therefore Nortier and I must escape that night. My decision was already taken when I heard the new sound.

It was late afternoon. The strip of sky seen through the window had deepened in colour. I moved the chair against the wall and by standing on the back I was able to reach the ledge of the window. I hauled myself up, like chinning the bar in the gym, and looked out. The rays of the setting sun caught the plane as it sank towards the landing strip inside the camp's fence. It was coming from the east, from Libya. It was an ugly duckling of a thing. 'A Renault 4 with wings' had been Nortier's description of a Skyvan. Exactly. I let myself down to rest my shoulder muscles. The engine note changed as the aircraft landed, taxied and halted. The engines were closed down.

When I next chinned myself to the ledge a man was walking beside the Skyvan. The sun struck gold in his hair. Even at this distance he looked like the photo Ella had given me. He reached the rear of the plane and swung open the tail-end doors.

I had to rest again. I was growing old. I shouldn't tire so quickly.

I looked again and Major Fellah was striding to the plane. He vanished inside the tail. I waited until my muscles screamed but he didn't come out.

There was cramp in my arms from the effort. It was hours since I had eaten and then it had only been couscous and vegetables. I needed sucrose for a burst of energy and protein to feed the muscles for a prolonged effort. I should ring room service.

A sudden wail reached out from the village. The muezzin called the faithful to prayer.

Up again. The sun had gone from the landing strip, the light fading fast. I felt cold and it wasn't just the setting of the sun. Fellah and Borries were walking away from the Skyvan. They had inspected the cargo, what Crevecoeur had called the *matériel de guerre*. But it wasn't being unloaded. Borries's job would be to deliver it to the towns where Skorpion cells waited. No one would question the Skyvan's arrival at any airport: it was Tunisian registered. Borries would unload whatever it was and fly on. Perhaps tomorrow was the day. At Major Fellah's signal Skorpion would strike, unleashing terror.

He was standing in the doctor's position but he'd come as a priest. He'd come to hear a final confession.

Or perhaps he felt guilt at our approaching deaths. He had come to confess himself.

'Major Fellah said he was going to provoke terror. *You* said he was a great leader with much to achieve. What's he going to achieve apart from the deaths of a lot of people?'

Jaafar coughed. There were twin spots of red on his cheeks like a Russian doll. He had a handkerchief to his mouth and he looked at it after he coughed.

'A revolution needs a deep sense of grievance,' I went on. 'It needs a philosophy. If it doesn't have that then it's no more than a bunch of killers, like the IRA. There are groups all over the world who claim they are liberation fronts. They want to free their country from this or that. Perhaps they don't mind how they do it: bombs, shooting. They say they regret the deaths but that they are necessary. I'll tell you this about Fellah: in the beginning he may have had an ideal but now he's slipped over the edge. He's a terrorist. He believes in blood, pain and killing for its own sake. He likes to torture. He could have used red-hot needles under my nails but he'd had a better idea. He came with a scorpion because he enjoyed watching it on me. If I'd been a man he'd have used his fists. But a scorpion promised excitement: a woman's body, her naked skin, the soft flesh he wanted to see hurt. He was playing with me. I was a toy to a murderer.'

Jaafar had gone very still. The colour had spread out on his cheeks as I ran on. If he'd been stronger he would have hit me.

'You are a danger to us,' he said. 'You are lucky you have been treated so well.'

His eyes had grown black with anger. He turned for the door and changed his mind and came back to me.

'I hate the West. I told you I had lived in Washington. Of all Western countries, I hate America the most. It is a society without culture or compassion. The system is wasteful and corrupt. It is quite beyond hope. Let me tell you about the time I had just taken up my post at the embassy. Someone from the State Department took me to dinner. "Entertained" is the word. I wasn't entertained. The restaurant was the product of a sick society. You had to bribe the head waiter even to get a table. The diners hadn't come because they were hungry but because they wanted to impress a business contact or a politican or a woman. The waiters despised the diners and banged the plates on the tables. And the waiters were not just waiters: they sang and went on roller skates. Everything was arranged to distract people from thinking about the obscenity of such a place. I was served a steak that was bigger than the meat the poorest of our poor eat in a whole year. Even the greediest of these diners couldn't finish their food. I saw men stub out cigars in their steaks. At the table next to ours a woman was given a plastic bag. "Is she taking the food home for her children?" I asked. The man who was entertaining me laughed. "No, to feed her dogs." '

'In every big city in every country in the world . . .' I began.

'No.' He was insistent. 'Rich Romans used to vomit so they could eat again. The Roman empire rotted from within. These Americans used their steaks as ashtrays or dogfood. You cannot defend that.'

I didn't want to defend it.

'That is why our movement is necessary. We must stop our country becoming Westernized. It is corrupting our people. For too long Islam has been sleeping. Now it is waking everywhere. We draw our strength from the true faith.'

But I thought of Major Fellah walking away from the Skyvan with Borries. The muezzin had sounded and Fellah had ignored the call to prayers. He worshipped power.

'Nothing but a revolution has any chance of succeeding,' Jaafar said. 'We are fortunate: we have a certain well-wisher in Libya. Major Fellah will give the order and it will be obvious to everyone that the current regime is finished. He will launch his March of the Masses from here. We will march north, the army and the people together. It will begin in Borj Mechaab as a small stream and it will grow into a river. The Islamic People's Republic will spread like floodwater. Long before the March reaches Tunis, it will be obvious we are the true expression of the people.'

He stopped. He'd run out of breath. His eyes dropped. He didn't look at me in the way that Crevecoeur did, more the way Nortier did, not seeing my body. His eyes climbed back to my face, making an Everest of the journey.

'I'll give you a warning. Perhaps you'll heed it. Major Fellah is concerned that you are not merely a spy but a saboteur. Or perhaps you have some means of calling in saboteurs.'

'What could I sabotage? What was in the plane?'

Jaafar considered the question but didn't answer it.

'Major Fellah will be seeing you again. He will make you talk this time. There is no doubt. He says electrodes never fail.'

170

17

◆

The flash had something of the colour of ice in it.

When they attach electrodes to a man they do it to his genitals. It's not just to produce the most intense physical pain. It's to add a psychological twist: the horror of impotence. Even before the current is switched on a man can look down and be haunted by the emasculation to come. Once the switch is thrown, an unseen power will attack his nervous system and he knows the pain will be unendurable. Except he will endure it. If he has nothing to tell, like Nortier, he has no choice.

Together with the flash came a noise like hot fat spitting. There was anger in that crackle.

With a woman there are practical problems that call for a modified technique. In the Bouboulinas Street building a Security Captain called Papadiamantis developed a special probe that replaced one of the metal clips. He even gave it a pet name: the Iron Tampax. He used to laugh about it. That was during the Greek Colonels' regime. Papadiamantis is dead now.

I caught that back-of-the-throat smell which electricity causes.

Major Fellah would have his own way. Since he had a man and a woman to play with, he would indulge his fantasies.

The flash and crackle lasted a fraction of a second. The cell was plunged in darkness. Not only my cell but outside in the corridor and some part of the fort, depending on the extent of the circuit. I could hear soldiers in the distance whistle in derision. The guard outside my door scraped his feet. I didn't think he'd come in this time.

If he did come in and had a flashlamp he'd find me standing on the bed to reach the light socket, pushing the bulb in. Like Levis, my slacks had a metal rivet. I made the short circuit with this.

They never think to take everything away from you.

The army camp must have its own generator, in some shed beyond the fort's walls. A fuse would have blown in the box. It would take time for the proper man to be found to replace it and I waited with my mind a jumble of thoughts: what day of the week was it and was Michel still at his cousin's wedding and was he missing me and what the hell was Crevecoeur doing and was Nortier mentally so tough because of his struggle against blindness and if we picked a Magirus truck we could crash the gate but only if I was physically big enough to drive the brute and was there a public phone in the village and would anyone in Tunis believe a ranting woman who talked of a revolution being unleashed and I would love a hot bath and clean clothes because I was fouled with sweat and . . .

It took close on ten minutes.

The lights came on outside and I pressed the rivet home again. In the darkness I could hear renewed jeering and a grunt from the guard at the door. They were quicker the second time because there was a man right by the fuse box. I pressed in the rivet a third time and darkness returned. If the bulb had been the screw type, I could have screwed the rivet tight to make sure the lights were permanently off. The bulb was the bayonet kind and the rivet prevented it plunging in far enough to lock. But after three black-outs even a military mind gives up and searches for the source of the short circuit.

Conditions in the fort were now perfect. Soldiers shouted and stamped their feet. There were catcalls and laughs. It was a holiday for them, a break in the tension before Major Fellah launched his offensive.

Standing on the bunk I was able to reach the high window with the chair. I jabbed with a leg and smashed the pane of glass.

Major Fellah must have barked out his order: the prisoner will be guarded at all times. It made things much easier for me. At the sound of breaking glass the guard shouted and banged a fist on the door. He could have called for help. He could have gone to fetch a flashlight. But he simply unlocked the door and came in. He stood a moment, an uncertain hulk framed by the dim illumination – there were lights down the corridor on a different circuit.

He spoke in Arabic and then in thick French: "*Moiselle, vous êtes toujours là?*"

I was still there, breathing through an open mouth.

He took a step forward and trod on broken glass and then I didn't need to worry any more. He took two more crunching steps and halted to stare at the high window. He was a big man who'd had little cause to use his brain. Now he was trying to reconcile the impossible: window broken, prisoner absent, but bars intact. He was still gazing up when I rose from behind the bunk and struck the back of his head with the chair. He slid to the floor like someone disappearing through an open manhole. The only sound had been the crack of wood on bone and a scuttering of broken glass as his body keeled over.

Never believe the indestructible heroes in the pulp magazines. The brain impacts against the inside of the skull and that's what causes unconsciousness. There's nearly always a degree of brain damage. There can be temporary amnesia or the sense of balance can be upset or a particular motor-function lost. Sometimes the damage is permanent.

I locked the door behind me.

Nortier had been taken to a cell round the corner to the left. Not far, but it was enemy territory I crept through. To the right some kind of soldiers' mess: stamping of boots on floorboards, drumming of spoons against metal mugs. I could hear orders being shouted and I knew that minutes were precious because they'd be sending men to try and locate the fault in the circuit, also to check the prisoners were secure.

At the right angle in the corridor I paused. It was deep twilit gloom where I stood. Ahead it looked midnight. There was a single pinpoint of light sweeping in a curve. It brightened on a face and dropped. The soldier outside Nortier's cell, smoking as guards always do. Humming started. It was a broken tune, keeping up his spirits in the dark.

The corridor ran right to the end of the fort. A distant square of dark grey showed where a window gave onto the night outside. I knew what I had to do. I was carrying the solid iron key of my cell and I had to hurl this as far down the corridor as I could because the clatter it made is what the guard would go to investigate. The key to Nortier's cell would be in the door and I would unlock it and that, in bald words, was phase one of escaping. No clever tricks. It relied on the soldier's brain running like a train on rails: noise, unexplained, duty to challenge it.

I was moving away from the wall to give myself maximum room to hurl the key when the lights came on again. The guard stopped his humming and turned his head sharply and saw me ten metres from him. I was gripping the key in my right hand, arm drawn back to throw, and I simply held it out, moving steadily forward, giving him no time to think.

He knocked the chair over getting to his feet.

I spoke in French. 'Major Fellah sent me to fetch the blind one.'

He had no gun, no cosh. But he was twenty kilos heavier than me.

He spoke in Arabic, a short staccato burst. We had no language in common. He dropped his cigarette and squared his body up to me and I knew I was heading for a brick wall unless I was nimble.

'Major Fellah,' I said, tapping at my shoulder where his insignia had been, 'Major Fellah,' putting on my winning smile and moving forward because it is damn difficult to start again once you've lost momentum, 'Major Fellah wants to see Monsieur Nortier,' making unlocking motions with the key, 'Major Fellah,' keeping up the incantation because the name must register, only it would help if I knew the Arabic for Major, and then pointing at the door and there the thing was, the key in its hole.

Just as well. Mine was only a prop for a storyline, mightn't have worked this lock.

I said something to the soldier, didn't matter what, he couldn't understand. I stretched out my hand and physically forced him to accept my key, nodding and smiling all the time. Oh we were such pals and the kindly Major had sent me because we had patched up our little difficulties and now I was just going to unlock the cell door. He frowned. His brain simply couldn't cope. I, a prisoner, had appeared out of the darkness with a key and in twenty-five seconds had manoeuvred him into a position where he'd appear foolish to himself if he tried to stand in my way. It was pride, that's all, the heart of so many confidence tricks.

I unlocked the door.

'Okay, we're on our way but we're not talking about it yet.'

Nortier was standing with his back to the wall. He was puzzling it all out. His mouth opened and he drew a breath to ask what was going on and I had to be quick. I whirled on the soldier and said: 'Where is he? Where has Nortier gone? Has he escaped? Major Fellah wants to see him. *Where is he*?'

It was the tone of voice that got through to the soldier, the worried arch of my eyebrows and the thumb jerking in through the open door. He moved forward to see what was worrying me. I stepped to one side, stumbled against the chair, leant down to set it upright and as he passed me I swung. He saw the chair coming out of the corner of his eye and at the last moment he began raising an elbow to fend it off. The chair landed squarely on his occipital bone. For the second time in five minutes a brain impacted against the inside of a skull. They must have considered the risks before they became soldiers. A woman wielding a wooden chair wasn't among them.

The soldier lay slumped across the bunk and Nortier began asking a question and I went and grabbed his wrist.

'Come on. There's no time. We've got to get out now.'

'How did . . .?'

'Later.'

I closed and locked the door and for a moment we stood together in the corridor. With the electricity restored, the rowdiness was subsiding. Did Fellah know about the power cut? Had his office been affected? Would he send someone to check on us? I tugged at Nortier and set off. The corridor echoed to our feet. Years ago the walls had been plastered and painted cream. Now the plaster was pitted and the paint scuffed and the army had no money to spare on aesthetics for soldiers. They had no money to spare on high-wattage bulbs either and we were half way down the corridor before I saw the window at the end was barred.

'Tell me how . . .'

'I short-circuited the lights,' I told him. 'I knocked out both guards and locked them in our cells.'

It made me out to be Wonderwoman. Nortier had to be told something. It was unreasonable to expect him to be kept in the dark. But it simply opened the way to more questions.

'How long . . .?'

Footsteps were coming to meet us. They grew louder than our own shoes. They became a roll of drums on wooden stairs. I cut Nortier short as a sergeant with a detail of four men came into view.

'Soldiers. If they've been sent to check on us, it's the end of the line. I can't handle five.'

Five pairs of eyes were on us. The sergeant pushed in front of his men.

'The sergeant weighs as much as both of us. You've got to speak to him, stop him thinking we've escaped.'

'Me?'

'You speak Arabic. Also you're the man.'

'What . . .'

'Do it.'

Nortier raised his voice. He didn't say much, a couple of sentences. The sergeant looked puzzled and asked a question. Nortier was sharp with him. We edged our way past the soldiers and turned up the staircase. Sweat had come on Nortier's wrist, or was it my fingers?

'He believed you, whatever you said.'

'I told him to go into the yard and wait by the place of execution. Major Fellah's orders. Wait and don't move.'

'You sounded convincing.'

'I'm fluent but I'll always sound French. Why are we going upstairs?'

'Higher up the windows shouldn't be barred.'

'If they're so high, how do we get to the ground?'

'For God's sake, the entrance we came in is guarded.' I pushed on ahead of him. 'A window is the only way. Let's just go and see.'

Nortier couldn't, of course. No more than he could see, at the bend of the stairs, that it was Major Fellah coming down.

I thought of Einstein.

The brain is a crazy thing, sometimes paralysed, sometimes leaping. Why should I think of Einstein?

He said time is relative.

The seconds were eternal while Major Fellah and I confronted each other. Behind me, round the bend of the stairs, was the shuffle of shoes on wood. Nortier was taking his time, being careful with steps he didn't know. Major Fellah always talked in a shout and it meant he needed a lungful of air. His mouth opened and his chest expanded and maybe it was to yell at me or maybe it was to bellow for assistance. There was no time for working out any tactic more complicated than turning and saying round the bend in the stairs:

'Monsieur Jaafar, it's all right. Major Fellah is here.'

Nortier muttered: 'What?'

It was cathedral grey on the stairs. I could make out confusion on Fellah's face. He checked his first impulse to bellow and queried: 'Jaafar?' He was a man who thought with his body and he continued down the steps. I pressed back against the wall and angled my head towards the bend in the stairs. But Fellah stopped a couple of steps above me, some doubt beginning to nag at him.

The shuffle of shoes on wood started again. Major Fellah unbuttoned his holster and got his pistol out. There are times when you feel even to look at a dangerous animal will provoke it. Fellah was one hundred per cent animal. I kept my head averted, just observing that his gaze shifted from me to the landing. He barked out a question in Arabic.

Nortier's footsteps stopped. Then he did a very intelligent thing. He coughed.

It was the dry rasp of someone coughing his life away and Fellah called out again in Arabic. Another paroxysm and suddenly Fellah was coming down past me, grunting to himself, angry because the evidence of his ears persuaded him it was Jaafar but the man wouldn't answer.

A flight of steps is the worst terrain. If your only weapon is your body, the narrowness constricts you. There can be none of the jump movements of savate because of the near certainty you'll lose your footing when you land. Judo is no better: the hip and shoulder and ankle throws depend primarily on perfect balance, which is denied. A *seoinage*, for instance, would have ended up with me at the bottom of the heap, crushed by his weight, vulnerable to his superior strength. Strangely, the position that offers the best hope to the unarmed person is on a lower level because leaning forward there is the opponent's ankle to work with; or reaching up you can grasp a wrist and give a tug and leave the rest to gravity. Also, being above you, your opponent is psychologically over-confident.

An armed person, of course, can simply shoot.

I had to be quick. Surprise is a powerful weapon but it explodes and is gone in a fraction of a second.

I launched myself at the precise moment Major Fellah rounded the corner when his brain would be fully occupied with the evidence of his eyes: that Jaafar was nowhere in sight and both prisoners were loose. I kicked at his right elbow and knew the gun had gone flying and then I was dropping on my feet in the only flat area, the little landing at the turn of the stairs. Momentum carried me to the wall and I kicked myself back off it, twisting to face Fellah whose elbow was still high in the air from the impact of my shoe. I had a simple choice: I could pass him and pull his wrist from below or I could push him from above. I struck with both fists between his shoulders and he went down the steps with a shout, cartwheeling because I had hit him so high.

He lay with an arm flung out, a dramatic gesture, like some forgotten soldier in the Flanders mud. But he'd only blacked out. His breath came in jerks through his mouth.

I took Nortier's hand to guide him along the corridor of the next floor. There was the sound of voices through closed doors. One door had no voices and no strip of light at the bottom. It was the ante-room to a dental surgery, pink and blue posters on the wall demonstrating how to use a toothbrush.

There is no such thing as luck. You create your own luck. If this door had been no good, I'd have tried another room and another until I created my own luck. But it was perfect, with an unbarred window that overlooked the grounds of the camp on the side away from the barracks. Again, I might have had to fashion a rope from towels and surgical aprons. But, call it luck, this side of the fort was used as a transport park: against the wall was a line of Mercedes-Benz four-tonners, their canvas tops a jump down from the window.

'Hang from the window ledge and let go,' I whispered. It was no distance to drop, but it takes courage when you can't see that with your own eyes.

'And then?' Nortier asked.

It was a Land-Rover, short wheelbase version. It couldn't reach 100 kph but there was no question of a race.

I rejected the idea of taking a truck. A four-tonner would be good for crashing the gate and would even provide cover if the sentries had been issued with live ammunition. Since this was Skorpion and a revolution in the making, it was highly probable they would shoot. The truck was a big target and this would be in our favour for they would be attracted by the bulk of it rather than aim at the tyres. But what could we do with a truck? We couldn't hide it in the village. We couldn't disguise it in the desert. We could go north on the road to Remada or south for another hundred kilometres to the border post with Algeria and Libya. Either way we could be picked off at will, a lumbering target on a narrow dirt road.

'There's a Land-Rover,' I murmured. 'We'll take that.'

From now on I'd have to play it by ear. The best scenario I could foresee was that the sentries would simply open the gate and I'd drive through. After all, the sentries were to keep intruders out. Once you were inside you were legitimate and could go out at will. If they didn't open the gate but it looked flimsy I could put the headlights on mainbeam to dazzle the sentries and crash through. They would be semi-blinded for some seconds and would shoot wild. The worst scenario was that the gate was locked and was solid and we had to halt while the sentries looked us over. One sentry would be enough of a problem. I remembered there were two.

'Where is the Land-Rover?'

'It's parked by some huts between the fort and the perimeter fence.'

I took Nortier's hand. It was cold with sweat. I checked

all round again: lights in the windows on the upper floor of the fort, humps of tents over to the right, two lights above the gate, a line of eucalyptus, nothing visible of the village except a minaret poking up to heaven. That damn dog was barking again. Mutters of soldiers' voices carrying on the still air, not in alarm. A feeling of the night before a battle.

We didn't have long before our absence was noted. I had knocked out three men bigger than myself in under fifteen minutes and I felt drained, the adrenalin no longer pumping through my system. Couldn't rest yet. We moved out of the cover of a truck and walked diagonally away from the fort.

'What sort of night is it?'

'Three-quarters moon. Cloudless sky. I can see stars away from the moon.'

'Can you see the fence?'

I'd thought about the fence. There was barbed wire on top but that was no particular problem. Suppose we hopped the wire – what then?

'All right,' I said, 'we could climb the fence but we can't get out of Borj Mechaab quickly enough on foot. Where could we go without transport?'

'I wasn't thinking of walking. Do you have good night vision?'

'Yes.'

He pulled me to a stop.

'Can you see the perimeter fence clearly?'

'Yes.'

'Describe the fence posts to me.'

'Straight up from the ground for a couple of metres, then at an outward angle of forty-five degrees. The posts are square, fairly substantial, made of concrete, eight or ten metres apart. All right?'

'How many posts can you see?'

The moon made tarnished silver of them. I counted until they faded into a blur.

'Eight, nine, maybe ten.'

He was quiet a moment, thinking. There was a tremble to the hand that was in mine.

'Suzanne, how do you rate our chances in the Land-Rover?'

'Higher than if we stay.'

Somewhere in the fort there was a shout.

'I don't think they're high.' His hand squeezed mine. 'I think our only hope is this: you be my hands and eyes. You read the dials and move the controls. I'll shout out the orders. We'll take the Skyvan.'

Reckless, unhinged, crazy . . .

I was searching for the right word when a bell began ringing in the sentry-post by the gate. The decision was made for us.

18

There are times when you are invisible if you are obvious.

A string of lights came on along the perimeter fence and voices were raised in the fort and the alarm bell still shrilled at the gate. We walked as if it was Sunday afternoon away from the fort and across to the Land-Rover. We were blessed with the key hanging from the ignition. I started up and drove on sidelights all down one side of the fort and out past the radio hut and stopped a short way off from the Skyvan.

It must be the ugliest plane in the world. With the ugliest cargo. I was sure it hadn't been unloaded. Borries was due to fly it out, maybe tomorrow. Except I was going to fly it out tonight or leave it spread out among the eucalyptus trees. There were more of Einstein's seconds while I stared at the plane.

'Come on.'

If anyone was turned in our direction, we were now in full view as we crossed towards the Skyvan.

'I've never flown a Skyvan,' Nortier said.

Jesus, two of us.

'I haven't even seen the layout of the cockpit.'

'How the hell can we fly it then?'

'If you've driven a Ford, you can drive a Fiat. Same principle.'

'But I've never flown anything.'

'There's a central column you hold. Push it forward and it puts the nose down and the airspeed increases. Pull it back and the nose comes up and the airspeed drops. Move it to the left . . .'

I stopped him. 'This isn't escaping, this is suicide.' I didn't want a sixty second flying lesson. Or to try and take off in the dark. Or to have a blind man as an instructor.

But a searchlight on top of the fort was switched on and began a sweep round the grounds of the camp, running along the perimeter fence, darting among the trees. There's a simple logic to a searchlight. Its name says it all. I didn't want to be discovered because it would result in my death. That was one hundred per cent certain. The Skyvan offered a chance, even if it was only a one per cent chance.

Steps led up to a door set in the fuselage. We climbed in, I drew up the steps and shut the door. In the payload section were the crates that Skorpion had been waiting for. I saw them and turned aside. A bulkhead and a curtain shut off the crew cabin. A sign on the bulkhead read: *Do not exceed 170 kph with the cargo doors open.* We pushed through the curtain.

'Take the left hand seat.'

I sat down and was confronted with an array of knobs, levers, switches, dials, instruments, headphones, column, pedals and knew at once I'd never be able to take off. My hands had started to shake, delayed reaction to the physical encounters with three men whose profession was fighting, and those hands would be unable to control this machine.

I stared at my hands and heard a fierce voice in my head: Those hands will not control a damn thing, your brain will. It will give the orders and your hands will obey and you will fly. You will take the one per cent chance and succeed.

Nortier was still standing and doing a curious thing, running his fingers over the instrument panel and the controls and the screen. He was rediscovering the body of a loved one. He sat in the seat on my right and fumbled for the restraint belt. As I locked mine I felt trapped and the machine overwhelming me and I had to force it back, impose my will on it.

'Find the master switch,' Nortier said.

It was dark in the cockpit. I undid the belt again. I strained forward and flicked switches and nothing happened and I knew this plane was never going to fly. I had to order myself: Find it.

Pinpoint lights, dials, ceiling lights sprang to life.

'Vital instruments in front of you: airspeed, artificial horizon, vetical speed, turn and slip, direction, altimeter.'

'Jesus.'

'Make sure you can identify them.'

Some had names, others had symbols. What the hell was the one with the outline of a plane?

He pressed on: 'A Skyvan shouldn't need auxiliary power, so find the ignition switches.'

If anybody had been looking, they'd have seen us walking across from the Land-Rover. Again, if anybody had been looking, they'd have seen the glow through the windows as the interior lights came on. But looking or not they'd hear the engines start. We would be pinpointed precisely. I was hesitating and he prompted me.

'A switch, a button.'

Panic was setting in again because once the engines were started we were committed to taking off.

'And then?'

'You've got to start the engines now. They need to warm.'

'We won't have the time.'

'Five minutes, three minutes minimum. You'll get power failure otherwise.'

I peered ahead through the front screen. Dust and insect splats cut visibility. A silver track beckoned, like a moonpath on water. Three minutes, three Einstein minutes.

I searched and pressed and the port engine turned over without firing. The air was cold and the engine was sluggish and shouldn't there be a choke? Then the night broke up as it caught. I pressed again while a whole stream of information was coming in from needles that flickered and the starboard engine caught and the roar was ten times louder than any aircraft I'd ever been in. They'd hear it in the fort. My nerves said they'd hear it in Tripoli. Nortier was talking but all my ears could pick up was the thunder of the engines and he was insisting, shouting at me.

'What?'

'Oil pressure. Is there a positive reading?'

Oil pressure gauge? I blinked at the dials.

'Push the throttle forward.'

'Which is the throttle?'

He leant across and fumbled and the engine note deepened a degree. I followed his hand and eased the throttle further.

'My guess is you want 11 or 1200 rpm to warm the engines. Have you found the dial?'

There was newspaper taped over the window on my side. To keep the sun off? I ripped it away and looked back at the fort. Figures were rounding a corner a couple of hundred metres away and I yelled: 'They know we're in the plane.'

'Check the oil temperature gauge. You'll see a minimum figure marked. Above that means the warmed oil is circulating.'

'Nortier, how do I fly the damn thing?'

'You'll find a dial directly in front of you: artificial horizon. It's night. You're going to be flying blind. You'll need the AH to survive. Have you found it?'

Headlights were switched on near the fort. I was still twisted to look. The headlights began to move and curved round towards us, their beam swinging across the roof of the cockpit like a lighthouse.

'They're coming.'

'Have you located the AH instrument?'

'Shit, we've got to move.'

'The engines aren't warmed.'

'*Now*.'

'Release the brakes, both wheels.'

'Where are the brakes?'

'Look for heelbrakes. Or handbrakes. I don't know the type.'

Brakes released. We began to roll. A minor miracle. Why had the Agency never taught me to fly? I could have managed one hundred thousand and one things. The hell with the muzzle velocity of a Walther. I should have learnt about lift and drag and the artificial horizon.

'Increase the power. Not too much. What's your visibility ahead?'

Too much happening in the cockpit, and light growing stronger as the car or Land-Rover closed the gap. Strange thrumming noise from the tyres as we rolled faster. I looked ahead.

'I can see right down the runway. Trees at the end.'

'They've laid down a metal lattice strip. Keep on it.'

I didn't even know how to steer. I asked.

'Pedals for the rudder. Left pedal moves you left, right pedal moves you right.'

Idiotproof.

My head suddenly threw a shadow. A spotlight had been switched on us.

'We've got to go for take-off.'

'The engines still aren't . . .'

'I'm pushing the throttle in. We can't stay on the ground. How do I get the bloody thing to unstick?'

'Smooth with the throttle. Don't flood.'

The engines grew louder. There was pressure from the back of the seat as we picked up speed.

'What's the airspeed?'

Airspeed? We were glued to the ground. I looked across the dials.

'25.'

'Think of it as driving a car. Point it straight down the road. Keep accelerating. Don't worry about getting airborne. Leave that to the machine. It's designed to fly. Just have faith.'

Jesus.

'Speed?'

'30.'

'Push the throttle right in.'

A roar. Then it felt as if we were tearing apart, roughness to the left.

'Right pedal. *Gently*. Get back on the track. Speed?'

'35.'

The needle had stuck. I was sure of it.

I had flown a plane before. Once, four summers ago. M borrowed a Cessna from a buddy in State and we flew from Washington to the Smokies. I was in the right-hand seat and when we were safely up he told me I was captain for the flight and I pushed the column forward into a shallow dive and eased it back into a gentle climb and said: Thanks a lot but the next time we go away for a dirty week-end, let's fly TWA.

'40.'

'I don't know the take-off speed. It's an STOL aircraft. It could be as low as 65 knots. We'll take it to 80.'

We ran off the perforated strip to the left again and I corrected and we ran off the other side. Ahead the trees were much closer. I looked across Nortier and we hardly seemed to be moving. I looked left and there was a jeep just beyond the wingtip.

'How do I take it up?'

'Speed?'

'50.'

'Too slow.'

'They're trying to run us off the strip.'

'It's the load in the back slowing us.'

'Nortier,' I had glanced out again, 'somebody's shooting.'

There were no flashes but somebody stood up in the back of the jeep, a submachine gun catching the moon. I waited for bullets smashing the glass but it's impossible to aim standing up in a jeep, even at pointblank range. Somewhere behind me was the ring of metal on metal. Twenty rounds, thirty rounds, then he'd have to put in a new clip.

'55.'

I looked again and the jeep was closing in, right under the wing. The soldier was jabbing his gun at the cowling of the engine or at the propeller itself. It would take his arm off. It would take us off the runway.

'Speed?'

'60.'

The jeep began to fall back.

Thumping came from below as the Skyvan veered off the strip. I was fighting with the pedals and holding the column steady and flicking my eyes across the dials and up to the trees looming closer.

'65.'

A window shattered on Nortier's side and I saw a big black car racing diagonally across the airfield to cut us off. A soldier in the back was leaning a rifle through a window.

'We've *got* to go up.'

'Ease the column back. Gently. Don't stall us.'

I had jerked, wanting to be up in the damn sky, and I put the column too far forward, overcorrecting, thudding back on the strip, then easing back again with the speed still rising and the tyre thrum ceasing and we were up, up, up with the fine branches of tamarisks brushing our belly and the line of eucalyptus racing towards us and then under us.

We were flying. The one per center had come off.

'You've made it.'

Nortier wasn't elated. His voice was dulled. He was drained. He could have done it himself and instead he'd had to talk up a woman who couldn't even drive the plane straight down the strip.

A hundred questions threw themselves at me. What height? Direction? Speed? One nagged more than any: How do I bring the plane down? I could sit here with the yoke in my hands, feel the rush of the wind over the ailerons and rudder, throb to the engines, see needles flicker and fool myself I was in command. But how do I bring us down again without stubbing the Skyvan into the earth nose first? Another one per center lay ahead.

I looked back and down. We weren't high but we seemed to have put a good distance between us and Borj Mechaab. There was a cluster of lights in the village. A necklace of lamps marked the perimeter fence of the camp. The fort glowed in patches, like a jigsaw half completed. Headlamps of jeeps and trucks were on the move.

We hit turbulence and the engine note changed. I swung back to look at the dials, double and treble-banked. The regular drone returned. I must not panic. I glanced at Nortier. His eyes were shut. He might have been asleep except for his lips moving. A prayer, curses, instructions he was rehearsing – there was no telling.

I hunched round and Borj Mechaab had vanished. Like a bad dream, it haunted me. What was Major Fellah doing? Half an hour ago he had two prisoners he was about to interrogate, a planeload of weaponry, a revolution poised on the brink. Everything he was trying to achieve was now threatened. He wouldn't reach for a cigarette and shrug it off. He was a military commander and this was a crisis and he would be giving orders. *Call Mohamed at Remada and tell him to take command of the radar and when an unauthorized plane appears on the screen send up an interceptor. Tell him the Skyvan must be forced to return. If its pilot is stubborn, then the plane must be destroyed. Mohamed must do this without fail or Skorpion's revolution will be in extreme hazard.*

188

Nortier shifted in his seat and said: 'There are three instruments it is vital you monitor.' His voice was firm again. I suppose he'd been running through the dozens of actions that had once been automatic to him. 'Altitude, gyro compass, artificial horizon. I can't teach you to fly in one lesson. Learning to fly is not like making instant coffee. But I can tell you enough to keep the plane in the air.'

But how do I bring it to earth? I bit back the question.

The night was ours. The sky was dark with even the moon hidden by the cockpit roof. I had levelled off and reduced speed, but the dials wouldn't leave me alone. There were continual changes, the airspeed creeping up because the nose went down, cutting back on the throttle when I should have been pulling back the column, airspeed dropping and losing height, correction, over-correction. Nortier began to explain trimming but I cut him short: I'd do it the hard way.

Keep busy. No time to brood. But I did.

We were heading north-north-west. This would take us parallel to the Algerian border but it would also by-pass Remada, just in case Major Fellah got in touch with the camp.

The air up here was cold and I shivered.

A bumble bee. The image rose up in my mind. A bumble bee cannot fly. Taking into consideration its weight, wing-span, muscular motor power and general aerodynamic crudity, it is impossible for a bumble bee to become airborne. But the clever scientists who proved this neglected to tell the bumble bee, which goes on doing the impossible. Our Skyvan was a squat heavy bumble bee. It had lumbered along the ground and I had eased back on the column and we had taken flight. Next time I came across a bumble bee I would stare and remember.

How did a bumble bee land?

'What's your heading?'

I'd strayed five degrees further west which would have meant an Algerian interceptor being put up. I touched the right pedal and over-corrected and used the left pedal.

'Altitude?'

'Eighteen?' Odd sort of figure.

'British aircraft. Eighteen hundred feet.'

The ground below was silvered with moonlight. Darker patches showed rocks or scrub.

'It looks closer than that.'

'The altimeter can be set to height above sea level or height above destination. Tripoli is on the sea so Borries must have decided to stay with that setting.'

The bumble bee droned on.

'About where we go once we're past Remada,' I said. 'Gabès is closest but its airport is most likely closed after dark. Sfax is crawling with members of Skorpion. They're probably lining the runway. Tunis is our best chance. Also we have to warn the authorities there.'

He turned that over. I think he wanted to get back to Sfax. That was his home. But he said: 'Agreed. Provided we have enough fuel.'

I searched for the dial and said: 'The fuel gauge is broken.'

'Broken? How do you mean broken?'

'It reads zero. We've been airborne fifteen minutes or so. Borries is a careful pilot and he would never have run the tanks so low. Therefore the gauge must be giving a faulty reading.'

That was logic. Or maybe it was whistling in the dark.

We neither of us spoke. I was listening to the note of the engines. In my head I heard the echo of my voice and the logic sounded fainter and fainter.

Nortier said: 'Borries was a careful pilot. He would never have flown with a faulty gauge.' That was his logic, better logic.

There's a saying that M told me about: There are old pilots and there are bold pilots but there are no old bold pilots. I remembered it at that moment.

'Assuming he flew from Tripoli,' Nortier said, 'he'd have filled up there so the gauge should show at least half full.'

I looked out and there was only a wilderness to see. Far to the right was a line of low hills. Somewhere beyond that ridge was Remada. Was there a jet with its engines warmed and its pilot waiting at the controls?

Silence, except from the bumble bee.

I checked the dials again and said: 'The fuel gauge reads below zero.'

'Then it's not broken. The tanks have been shot through and they're emptying out. Put the nose down.'

'Do what?'

Panic was switched on. It was a light flooding every dark corner. Landing in Tunis had been several hundred kilometres in the future. Putting down here was sudden death.

I had to force the panic out, switch it off.

'We're going to run dry. We have to make a forced landing. It's better to do that with a powered approach while we still have the option.'

I eased the column forward and saw the airspeed indicator creep up.

'Close the throttle.'

'How far?'

'Almost completely. You want just a trickle of power.'

The engine note died away and the airspeed stopped climbing. I was concentrating on the artificial horizon until I looked up and there the real horizon lay a hand's breadth above the crash pad on top of the instrument panel.

Crash pad, matter of life or death when you do a crash landing. Never mind Nortier's 'forced landing'. I was going to put this machine down for the first time ever, on rough ground, with no runway lights. My one per center.

'Altitude?'

'Six on the dial.'

'Can you judge the height visually?'

'Very low. Perhaps a hundred metres.'

'What's the ground like?'

'Flat.'

I stared down. I couldn't take my eyes away. The engine note was a murmur and I could hear the windrush. The moon was high and we chased our shadow. I fixed on the shadow because it's hard to tell conditions at night from up in the sky. Did the shadow run smoothly? Did it jump at a hillock or a rock? As I watched it grew bigger.

'What's it like ahead?'

I forced my eyes ahead. I strained to see what our chances were. I couldn't tell.

'Flat.'

'Keep going down. When you estimate you're ten metres

off the ground, tell me. Level out and hold off while your speed drops. Don't worry, I'll talk you through.'

I was going to crash the Skyvan. I was going to kill us both. I wouldn't live to tell Crevecoeur about the Skorpion base or warn the Tunisian authorities. Major Fellah would get hold of new weapons and the revolution would be unleashed because the Agency never taught me to fly. Oh, I had flown with Michel, soared with passion, floated high above the bed. But I hadn't learned to pilot an aircraft. Michel and I would never make love again, because the ground was tearing up.

'Ten metres.'

'What's it like?'

'Still flat. Bit of grass.'

'Open the throttle a little. A little more. Lower the flaps. If you see any rocks ahead, ease the column back because you still have power. You're going to sink down onto the main wheels and let them take the weight of the plane. Don't worry about braking; that will slow you. After a few seconds the nose-wheel . . .'

Then it all went. The engines faltered and died. The vibration we'd been living with stopped. Life was going out of the plane, I could feel it draining away. The sharp line of the horizon crept up the front screen as the nose sank down and I pulled the column back to get the nose up and . . .

'Don't pull the column back,' Nortier shouted.

The Skyvan was tilting left and I put the column right and nothing happened. The controls had gone soggy.

'Push the column forward. You're losing speed.'

Ground very close. Rushing past left and right, like shooting rapids.

Ground *higher* than me and I understood it was a rock outcrop and I pulled back on the column and there was nothing to lift us.

Nortier made a grab but it was useless. We hit the ground and it was a hammer blow and we were up again and down and something snapped like a bone breaking. There was sudden hammering all through the aircraft and it died with a shudder, bouncing on one wheel and lurching up and over on the nose-wheel. There was pain across my chest as the safety belt bit deep and a shattering of glass and an avalanche to the rear where the payload broke loose and slammed against the bulkhead and a scream from Nortier or a scream from me and a final thought before the night swept in and filled my mind with blackness:

I crashed the bumble bee.

19

The beast loomed over me.

I must get away.

The beast looked on me as carrion flesh and would pick my bones until they were clean and white. The beast was huge, bigger than an elephant, bigger than a tyrannosaurus.

I began moving, crawling, grit sharp on my hands and knees. The beast stayed still, dark and menacing. It couldn't move because one limb was snapped off, jagged bone sticking out from its body.

If the beast couldn't pursue me, I could relax my efforts. Rest, sleep, no need to worry, nothing matters in this world. Eyes closed.

The beast was crying out.

'Suzanne? Suzanne?'

Not my name. My name is Cody. Don't tell Major Fellah.

'Suzanne!'

It was a voice I knew, Nortier's voice. He was inside the beast, swallowed alive. I saw a hole in the beast's ribs and a shadow heaving. I closed my eyes and thought about this. It wasn't a whale or a dinosaur Nortier was escaping from. It was a plane. I shook my head but it still seemed to be filled with night and craziness. It was the Skyvan and I had crashed it and a wing had been torn off. Images raced through my brain: rocks flashing past, dials, controls, horizon skewing as the plane tipped, a maelstrom, darkness. That was all. I had no memory of getting out of the Skyvan. I couldn't have been thrown free because of the safety belt and the narrow configuration of the windows. I had blacked out and come part way conscious. Perhaps this had happened two or three times while I struggled to crawl free. It is a primitive instinct to flee a place of danger.

Danger, fire.

'Suzanne, are you all right?'

'I'm coming.'

Must get Nortier away. The Skyvan could be a fireball in seconds.

I shook my head. Why couldn't I shake the loose connections together? There was no fire danger because there was no fuel. Every last teaspoonful had gone.

'Where are you?'

'I'm coming.'

I rose to my feet and stumbled. When I closed my eyes I saw fireworks and raged: No, you're not blacking out again, too much to do.

The Skyvan had lost its nose-wheel and a mainwheel and a wing and it lay marooned with its good wing at an angle of thirty degrees. Nortier was squatting in the open door.

'Jump,' I said. 'It's not far.'

'Help me, will you?'

I reached up and found his hands and he came to earth with a gasp.

'Are you all right?'

He was frowning. There was enough light to see that. He said: 'A certain amount of pain.'

It made me pause. It wasn't the words, which sounded so prissy in French. *A certain amount of pain*, where an Englishman would have said: *It hurts like hell*, or, *I've creased something*. It was the tone of voice, withdrawing from me, blaming me for the mess we were in.

'Where's the pain?'

He pointed to the right side of his chest. When I put a hand on his shirt he shied away. He said: 'Don't touch it.' And then as if he didn't want to talk about it any more: 'What happened with the plane?'

'I crashed it.'

'I know that. I meant before. You lost power but you could still have brought it down.'

'I've never flown the bloody thing before. What do you expect?'

He turned away from me. That was his answer. He turned away and coughed and fell silent. So I'd crashed the plane and Nortier's chest hurt and we were in the deep south of

195

the country with no transport and a revolution sharpening its claws at our heels. But I still didn't like his tone of voice.

The Skyvan had finished up at the foot of a hillock and I began to move.

'Where are you going?'

'To see if there's any sign of life around.'

There were rocks and tufts of weed and sand and loose pebbles. I climbed slowly, testing each step before I put my full weight down. I still felt muzzy. Something had hit my head during those final seconds in the cockpit. Perhaps it had been Nortier's elbow as he wrestled the controls away from me. At the top of the knoll were three rocks left over from a giant's picnic. I wanted to sit down. But I thought of scorpions, how they rested in cracks in rocks.

'What can you see?'

'Nothing. A lot of it.'

Heard a lot of nothing too. Sound carries in desert regions because there are no trees, no bushes, not even water vapour in the air to deaden it. I looked over to the east and wondered if the Skyvan had suddenly vanished from some radar screen in Remada and if friends of Major Fellah would come on the prowl. To the south was the crashed plane and a grouping of rocks and, far off, a darkish area that might be the dried up course of a *oued*. To the west, nothing. Algeria lay that way, desert for a thousand kilometres until Morocco and the Atlantic ocean. To the north, nothing visible. It was a moonscape, flat and empty.

There was no sign of human life in any direction. There was only us.

It was getting low in the sky. It looked like an orange with a bite taken out.

I'd slept for three hours because my body and brain wouldn't take any more. While I slept my unconscious had worked on the problem and come up with the answer. It was so obvious, why hadn't I thought of it before? Too overwhelmed by the disaster.

I got up from the patch of sand that was my bed and went to the Skyvan. I made a jump for it and got my hands on the sill of the open door and hauled myself up. My shoulder muscles screamed in protest – tension and cold had made them stiff. I moved into the cockpit, stumbling over something that had broken loose. Pale light came through the windows. I stared out a moment because I expected the moon to be silver. It was golden and its outline wasn't quite sharp. I lowered myself into the pilot's seat. The dials in their ranks looked like the faces of dead animals. I found the master switch and clicked and clicked again and the dials didn't come to life. So I moved to Nortier's seat and put on the earphones and reached for the switch and flicked it, though I already knew what response I would get.

There was silence in my ears. I wanted a hum or static or better still a human voice.

Cody?

Receiving you.

Can you give me your co-ordinates?

One hundred and twenty kilometres north-north-west of Borj Mechaab, one hundred and ten kilometres due west of Remada.

Just a moment, Cody, I'm plotting your position.

Who am I speaking to?

A friend.

Did Crevecoeur alert you?

Is he a friend of yours, Cody?

Can you come and get us? The Skyvan is busted and Nortier has been hurt and we need to get out before sunrise.

Why is that?

Because they'll start looking for us at first light. If there's no report of our landing at Tunis or Sfax or Tozeur or some other airport, they'll assume we came down en route.

I'm sorry, Cody, we cannot help you. You'll have to get out through your own efforts.

But how? There's nothing but desert round us. The nearest army bases must be assumed hostile. They'll be sending helicopters to sweep along our known flight path.

Isn't that what you've been trained for: to survive?

But how?

Good luck, Cody. Or goodbye.

Just a minute. Don't close the transmission. Come back.

The radio was dead. I'd crashed the Skyvan and wrecked

197

the electrical circuits, and the dials, the lights, the radio, everything was gone. I couldn't call for help.

I climbed up the slope of the aircraft and jumped to the ground. Nortier was sitting hunched against a rock. He said: 'Where have you been?'

'Trying the radio. It's smashed.'

'How do we get help?' When I didn't answer he rose to his feet. He did it slowly, like a man with a crippling disease. 'If we can't call for help, how do we get out of here?'

'I'll have to think about that.'

'How do we get out of here alive?'

He began to cough and shrank visibly. When the spasm passed, he was silent. The whole night was silent except for the whisper of sand. A breeze had sprung up and the sand drifted over our shoes and grated against the broken wing of the Skyvan.

Before dawn I realized why the moon had turned to gold: sand had coloured it and blurred its outline. The breeze grew into a wind, coming from the west, a gift from Algeria. Nortier and I lay on the ground between the rocks with our faces turned away from the stinging sand. It invaded our clothes, rubbing into every pore.

A refrain ran through my head: one hundred and ten kilometres from Remada, one hundred and twenty kilometres from Borj Mechaab, a cold welcome in each. All round us was desert and the desert was dangerous. This sand was a warning. It could kill us, bury us alive. It wasn't even a sandstorm, which is as terrifying as a blizzard, darkening the sky with columns of sand five and seven thousand metres high. This was its little sister called sandsweep. Sandsweep grates in your eyes and muddles your brain and drifts over everything.

'Does it hurt?'

'What?'

'Your chest. Does it hurt?'

'Of course it does.'

'All the time or only when you move?'

'All the time. More when I move.'

'A stabbing pain? A continuous ache?'

'It hurts.'

The wind whipped his words away. We lay still, waiting for it to grow light, waiting for the wind to die, our mouths shut against the sand. We had nothing to say to each other.

Dawn came slowly, dulled by the flying sand. Its muezzin was the wind howling across the sharp edges of the Skyvan. When the light was strong enough I climbed the hillock again and checked in every direction. There was no indication of life anywhere, no flock of goats nibbling at desert weed, no low-pitched tents of nomads, no string of camels. We had crashed on an eroded plateau, arid and desolate. The sky was pale blue above; towards the horizon it was greyish, dirtied by the sandsweep. I turned full circle again: nothing. I looked down at the wrecked plane. It had ended up between groups of rocks with its nose against the slope of the hillside. It was almost totally hidden, except from above.

As the sun rose, the wind mysteriously died away. I came back down to Nortier and saw the first living thing in this place. Long ago nomads had passed this way and goat droppings lay scattered about. A beetle was rolling a pellet of dried dung up the hill towards a rock. To the beetle it must have seemed like conquering Mont Blanc and half way up to the rock the dung slipped out of its grasp and rolled to the bottom. The beetle was browny-black with a shine to its hard casing. If it had been human you would have said the shine was sweat. It went down the slope in jerky movements, searching for its dung.

Nortier said to me: 'Are there any painkillers in the plane? There should be a first aid kit.'

'Does it hurt that much?'

No answer. It was a weakness he didn't want to discuss. I clambered up into the Skyvan. Now that full daylight had come I could assess the damage and the potential for survival. I looked first in the payload section. I don't know what I expected. Stacks of machine guns? Flame throwers? Boxes of grenades? There were ten crates. They had been placed five to each sidewall of the plane and strapped to stanchions. The crates on the starboard side had snapped their ropes and slammed against the bulkhead as we crash-landed.

The crates were of metal, somewhat larger than coffins.

The metal was painted dull grey with the letters CEA and serial numbers stencilled in white. Someone had made a later addition, hand-blocking in large letters: *Machines agricoles*. You'd think they'd invent new lies, wouldn't you? So what did they contain that was so vital to Skorpion? I wanted to find out. I wanted to know very badly what Borries had flown in and what Crevecoeur was so edgy about and why it was worth killing so many people to protect the secret and what terror would be unleashed.

I would open one of those crates. I was like a cat with burning curiosity. But the more I inspected the crates, the more baffled I was. The lids had no external hinges to be worked on. The metal was unyielding steel. There was no crack I could insert a jemmy into. Each crate had two sunken locks and they were much more serious than the lock to my apartment. Hopeless. These crates were designed to withstand tampering.

Nortier had been shouting outside and I scrambled to the open door. 'There's a plane over there, a small one.'

It made no more noise than a wasp in the next room. I searched and found it a long way off to the east. It was almost invisible against the bright morning sky.

'It's low,' I said and went on watching. It was hard to be certain but it seemed to be following a parallel track to the one we'd taken, except it was eight or ten kilometres away.

'Is it searching for us?'

'It's possible.'

'A rescue plane?'

Did he believe that? I turned aside and went into the cockpit where our dream of flight to safety died during the night. Dials were smashed where struts had come through the control panel. Glass crunched underfoot. I tried the radio again, just in case, the way a drunk tips up an empty bottle, just in case. There were lockers by each seat and I rifled the contents. Between the cockpit and the payload section was a toilet. It was a little bit of Germany with its soap and towel and a bottle labelled Kölnwasser that had fallen on the floor but not broken. Once the toilet door was open it wouldn't close again, because of the angle of the plane. I left it as it was and jumped to the ground and went over to Nortier.

'Any hint of the aircraft coming back?'

'No,' he said.

I curved my hands to form two tubes and held them to my eyes like binoculars. They didn't magnify but they shielded out the worst of the glare. I gazed at the whole rim of the sky from south-east to north-east and it was empty. But the plane could come back. It could fly directly over us. If it was searching for Nortier and me it certainly wasn't friendly. It had been put up by Major Fellah.

'Did you find the first aid box?'

His face was pale: fatigue, tension, pain. His voice was on edge and at least part of that was because he felt helpless. He depended on me. He hated that.

'No painkillers.'

'Oh.' He clammed up.

Was it the same beetle? It had retrieved its dung, its possession, its pride, and started on the long climb back. I watched. I suppose a beetle doesn't possess patience, it is simply programmed to behave like that.

'Show me your chest, where it hurts.'

'There's nothing to see,' he said. 'There's no cut. I can't feel blood.'

'I still want to look.'

He unbuttoned his shirt and lifted it aside. There was a slight abrasion and a smear of red, nothing serious. But the flesh was badly puffed and bruised.

'Can you lift your right arm?'

He raised it about a third of the way to the horizontal. No more. He made a face. Poor man; it hurt more than he wanted to let on.

'You've fractured a rib, maybe more than one. That's what it looks like.'

'Are you some kind of doctor?'

My father had been. What did it matter? Nortier would believe me or not, depending on his mood. At present his mood was against me. He'd had a vision of flying, with me an extension of his former pilot self. His vision had come crashing to earth, with me at the controls.

I hauled myself into the plane again and uncoupled one of the seat-belts and came back to Nortier. I strapped up his chest. It was the best I could do to keep the broken bones from grating.

'Listen, Nortier, can you walk?'

'Walk?'

He took a couple of steps and shuffled back again, as if this was another amateur medical test. My attention was caught by movement on the ground. It had lost its precious dung again. Its whole fortune was this dry pellet and then I stopped the train of thought because there aren't any useful parallels between a dung beetle and a human being.

'I mean, can you walk a hundred kilometres across the desert?'

Except you keep shoving this shit up a hill and it rolls down to the bottom and you have to start all over again.

20

The enemy was in the sky.

It stared, unblinking. It was going to be our constant companion for fourteen hours out of twenty-four.

In its centre the sun reaches a temperature of ten million degrees, 'give or take a thousand or two'. It had been a well-fed astronomer from Cambridge who told me that, one of the series of smoothies my mother had pushed at me. He had been pleased at his little academic joke. He wasn't here now. In the shade it must already be nudging thirty-five. The only shade was under the body of the plane. Out in the open the temperature was raised by a killing margin. The sun was waiting for us.

'The thing is,' I said, 'we have a choice. We can sit here and hope to be found or we can walk.'

Nortier turned to face me. I still found it disconcerting, his habit of staring at me with blind eyes. 'You call that a choice?'

At once I understood it was going to be infinitely harder. That one sentence and the tone of voice told me that. It would be my willpower that brought us out alive because he had resigned himself to death. More, he blamed me for it. But I laid the possibilities before him.

'There's water on the plane. The tap in the toilet works so there'll be however much the tank holds. I don't know how much that is – say enough water for ten days provided we stay out of the sun and keep very still. Then there follows a certain period while the body dehydrates. All told let us assume a fortnight. We do what we can to draw attention to ourselves. We can scratch SOS in huge letters on the ground. We can drain the sump and make a fire with oil and rags: on a still day the black smoke will rise high. We can unbolt a wing panel and scrape the paint off to bare metal and tilt the panel to reflect the sun at any passing plane. The question is: how likely is there to be a passing plane that's friendly? There's some evidence of nomads, so what are our chances of a camel train in the next two weeks?'

'Two weeks,' he said. Nothing moved in his face. 'We have no food.'

'Food is not important. Water is the limiting factor. Not having food is a good thing because digesting it requires water. Also, it is one less thing to carry if we walk.'

'Good God, how can we walk? It's a furnace out there.'

'It drops to near freezing at night. Remember how we were shivering before dawn? We travel in the dark. The exercise keeps us warm and we avoid the sun. We take the curtain from the cockpit entrance to shelter under during the day.'

So simple. We were going for a week-end hike, like I used to with my father.

He said: 'Where would you aim for?'

'We can't go east or south because if they are searching for us that's the first area they'll check. Algeria is to the west and there's nothing but desert for hundreds of kilometres. We go north. We have to. There's a chart in the cockpit and it shows a string of places round the Chott el Jerid.'

'Kebili, Douz, Zaafrane, Sabria.' He recited the names in the flat voice of a station announcer. 'You've worked out our position on the map? You know what heading to take?'

'If we go due north we must hit something, a village, a road.'

'You've got a compass?'

'The gyro compass is smashed. I'll go by the stars.'

'A hundred kilometres, you said?'

'Four nights' march,' I told him.

His face seemed to close up and I know he'd died a little more. In truth I reckoned it was more like a hundred and twenty kilometres and five nights' march, if we were lucky. Nothing to be gained by adding to his fatalism. It would be slow at first, because of carrying the water, agonizing at the end because of the lack of it. More: we'd be staggering without food to fuel our bodies.

'Why did you come?'

He didn't stir. I had to get some response out of him. I

204

had to put a spark back or he'd simply lie on the ground and wait for – what? Thirst-madness? Fellah?

'I said, why did you come?'

'I didn't know this would be the end.'

The rot had spread further than I thought and I shouted in his face: 'Why the hell did you want to go to Borj Mechaab in the first place? What interested you? What jolted you out of your cosy little routine and parish pump politics and scoops on glider races to Gafsa? Moral outrage? Good story? Like a dog after me?'

'After you?' He moved at last. 'You think you're so fascinating?'

'I don't know. What did you smell? A world exclusive? Mercenaries, mysterious plane, camp commander held at gunpoint? Maybe you sniffed something more personal. But I didn't force you to go to Borj Mechaab.'

'You're crazy. I wasn't running after you.'

'Taking my arm when we walked. Inviting me to your apartment for the night.'

He scrambled to his feet. He forgot the pain in his chest. 'For God's sake.' He took a few steps until the sun hit him.

'All right, you saw a story. And it's got bigger. Executions, a revolution, Libyan involvement. Who's going to know unless you get away from here? Perhaps they won't believe you – say the sun fried your brains. But first you've got to get your story out. Either you walk with me or you stay here and wait for the vultures. Because if you stay on your own you don't stand a chance. Simple as that. Suppose you heard an aircraft and lit a fire. More than likely it would bring Major Fellah down on you. Because you escaped he'll never accept you're a simple reporter. You're a spy who's been left behind because you're wounded while I go for help. Fellah will have his fun with electrodes while you scream it's all my doing. He won't believe a word. I'll tell you how it ends. He'll tie you to a tree and pin a white card over your heart for them to aim at.'

I was shaking. I was angry with him. Angry with myself too. Couldn't understand that.

Nortier stretched out on the ground again. He couldn't turn his whole body away from me because that would mean

205

lying on his broken ribs. He turned his face away. A schoolgirl will do that, making a drama out of a slight.

You could roast meat inside the Skyvan. I was the meat.

There was no screwdriver so I prised off the metal rim surrounding one of the dials and used that on the screws of the wall panel above the basin. Six of them came out after a struggle. The last two made the sweat pour off me. A power screwdriver had been used on the production line and these two screws wouldn't budge with the pressure and twist I could produce. The metal rim buckled so I dropped it and got my fingers behind the panel and wrenched it away

'Suzanne.'

It was better than I dared hope. There were two tanks, one to supply the hot tap and one the cold. Both were more than half full – eight or nine litres in each – and the tanks themselves were plastic. Plastic didn't corrode and was light. Weight was important in an aircraft. To me it was vital because I'd be carrying the tanks.

'Suze.'

He'd chopped my name down. It was as if the heat made two syllables unbearable where one would do.

Metal brackets fastened the water tanks to a laminated backing and I turned my attention to the nuts and bolts that secured them. I used the discarded metal rim, bending it to form an angle that would grip the nut. There was a tremble to my fingers. You wouldn't think that removing the plastic containers would take so much effort.

'Suze!'

Louder this time. Odd he called me that. Suze is the name of that French aperitif that leaves a bitter taste in your mouth.

'Can you hear them in there?'

I stumbled to the door and looked out. The tremble in my fingers hadn't been due to effort. It was vibration. I had felt it in the aircraft frame and thought it was my own nerves twitching, and all the time Nortier had been calling out to me because he couldn't see them but he could feel the vibrations even before he heard the sound. I counted them. Six, nine, twelve, fifteen helicopters. They were low and coming from the north and would pass us on the west side.

Or they wouldn't pass. They would see the downed Skyvan and sink to earth and our break for freedom would end here among these rocks.

I jumped down and went to stand beside Nortier. I put a hand on his shoulder. Partly it was to give him the reassurance of human contact, because he couldn't see the danger. Also there was a hint of restraint because he must be in two minds. A helicopter ride out of this place would be infinitely easier than a trek across the desert. It was at the end of the ride when the hard part began.

'Have they seen us?'

'No. They're holding their course.'

It would bring them within a couple of kilometres of our rocks. If we could see them, what was to stop them seeing us?

'Perhaps they're not searching for us,' Nortier said.

'Why else would they be here? At this time, in this place?'

'Coincidence?'

Even Nortier didn't like to suggest that. I couldn't accept it at all. You never put your trust in coincidence, not when your life is at stake.

Nortier tried again: 'It could be a military exercise totally unconnected with Skorpion.'

The helicopters were much closer now. Their course remained fixed towards the south.

'The Algerian border isn't far away,' Nortier went on. 'The army must do routine patrols.'

'Not with fifteen helicopters.'

One helicopter sets up a thrum as its rotor sweeps through the air so that you feel it inside you like a fast pulse. A squadron fills your whole body with continuous sensations. It drives all thoughts out of your head. You feel an animal panic to run and hide. Except the only hiding place was under the plane and that was no good. They were looking for the plane. Weren't they?

Doubts had been setting in. They kept a tight formation whereas a search patrol would have spread out. And although they were flying low they were also flying fast and that's no way to spot something the size and colour of the Skyvan.

There was a change in the pitch of the helicopters' engines

and I thought: They've sighted us, they're changing course. But it wasn't that. It was the Doppler shift. They'd passed the point directly in line with us and the lowering of the pitch was the effect.

Nortier noticed it too. 'They're going away.'

I watched a few seconds more, checking. 'Yes.'

There was a flash from the leading helicopter. Nortier said: 'What is it?'

How did he know? I must have gripped his shoulder tighter. God, my nerves were all over the place.

'Nothing. The sun reflecting off some glass.'

But in the first seconds, before my brain took over, my instinct said it was the flash of a gun.

I watched and Nortier listened while the squadron bore on south. They vanished into the haze near the horizon. Their sound lingered. The vibrations lasted longest and then nothing was left. Nortier was silent. Everything was silent. We were alone again, one hundred and twenty kilometres from safety. A trickle of sweat ran down my back. The sun, fear.

There are rules for survival in the city and rules for survival in the arctic and rules for survival in the desert. They drum them into you at the place in Virginia and send you out for practical experience in Alaska and Arizona.

Desert survival, rule one: Never abandon your vehicle because it is larger and easier to pick out than a human being. Plan to wait a week for rescue. Ration water accordingly. Keep movements to a minimum. Prepare emergency signals.

Rules were useless. Our friends wouldn't be looking for us because we had no friends. And it could be months before nomads chanced this way.

Our enemies could arrive at any moment. Major Fellah had planned to torture us because he believed we were spies. Now we'd escaped he wouldn't rest. We had to be prevented from warning the authorities that a coup was under way. Also he had to recover the crates we'd stolen. The crates were vital to him.

What was in those crates? Gas? Chemicals? Fellah had promised 'terror' would be unleashed. I laid an ear against

208

a crate as if I could hear a mechanism ticking. I sniffed all round the locks. I ran my fingertips over the smooth steel. I gave it up.

All I got from the crates was the rope that had been used to lash them to the stanchions. I set about fashioning two backpacks. Nortier's contained eight wrinkled dates found in a bag in the cockpit, a pile of rags soaked in engine oil and wrapped in a sheet of polythene, matches, a bandage and scissors out of the first aid box. I included the scissors because the time might come when thirst was unbearable and opening a vein is preferable to the kind of madness that has people eyeing each other as a source of liquid.

My pack was the two plastic tanks wrapped together in a length of curtain. The sun was well into its descent by the time preparations were done. Even these simple tasks had brought a rain of sweat from me and the level of one of the tanks had sunk. We had about fifteen litres left. I tested the weight of my pack. Fifteen kilos plus two for the tanks themselves plus another couple for the curtain and rope. Not a crippling weight when you're fit. But I was setting out tired, hungry and weak. I planned to rest once an hour to conserve strength.

'When do we start?' Nortier asked.

I looked up in the sky. 'Give it another hour.' It was the water I was thinking of. The sun would boil the water out of our bodies. Nortier knew what was on my mind.

'How much are we taking?'

'Water? We have one and a half litres each for five days.'

He got to his feet. You see an old man get up like that. 'One and a half litres a day? Are you serious?'

'I can't *make* the stuff,' I shouted. 'Can't you get it inside your head? That's all there is.' I stopped and closed my eyes and brought my temper under control. I mustn't shout. I mustn't get angry. It raised my body temperature and I would lose water through sweat. 'Fifteen litres is all we have. We'll rest during the heat of the day.'

'I know this country. I know what it's like out there. Have you any idea what the desert can do to you?'

Oh yes. I remembered, though not with pleasure. 'We'll

survive provided we don't move in the sun and there's no wind from Algeria to dehydrate us.'

'Three to four litres is the minimum. You can sweat out one and a half litres just by . . .'

'Also,' I interrupted, to shut him up, 'it's important to keep your mouth closed and breathe through your nose so your saliva doesn't dry up.' I decided to give him the survival lecture all in one go. 'Another thing, when you drink, don't gulp, moisten your mouth fully. Urinate as little as possible because that drains liquid out of the system. The same goes for defecation though you won't want to anyhow after a couple of days.'

We started. We aimed at a ridge some five kilometres away, the rocks at its top rosy in the setting sun.

But distance in the desert is deceptive. It was more like ten kilometres to the ridge and we rested four times on the hardpan, our breath coming like wind through pine trees. There were no trees, just a scattering of desert weed that snagged our ankles. It was dark long before we reached the ridge. The night sky dwarfed us.

Navigating by day is easy provided you don't wear a digital watch. You can always calculate south using the sun's position and the hour hand of your watch.

I hate night navigation. Never was any good at it. You're full of shit, the instructors would shout, nothing but shit, Cody, use the stars. And I would look up. A million stars up there. But stars are for lovers. Or that fat-chop astronomer from Cambridge.

'*Merde.*'

He'd stumbled again. It was a problem for Nortier, trying to make reasonable progress without turning his ankle. Also, the whole right side of his body had stiffened. He walked crookedly, either bumping into me or wandering away at a tangent.

'Look, I can't hold your hand for a hundred kilometres.'

'Thank you very much.' His tone was hard and precise.

I rearranged the cord that bound together the two water tanks and gave him an end to hold. He walked behind me at the end of a metre and a half of rope, linked like two packmules, plodding, saying nothing.

At the top of the ridge we rested again. Nortier wedged himself between two rocks, the pressure giving some ease to the throb in his chest. I sat apart. There were things that spent their lives under rocks and they crawled through the dark areas of my imagination. We each have a special fear and for me it had always been spiders. It is a fear beyond reasoning so it is no good arguing: Look, even a black widow isn't always fatal. It is the touch of the thing I dread more than the bite. Now I had a new terror: the scorpion. I could feel the tickle of it on my skin and I squirmed at the memory.

When he'd got his breath back he asked: 'What's it like ahead?'

I lifted my head and stared past him. 'It's dead.'

'Damn you, what's it like?'

I could prepare myself mentally for what lay ahead. He was helpless. I must try to understand, try to help.

'It's the starlight that does it,' I said. 'It makes everything look dead. The world is ghost-coloured. There are some dark ghosts and some light ghosts. We descend from here through more rocks to a lower level of the plain and that looks like more of what we've been through, with those hummocks of weed that trip us. I can make out a couple of pools of darkness far ahead. My guess is they are depressions or maybe the bed of a dried-up *oued*. On the horizon is another ridge and I can't see beyond that.'

'Is it high? That next ridge, is it high?'

'It's hard to tell. You can only judge how high something is when you know how far away it is. I can't estimate the distance. But we've got to make that ridge by sunrise.'

The wind had dropped and it was cold, the daytime heat radiating away in the clear air. There were no lights anywhere. Nortier and I were adrift under the stars, the only living things, except for what had crawled under the rocks.

When we walked there were a dozen different noises: footfalls, a pebble dislodged, desert weed against shoes, breath through nostrils, clothes rubbing.

When we rested it was in a deaf person's world. The

stillness was absolute. There is the silence of snow but that is when sound is muffled. This silence was clear like spring water is clear.

We didn't speak. Mustn't let the saliva dry in our mouths, mustn't squander the water of life. What was he thinking of? If I turned to look at him he was a hunchback with a private anger. A wounded man is like a child or an old person: his own needs are the only ones that exist.

He blamed me. I was sure of it. I had enlisted his help, convinced him of the existence of Skorpion, driven him south to fall into the hands of Major Fellah. Then Nortier had had a vision of escape. Call it a blind man's vision, summoning up his inner powers and using me as his instrument. The Skyvan had failed him. More than that, I had failed him.

Now he trailed behind me at the end of a piece of rope. That was his lifeline across the desert.

Was he thinking about me? Or about his pain? Or the possibility of death?

Would he forgive me?

Dawn cracked open the sky at the horizon. It was indigo, lightening to pale blue. There was a dusting of high clouds, no more than wisps. They turned pink and then lemon as they caught the sun and then they vanished. The enemy reared up. Within quarter of an hour the coldness of the night had gone.

Nortier jerked on the cord and I turned to see why he had stopped.

'Must rest, Suze.'

The rays of the sun were full on his face. Four days growth of beard shadowed his cheeks and jawline. Fatigue blotched the skin under his eyes.

'We can't afford to rest here.'

'Why not? There's nothing to go on for. The Sahara Hilton isn't over the next ridge.'

'There's no shelter from the sun. Also, if anyone comes looking, we're totally exposed out in the open.'

'Half an hour.'

'Jesus, in half an hour you'll be able to fry an egg in the sun.'

'Five minutes,' he said and dropped to the ground to end the argument.

Anger closed his face. Or exhaustion. Maybe it was just the sulks. We squatted in the dirt like animals. I took an oily rag out of his pack and smeared black on our cheeks to cut down the glare reflected off the skin. Five minutes didn't last long. I pulled him to his feet and we moved again.

We made camp half way up the ridge, sheltering between two boulders with the curtain stretched tight on top and weighted with stones. The climb had cost a lot of sweat. I drank water that was lukewarm and didn't quench my thirst.

'How far have we come?'

'It could be twenty-five kilometres.'

My back said it was further. My stomach muscles ached from counter-balancing the nineteen kilo load. Next night it would be sixteen kilos. The night after I would discard one tank completely. But I would be weaker by then. Much. Also, both shoulders had rubbed raw. The thing about pain is not just that it is unpleasant; countering it for long periods saps your stamina.

We lay in the shade of the curtain and let sleep come.

'Wake up, wake up.'

Nortier was shaking me. I'd heard the noise but it had got tangled with my dream: they were digging up rue St-André-des-Arts again, always practising outside my window. Crevecoeur was using a pneumatic drill and suddenly he upped it and it turned into a machine gun he fired at my apartment. That was what I heard.

'It's an aircraft. Get the rags. No, I've found them. Where are the matches?'

Crevecoeur faded from my mind, the image of the machine gun remaining. Nortier was on his feet, waving his left arm in sweeping gestures at the sky. I grabbed his other arm to pull him down and he yelled at the pain of it.

'Damn you, why aren't you signalling? You want us to stay out here until we die of thirst?'

'We don't have any friends looking for us. We only have enemies.'

It was a light aircraft between us and the first ridge we had climbed in the night. It was low but seemed to be making normal progress. It was heading west and in ten minutes or so would cross the line on the map that divided Tunisia from Algeria, unless it turned back.

Was it searching for us? Keeping low to escape detection? I watched it until it dissolved in the heat haze.

Nortier was mumbling. I could just catch the words: '*La vache, la vache.*' It could be me he muttered about, it could be the general bloodiness of life.

A tiny breeze got up. It wasn't cooling. It simply puffed hot air over our skin, sucking moisture out. I could feel the sun trying to get at us through the curtain. How thick was the material? Three millimetres? That was all that separated us from death.

Nortier got to his feet and wandered away.

'Where are you going?'

He swung back. 'I'm going to have a piss. Is that all right? I don't have to save it? I have your permission?' The questions whined.

The afternoon was longer and hotter than the morning.

I stopped.

'What is it?'

'Just checking. I think we're heading too much to the north-east.'

Polaris low on the horizon, Plough pointing. With my head level and face dead in line I should be able to make out . . . Gone out of my mind. What was the constellation called? Steady; getting confused. Physical weakness beginning to affect mental alertness. Forget about the stupid names. Practical applications: I had to turn my body as much as ten degrees and a correction of that magnitude when you've got a hundred kilometres to go is serious.

About midnight we passed a patch of scrubby thorn. Counted them. Six bushes. Enough to nourish a handful of snails. Not enough for a man or a goat. On again. The going was easier here, the desert weed had thinned out.

Look again at the stars. There are stars you can see and stars you can't. Some degenerate and collapse on themselves

214

under a phenomenal force of gravity. This is what the astronomer from Cambridge told me, his small talk. The atoms pack tighter and tighter together, matter collapsing on itself until thousands of tons are reduced to something no bigger than a pinhead, collapsing so far and developing such a power of gravity that not even light waves can escape. In the end even space bends and folds in on itself under this incredible force. All that remains is a hole in the universe from which no light escapes. A black hole. That is the way I pictured Crevecoeur.

I checked again and we were on course. There was something different about the sweep of land that rose in front. It looked as inhospitable as a glacier and the closer we got the smoother its appearance. The slope began abruptly and I climbed two paces and knew our luck had run out. We had left the hardpan behind and were into soft shifting sand. Each step was twice as tiring. By the time we reached the top of the dune we were struggling for breath as if we were in the Himalayas. Our mountain had been all of thirty metres high.

We sank down. When Nortier's lungs had stopped pumping he asked: 'What can you see ahead?'

'It looks like the tide has gone out a long way.'

Abruptly the anger boiled over in him. 'Why don't you tell me? Why? Why? Why? You want to play God and keep me under your control. You act as if you . . .'

I found I was shaking him, my hands on his shoulders, his head jerking. Words tumbled out of me. 'You're always shouting or whining, always on at me like a spoilt brat. I'm not mothering you, do you understand? I'm just trying to keep us alive. You shouldn't have come, your own damn fault. Skorpion are bastards, you knew that beforehand, bombing a plane, burning a hotel, killing anyone who gets in their way. I didn't twist your arm to make you come. You wanted to because you sensed a story. I didn't simper and wear perfume and boost your ego with flattery and rub my body against you and all the rest. You're welcome to sit here and wait for a miracle to happen. Don't expect me to stay. When the water's finished you'll go crazy and it's a terrible end. You'll blame me but I'm not going to be here to listen to the rattle in your throat. I'll be far away. I'll be on my own. I'll be free. I'll . . .'

No point in regrets. I'd said it now. Some things were true, some of it was just hurtful. The poison inside had all come out. My arms fell away from him and I felt drained.

The silence was terrible. No insect, no night animal, no bat, no stirring leaf. There was small comfort in the sound of our bodies breathing and moving. The immense silence all round made dwarfs of us humans.

I had experienced worse than this. At the place in Virginia there is a room called the Dead Chamber that provides absolute insulation against ambient noise and light. You hear nothing, see nothing. It is part of the schedule on stress-immunization: total sensory deprivation. I had survived that and knew I could survive this. But Steven Bull, in my time, had been in the Dead Chamber and when he came out he pronounced it a failure because there had been continual noise.

'What did you hear, Steve?'

'There were two sounds. Someone out here was hammering a nail into the wall.'

'That was the beat of your heart.'

'And there was a constant screech, like metal on metal.'

'Steve, that was the blood in your veins near your aural nerves.'

'It was what?'

Some can stand their nails being torn out but break on a few words. It is the terror of the imagination. Bull could not bear the idea of listening to his own blood. When they tried to put him back for Phase 2 training he ran away through a fourth floor window.

The silence here didn't have that absolute quality because another person shared it. I tried to see into his face but it was still closed to me. He'd been full of resourcefulness when I'd met him. He'd been on his own ground, had his own strength, digging and probing for the missing Borries. Here he could no longer cope, he relied on me, felt diminished by it. He was resigned to death like a tribesman struck down by voodoo. I gripped his hand, wanting my voodoo to be stronger, trying to communicate my willpower.

He said again: 'What can you see ahead?'

His voice was calm, and mine too, as if nothing had passed between us.

'People say the real Sahara is like an ocean and they're right. It's a sand-sea where you can be shipwrecked and drown. It has no features. There's nothing all the way to the horizon. All I can make out in the starlight is a little irregularity and I expect that's because of dunes. They're like ocean swell, none very high. It's the same old ghost colour. And that's all there is to be said.'

Night Two finished. We hadn't covered so much ground. Our feet dragged across the sand. Climbing the smallest dune left our bodies racked. After the liberation of Auschwitz, living skeletons tottered out. We swayed like that. Our bodies had weakened: it was sixty hours since we'd eaten, except for the handful of dates. The sand was fine and loosely packed on the sloping sides of the dunes. You put a foot down and it slipped back under your weight, the sand shifting, gliding, tumbling down. Two-thirds of the effort was wasted. A dune only five metres high brought the breath hissing. Sweat trickled even in the cold night air, precious liquid lost, precious little gained.

We reached a patch of hard crust with a dusting of desert weed and rocks piled like a cairn. I was too exhausted to worry about scorpions. We pitched our shelter as full day broke and the enemy rode in triumph up into the blue.

'How far?'

I shook my head. Useless, he couldn't see. 'Don't know.' I didn't want to think about it or waste energy speaking.

Before the sun climbed above the rim of the curtain, it lit up his features. He had the face of the war-wounded: the stubble, the sockets of the eyes, the gaunt cheeks, the hollows of his temples. You saw the thinness of the living flesh. You saw the skull underneath.

In the late afternoon when the sun was in its last hour, I climbed the cairn of rocks and scanned ahead. A large dune, a hill of sand, lay some way off. I wondered, quite simply, if Nortier had the strength to reach the top. Once during the previous night he'd tripped and lain on the ground coughing. He'd wiped his mouth with the back of his hand and left behind a smear of something dark. If he had begun coughing blood, what could I do? I had no drugs. The bandage was no use. He should be in hospital, in the intensive care unit. Instead he faced three nights' march. That was the minimum now, unless we ran across a camel train out of one of the villages. The water position was growing acute. One tank had been emptied and discarded. Less weight to carry, less water left. Also, Nortier was running a fever and craved extra water. I cut down on my own ration. My tongue was rough and made an ugly rasp against the roof of my mouth.

Don't think about it.

Think about reaching Douz, Zaafrane, Sabria. There is a limited number of kilometres to cover and a finite number of hours, so take them one at a time.

Time to start.

It had been designed by Pininfarina.

The dune loomed above us, sand piled higher and higher by the wind from Algeria. It might be seventy metres high, more even, with gentle curves ending in sharp edges, the way the Italians sculpt their cars. We could no longer walk; we had to crawl up it on hands and knees. Sand shifted and grated under our movements with a sound like tiny maracas.

'Please,' he gasped. 'Suze, please.'

Rest. I held the tank to his lips because he couldn't steady it himself. A dribble came from the corner of his mouth. Wasted. It was slightly darkened. Roman legions, the French Foreign Legion, Rommel's and Montgomery's divisions, all spilled their blood in this sand. Nortier's name was the latest in a long roll-call.

'Come on.'

Our shoes were off. Shoes were hopeless. They filled with sand that rubbed against the heel, blistering the skin. The sand filled up the space at the instep and between the toes until each foot was a leaden weight.

Wiggle your toes in the sand, you're on holiday.

'Pardon?'

'What do you mean, "Pardon?"? Didn't speak.'

Had I? That was worrying. Watch it. All right to mutter to yourself, broke the silence of the desert, but you should know when you're doing it. Only the mad never realize they're talking to themselves.

'Left hand, right knee, right hand, left knee.' I spoke it right out loud, sure of it. No response.

He sank back on his haunches and I couldn't get him to move. I gripped his hand, hauled, like trying to budge a mule. We stopped there, breath rasping. Five minutes.

'Don't give in now.'

The top was just ahead. We were over the worst, the slope was gentler. I got to my feet and tugged him upright. We'll make the top like champions. Ten steps, five steps, see that sharp edge and perhaps we'll find a nomad's campfire down the other side. We made it, lurched to a halt at the summit, muscles knotting, lungs pumping, triumph, kings of the castle. I lifted my eyes to gaze at the promised land when the world collapsed round us. The whole of the top crumbled because the far side was as sheer as a cliff and our weight started the landslide. Crashing down in an avalanche of sand, shouting in fright, tumbling in the blizzard of sand, mouth filling, grit in the eyes, drag of the rope against the raw flesh of my shoulders. A shock as my rolling finished, smashing into a rock, the tank jarring my spine. All round was the sound of sand falling, like small animals in the night. It died to silence.

'Antoine?'

I turned my head, searching for him. There was nothing but sand – under my body, over my head, a world of sand. I closed my eyes to concentrate my hearing. I caught a sound. He'd come to rest below me and was dry-sobbing.

'Antoine, are you all right?'

The sobbing went on. I felt it then, the trickle down my neck and shoulder. It must be my blood not his. Couldn't be his, blood doesn't fall uphill. Nothing wrong with my brain, worked it out like lightning. I eased myself up on my knees and began to feel for the wound. No bones broken. I was bruised and aching in a dozen places yet I couldn't find the cut. But my hand came away wet.

Then I was tearing at the ropes and I had the harness off my back so fast. I found it with my fingers: the rent in the plastic tank. Our life ebbed out on the sand.

There was a period when my brain refused to function. I lay back on the sand and stared up. The sky was black, the milky way was a veil, and we were lost.

Night Three was over. We had moved on from that dune of disaster and made camp where nomads had been before us. Living people had passed this way. You wouldn't have thought it possible. The only trace of them was soot marks on a circle of stones. There wasn't even any camel dung: that would be saved and dried to serve as fuel. They had left nothing to succour a dung beetle let alone a human.

If nomads had pitched camp there was a chance of water. No sign of a well. But a scattering of weed had grown after a long-ago storm and been browsed to the roots by camels. If rain had soaked into the sand, I could construct a solar still.

I worked slowly to conserve sweat. The storm had crusted the sand but underneath it was soft. I had no tools so I used my hands to scoop it out and raise a wall. The hole was a metre across, half as deep. Sandcastles on the beach. There was no container to collect water so I used a square of polythene sheeting to line a dip at the bottom. The rest of the polythene I stretched tight across the top, weighting round the circumference with sand. I placed a stone in the centre and the polythene sagged.

The principle is elementary.

The sun's rays heat inside the polythene like a greenhouse. The temperature rises until it is an oven, vaporizing the water soaked into the ground. When the air is saturated, the water vapour condenses on the underside of the plastic because it is cooler. This condensation trickles to the centre of the sheet where it is weighted by the stone and drops into the container below. The bigger your solar still, the more water you collect. Dig it the size of a bath and you can get a litre a day.

'Safe to drink too because it's distilled.' It had been Lieutenant Myers instructing us before we flew to Arizona.

'Guess what: you might get a snake crawl in and that's good eating, except for the head. Food and drink – you'll be dining at the Ritz.'

It had got a laugh.

Lieutenant, you should have been here. More than an hour I worked with the shirt over my head against sunstroke and a fingernail ripping in the sand. Come evening there was no water collected at the bottom, no condensation on the sheet. Not many laughs in that, Lieutenant.

The rent was down one seam, almost to the base of the tank. The level of water darkened the plastic. A litre remained. That's what I estimated.

'Thirsty,' he said, so I tipped the container against his lips. 'Still thirsty.'

I slammed the bung tight in the tank and dragged the harness over my shoulders.

'More,' he said.

'Let's get moving.'

'Suze . . .'

'What's Skorpion doing now?'

'Skorpion?'

'Major Fellah, Jaafar, Borries.'

He was silent. Perhaps he didn't want to think of them. It was better he remembered them than brooded on thirst.

'Don't know,' he said finally. 'They won't find us now we've come this far. There's too much desert to search. Also, by day we're under the curtain and that's like camouflage. We're safe.'

The Sahara was an ocean, undulating in gentle waves. How far was the shore? Fifty kilometres? And he said we were safe?

We moved slowly. The weight of water was replaced by the weight of Nortier leaning on me, his good arm round my shoulder. A knee had twisted in the landslide and he limped.

We walked, we rested, we walked. He asked: 'What are you wearing?'

'A striped matelot shirt and slacks the colour of the sand. Got them in Sfax. The rest of my things went up in the hotel blaze.'

221

'Do you always wear clothes like that? Slacks and jeans I mean? I can't picture you in a skirt.'

'I've got a closet full of skirts. Long skirts, short skirts, dresses. Lots of colours, Indian cotton, Thai silk, batik prints, flares and frills. I've got a black lacy number that froths like a bubble bath if I feel a bit wild. Which I do when the moon's full.'

'You like dancing?'

'If the mood's right. Do you?'

'The kind where you hold each other.'

He didn't say more. No need. You can be strangers one minute and a word or a gesture brings a new dimension. We had met in Sfax, been imprisoned in Borj Mechaab, crashed in the desert – and we'd stayed strangers. Now it had changed. All he'd said was he liked dancing, the kind where you hold each other. I was holding him.

'Suze, have you ever been married?'

'No.'

'Boy friend? Girl friend?'

'Michel.'

'Live together?'

'Sometimes. But I'm not good to be with twenty-four hours a day. I need space.'

'I understand,' he said.

He'd been the cat that walked alone. I'd had the feeling very strongly in Sfax. He'd had a kind of victory over his blindness and that gave him strength. He'd taken pride in what he could do on his own.

'It's all right now, isn't it?' He meant between us.

'Yes.'

He'd shouted and I'd raged back and that was behind us. It can happen like that. There's a barrier and you shout and like the walls of Jericho it comes tumbling down.

We sat side by side. He hadn't asked for a drink and I hadn't offered him one.

'The first time you've been in North Africa?'

'Yes,' I said.

'The Sahara is the simplest place in the world. It is cut to the bone.' His voice was thick, slurring the words. It was an effort for him to get anything out. 'Sky and earth and nothing else, no embellishment. It is perfect in its cleanness.' He spoke as if he was thinking of something else entirely from the sun and the dunes. Perhaps he was. He added: 'It is like a true passion: it can kill you.'

His arm round my shoulder, my arm round his waist. Like lovers along the *quais* in Paris, and strolling about as fast. He had grown feverish. Talk of the Sahara's beauty had been the start. After all he'd never *seen* the Sahara. When we'd walked on he'd said: 'You must have heard of the basilisk. The legend says it lives in the Sahara and its stare can turn a man to stone. That's where our basilisk lives, up there.' He spoke of the sun, jerking his head as a man does in a fever.

Now he muttered: 'Water, water.'

I moistened his lips.

The sand stopped as abruptly as it had begun and walking was easier. Desert weed had grown in patches and been grazed by goats. Their pellets littered the ground. The plants had seedheads like thin pea pods, tart on my tongue. They were long dried, no moisture in them. But I took heart from the bedouin who had passed through.

Sand again.

It was after midnight when I stopped.

'What is it?'

'I can't see the stars. I can't keep our course steady.' There was no feature in this sand-sea to get a fix on.

'Where have the stars gone?'

'Covered by cloud.'

'Will it rain?'

'We could be lucky.'

We lay on the ground and he said: 'I'm cold.'

I moved close, my arm across his belly, avoiding his inflamed chest. My body shook to his shivering. He said something. I had to put my ear to his lips.

'When we get back, do this again.'

I felt a hand move and rest on one of my breasts. His fingers trembled. Suddenly and inexplicably I began to sob. I hadn't cried for years and why now?

223

'Don't cry.'

'Antoine, I'm sorry, sorry.'

'Mustn't cry. Tears waste water.'

Made it worse. Nothing I could do. The tears came and then they lessened and then they stopped.

'I'm so cold.'

I put my lips on his forehead and it was feverish hot. Why had I kissed him? Because we'd shared hardship together and now we faced death together. That's all. Had to be all. Didn't love him. Couldn't. I'd cursed him and railed at him and I couldn't love him now.

I nursed him through the rest of Night Four.

It didn't rain.

The sun dispersed the cloud cover. The basilisk stared, a hammer at our heads. I erected the curtain to shelter us. Wind got up and eddies of blistering heat wafted in.

His lips moved. 'Water.'

'It's finished.'

'No more water?' The lips were cracked. Dried blood showed black.

'We'll move on tonight. Nomads have passed round here. Must be a well. We'll find it.'

At midday the heat was stunning. He stirred and said: 'What's that?'

I caught it, a whisper. I located it in the sky, the condensation trail of a jet. 'It's an aircraft.'

'Hurry. Light the rags.'

'Antoine, it's ten thousand metres up. It's Air France on the way to Cairo.'

He swallowed and it looked painful.

'Ring for the stewardess. I want a Ricard with lots of ice. Maybe a Kronenbourg, if it's really cold.'

'We'll order champagne,' I said. 'We're travelling first class.'

He turned his eyes on me. Calling the stewardess hadn't been a joke. There was confusion inside him and the struggle against it showed in his face.

'You're not a spy for Crevecoeur.'

224

There is a tone of voice between question and statement and he was using it. He had to get things straight in his mind. The wound, the exhaustion, the thirst, the fever had clouded his brain. He craved certainties.

'No more than you,' I said.

'Major Fellah and that dried up little man with the cough . . .'

'Jaafar.'

'Was that his name?'

What journalist forgets a name? It was another small sign.

'Yes.'

'They were convinced you were in Crevecoeur's pay.'

'Fellah would believe whatever justified his sadism. Jaafar is different. He thinks he is the philosopher of Skorpion. Really he's driven by hatred. Must be a positive side to him, but hatred of the West is what fuels him.' I broke off. So many words, so much effort. I tried again. 'I was seen in Crevecoeur's company, had driven him round Sfax, stayed in the same hotel. I was Crevecoeur's agent, had to be. Haven't you seen it? A man prides himself on his scepticism. But you can trick him into believing something because it fits in with his prejudices. Even you were half convinced I was Crevecoeur's agent. Isn't that so?'

Longest speech of my life. I lay back.

Antoine wouldn't speculate. He just wanted to get his understanding straight.

'But you weren't.'

'You know I wasn't.'

The light from the sun had gone opaque and the wind grew stronger. We talked in whispers, gusts snatching away the words. I think he said: 'I believe you.'

'I was Crevecoeur's lackey. They hungered to believe that. Major Fellah wanted his bit of fun and games and Jaafar wanted an imperialist plot. That's all.'

'The one with the cough . . .'

'Jaafar,' I encouraged. But he'd run out of words.

The sandstorm struck with sudden fury and I made a grab for the curtain. Sand as fine as talcum powder blew in our eyes and nostrils and found its way into every crevice of our bodies. I took off my shirt and covered our heads and the stuff worked its way through the fabric and grated hot and dry against our skin. I wrapped the curtain tight round us and still the stuff got in. I had my arms round Antoine while the sand roared and stung and blotted out all thought. He died in my arms. I don't know when. The shriek of the wind hid his end. When the fury slackened and the storm was only a dirty smudge on the horizon, I found the breath had been blown right out of him. His body felt colder than any grave.

I had brought him to this place. My old relationship with Crevecoeur and my clumsiness with the Skyvan had proved fatal. I had killed him.

No, others carried the guilt.

I laid his body out on the open sand. The sun could no longer burn him.

I put up the curtain and crawled under it. Oh, I missed him. I wanted him back. I wanted him to argue with me, to squabble, to frown like I'd seen him do so often. I wanted to see the smile that lit up his face. I hadn't seen that often enough. I could have made him smile more. I'm sure of it. Antoine, I whispered, I'm so sad without you. I'm alone.

I howled. I didn't cry. It was a wild animal's howl.

Antoine.

His hand moved. A muscle in his arm relaxed and his hand flopped over onto the sand and I scrambled out from my scrap of shade and crouched over him, my head to his chest, listening for a heartbeat. I touched the hand.

Cold, in spite of the sun.

'Antoine.'

Come back to me. I want to give you something. I want to give you my love. I want us to share the struggle. I don't want always to be alone.

All afternoon I huddled under the curtain. In the evening I scooped a shallow trench and laid his body in it and stood watching the brief dusk darken his face. Sandsweep was already sifting round him. By morning his body would be covered, as in any cemetery.

My face was in sorrow. No tears. My body could no longer grant such luxury. But in my chest was a sharp pain, the ache of separation.

At the top of the rise I turned but his grave was lost. He had no headstone.

Goodbye.

Once I sang. Wasn't much of a song.

> *Cody's body is a-drying on the sand*
> *Cody's body is a-drying on the sand*
> *Cody's body is a-drying on the sand*
> *But she damn well marches on.*

No loneliness like the desert. Not a prison cell. Not the Dead Chamber. Not the first second when you know your lover's betrayal. It's the loneliness of madness. Singing helped a little. Filled the silence, kept madness away another five steps, ten steps.

I no longer had him on the cord. His arm gone from my shoulder. Night Five should have been easier but loneliness is a terrible burden.

My body drying out. Hard physical effort at night, sweating it out under the enemy's eye by day. Short rations and then no rations, Antoine had it all. Expected my tongue and throat to rasp with dryness. Wasn't prepared for pain in my bladder and kidneys, cramp in my guts, ache in my lungs.

Why was I sitting on sand? Looking at feet. Feet most precious thing in the world. Blood everywhere but the sensation had gone. My brain had abandoned them. Wrong. Feet more valuable than brain. One step forward worth more than any thought. Award them Nobel Feet Prize.

Sand. One, two, three gullies eroded by wind. More sand. Cody in the land of No: no water, no well, no vegetation, no people.

Must remember to check sky. Wandered away to the right.

Ahead a glistening. Like water glistens. A lake of it under the moonlight. Stop feet, brain got work to do. This is Sahara, no glistening lakes. But – no mirages at night in Sahara. Mirages only in daylight. Close eyes, open eyes, lake beckoning. Can't be. Dream. Closing and opening my eyes in a dream. Force eyelids wide with fingers.

Lake still there, shining, reflecting moonlight.

Maybe it's real.

Suddenly I found the strength to crash forward until my feet reached the gleaming silver. It crackled as I stumbled in and lurched to a halt. On my knees. Why weren't my knees wet? Where were the ripples? Feel the water. Go on, reach out.

It was a small *chott*, the salt crystals reflecting the moon. Its dryness mocked me.

Night Five ended.

Winter grips the land. Summer lays it open.

My camp was on a ridge of eroded rock. Turning through east, south and west I saw dunes, rolling waves of sand. But to the north, far off, a beach-head of scrub. Check again. Remember the *chott*. The Sahara cruel in its tricks. It was scrub bleached the colour of frost by the onslaught of the sun. I crouched under the curtain and stared out. The heat dissolved the featureless landscape and the scrub melted and reformed. Like staring through a window streaked with rivulets of rain. Cooling rain, blowing out of a grey northern sky, splashing your face, slicking your hair, muddying your shoes.

My imagination awash.

Night Six.

Dunes, sand up, sand down, a track. Didn't see the track at first, saw the snake. It lay curled in the dirt. Then I registered a patch of hardpan and the track crossing it. A motorway, an *autobahn*, a six-lane Interstate through this desert. Picked out the scratching of a Land-Rover's tyres, the droppings of a camel, and a snake of a broken fan belt.

Feet stop. Brain think. A track joins two centres of life. Humans made this track and humans would be at either end. Even in the desert life was possible. Humans needed water, shelter, food. Humans would succour me.

Nobel Brain Prize.

Check the stars and check the track. North-west to south-east. I turned half-left and was king of the road. The track faint but visible in the moonlight. Hope, new sense of purpose. I forgot the pains that possessed every part of my body.

A sand dune and the track skirting it. I didn't even have to climb the dune. I could walk round it and as I did the track vanished. Wind had blown the desert over the track and buried it. Bedouin might know the course to follow but I would wander in vain, searching for the resurfaced track. I would be lost. So look to the stars again and correct course. North. Don't grieve for the track.

Slower now. My knees hadn't been so stiff before the track. My joints drying out. Cramp seized my abdomen and I doubled over.

Rest. Just rested. Then rest again because of cramp. A small voice inside my skull added another torture: perhaps my urine was seeping back into my body like foetid ditch water soaks back into a dry field.

First light. I became aware of a roaring in my ears. Puzzled, then I identified it. Really weird: how had Niagara got here? It was gushing, roaring, thundering, tumbling.

When I came round, the sun was already ten degrees above the horizon. I struggled with the curtain. It was all I carried now, except the scissors.

In the sun's clamour at midday I saw it. I wasn't fooled.

The lake floated near the horizon. My eyes were on the island in the centre. There were lush palm trees lapped by water.

Couldn't look away. My eyes kept returning to that water. Nothing else to think about. I didn't ask much. A glass, a spoonful, please. I was a beggar and a beggar never asks for lunch at the Ritz, just the price of a cup of coffee. I didn't beg even a cup of coffee, spray on my face would do.

I watched the shimmer of the mirage. Once I found myself on my feet, setting off towards it, not believing it was unreal. How can the world not be what it seems?

Between me and the unreal lake the sand had been scribbled on by giant fingers.

The mirage vanished in sections, like pieces of a jigsaw being lifted. Darkness grew out of the ground. Night Seven coming. Lake entirely gone and my brain had other thoughts. This came to me: I was at the beginning of Night Seven but I

229

might not reach the end. I might not want to. Scissors. I checked they were there. Pain all over. My body was made of skin and bone and pain.

Walking. No recollection of starting. I gave up navigation. Stars swinging. Hopeless.

Pain in my eyes acute. The eyeball needs moisture and mine were drying. Walking with lids closed, staggering. The sand wouldn't stay level. The sand coming up to hit me. Hit back. Fists in sand, punching like a butterfly. Opened my eyes. Crevecoeur was squatting on the ground and I faced him on all fours. Something to tell him. Vital.

'Do you know, Crevecoeur, that you are a certified one hundred per cent . . .'

'Yes?' he prompted.

'Not hundred per cent, thousand per cent.'

'What?'

'Doesn't matter.'

'You're a fool, Cody, stubborn as a stone. I told you to get out, said you were out of your depth. Of course you wouldn't listen. You're the big hero, you're invincible. So what have you achieved? You've crashed the Skyvan and caused the death of your journalist buddy. You loved Nortier in the end and you killed him. Soon you'll die yourself.'

'Shut up,' I screamed.

Punched him and he flew away, dirty raincoat flapping like crow's wings. I got up. Later I moved on. Left foot, right foot, left foot. Not possible. Means I've got two left feet. Right foot, left foot, right foot. Better. Got six feet. Walk anywhere with six feet.

Found him again. Couldn't escape me. My six feet better than his two feet. He was standing behind a palm tree, pretending to be a shadow.

'Listen, Crevecoeur, it's your fault. All those deaths in Sfax because Skorpion wanted to stop you. Major Fellah's threat of torture because of you.'

'I warned you not to play with the grown-ups.'

'No, you wanted me dead. You always have.'

'Absurd.'

'I've got proof.'

He waited. He laughed when I didn't say anything.

230

Couldn't seem to find the words. It's just I have a nose for the rottenness of his world.

He laughed again. Not a laugh, a cackle like a scared chicken. He flapped away into the depths of palm trees. He mustn't get away. Wanted to tell him something. Important. Skorpion. I knew where its base was. You drove south and drove south and skipped past the checkpoint on the road and went on until they came to pick you up in the big whirly-bird. Warning: watch out for the mad Major.

Come back.

Couldn't get the words out. Must go after him but the dog stood in my way. Dog was as skinny as Crevecoeur, ribs like fishbones. Did Crevecoeur's ribs stick out? In bed with him would be like making love to a skeleton. Rattle of dry bones.

Dog trying to tell me something. No, called barking. I can bark too. Good boy. Dog snapped its jaws at me, teeth like white slugs in the moonlight. Now hold on, fella, let's be pals.

The dog summoned ghosts. They stood in a circle, a chorus of them, saying something. No use. I don't speak Ghost. Not one damn word. Can't even pass the time of night.

'Where he vanished?' I asked the ghosts.

Ghosts weren't English-speaking ghosts. Try them in French.

'*Il est disparu, Monsieur Coeurcr . . . Cre . . .*' Hell with it. Tongue couldn't get itself round the bloody man's name. Better at barking.

Ghost put out its hand and I tried to knock it away and missed and tried again. Gave it up because I could hear Niagara again, pain in my ears where the blood roared and the glands throbbed. Roaring to one side too and it was a beast. Know the name. Called a camel. As I pitched forward and the stars span, hands caught me.

Good morning, Michel.

Should call you Esau, a hairy man, haven't shaved yet. Rasp of your bristles across my cheek. Ever kissed a man with a beard? No, don't suppose you have, not your fancy. It doesn't scratch, it just tickles. It's bristles in the morning before the razor's got at them that scrape my skin.

Not that I mind.

Pleases me. It's part of you.

Another thing, I've never told you this, another thing is that in bed in the morning there is this smell to you. Don't heave over like that, I'm not criticizing. I call it the peasant in you. Puts ideas of barns and haylofts and going behind hedges in my mind. The smell of a man. I like it, Michel. I like it before you have a shower.

Think I'll have another zizz now. Feel tired, aching in every imaginable place and some others. What were we doing last night?

I was on top. He was moving under my body, a long rhythmic beat, heaving to one side. Roughness against my cheek, odour in my nose. Michel, speaking frankly, I think you haven't bathed since I went away. Oh, just down to North Africa, sun and sand. Did you miss me? Liar.

Heat in my blood and a brightness across my eyelids. But none of the surge and explosion of love. I opened my eyes and looked and there was a line out there, milky blue on top and beige underneath. That line, it's called the horizon. It was dipping and swinging. No horizon like that in a bedroom.

My cheek lay flat on the rough surface. It wasn't his skin. It was grubby and patterned, grey and tan zigzags. A rug.

A noise, curious bubbling sound. Also a soft plop-plop.

Did I have the strength? Yes.

I turned and was face to face with a camel. It moved in a slouching gait while the head on its long neck was twisted right round to inspect me. A cynical eye, a curling lip, brown-stained teeth. Beyond the camel's head was sand, then toy trees and low buildings. A rope was round its neck. At the end of the rope a man in a *djellaba*. He looked back and saw my open eyes.

'*Saa'id*,' he said. He showed teeth the colour of the camel's.

21

Life returning was as hard as life departing. Organs and limbs cut off by desiccation were reconnected. Pain came flooding in with the water.

Faces pressed down. Hands gentled. Fingers touched. One finger was thin steel. Faces, hands, pain, everything floated away.

I didn't wake. I became aware.

I could see sunlight. This was benign stuff compared with the fire of the Sahara. A beam as solid as iron punched through a square window and lit a table in a corner of the room. There was a vase of flowers, not the sort that comes from the florist embalmed in cellophane but the kind you pick in a cottage garden. I stared at them, giving them names. There were ox-eye daisies, zinnias, cosmos, salvias of a colour I'd once heard a man at a party call 'Mexican whore red.'

What had been the man's name? Marty? Good, memory was returning.

Never mind that bar of sunlight. This room was cool. The walls had been whitewashed. It could be a cell in prison, except for the flowers.

'Where am I?'

'Kebili. The hospital.'

It was Crevecoeur's voice, altogether crisper in reality than in the meanderings of my dreams. I turned my head. He was perched on a chair. It *was* Crevecoeur, wasn't it? Not another hallucination?

'Why are you wearing that?'

'France and Tunisia have been holding joint military manoeuvres. I wanted to fit in.'

He was in khaki. He even wore a jacket with ribbons on his narrow chest.

'Where were you in combat? The corridors of the Ministry of the Interior?'

He didn't bother to answer. He got out a packet of Gitanes and lit one and looked round for an ashtray. There wasn't one. He got up and dragged his chair towards the table and dropped the spent match in the vase.

'How did I get here?'

'You walked.'

'After that?'

'You wandered into a village on the edge of the desert. It was a small place, a *bled*, no name that I know of. They slung you across a camel like a sack of wheat and took you into Douz. There's a doctor there but no hospital. He brought you into Kebili, this place.'

'How long have I been here?'

'Forty-eight hours.'

It was blank mostly. I had an impression of men in ghostly robes and of collapsing and the heaving journey on a camel. Then it was darkness. Like a thunderstorm, occasional flashes illuminated things. Somewhere there'd been a woman dressed in violent colours, as if she'd been gift-wrapped by a madman. Magenta and yellow and peacock blue and Irish green overflowed down her arms and legs. She wore silver at her throat and ears and squatted on the ground, watching over me.

'*A boire*,' I'd said. I had to make drinking motions.

She'd given me mint tea in a glass. I'd wanted a great pitcher of the stuff. But I couldn't drink even one glass. Too painful. She moistened my tongue. Her face was as proud as a hawk. She never spoke to me. Or if she did, it had vanished down the black hole of unconsciousness.

I remembered a huddle of stone buildings with blind walls. If the windows are in the courtyard there's less chance of sand blowing in. I remembered the amazing green of the oasis with a forest of palm trees and the sound of rushing water, whitewashed cubes of houses, soldiers at street corners. And the doctor. He'd worn a suit and tie and over the top a *burnous*, chocolate brown. I remembered the needle in my arm. I didn't feel it but I saw it slip in. I remembered nothing after that.

234

'How did you find me?' I asked Crevecoeur.

'You talked French so they contacted the French embassy. It was just rambling most of the time, according to the doctor. When they undressed you to put you to bed you got violent. You kept saying over and over: "My name is Suzanne Deschampsneufs. I'm not working for Chief Inspector Crevecoeur." Sometimes you varied it, "*le salaud Crevecoeur*".'

'You've been called worse.'

He shrugged and dropped his cigarette between the flower stems. It gave a brief hiss as it drowned. There was water in that vase, enough to have kept me alive for most of a day out in the desert. Crevecoeur was shaking his head.

'I warned you that you were getting out of your depth.'

'Go to hell.'

'From the look of your face, you've been there and back.'

A mirror hung on a nail above the washstand. He brought it to the bed and held it for me. I didn't want to look but Crevecoeur has a streak of sadism in him and wouldn't take it away. All right, just a peep. I snatched a glance at the mirror and away, but I'd seen too much. Worse than I expected. I had to look back. Had Michel ever kissed those lips? They were split and caked with blood. The eyes were shot through with red. The rims and lobes of my ears were rubbed raw. Cuts, abrasions, blisters covered my cheeks and neck. A bitten tomato for a nose. A dressing across one cheekbone hid something worse. Hair cropped to the skull to keep from getting in the wounds.

'Don't worry, it'll come back.'

'What will, Crevecoeur? What are you talking about?'

His glance flicked round my face and came to rest on my eyes. 'That certain something that attracts men. Even the ones who can't see.'

I broke away from his eyes. *Why did you come? Like a dog after me? What did you smell?* No, Antoine had scented a story, that was all. He was a newshound on a trail and it had ended out there in the desert.

'Nortier got his story but never got to file it.' Crevecoeur's voice was gentle, or gentle for him. 'Are you going to do it for him?'

He had no headstone. In a way it would be a marker over

him, something in his memory. Crevecoeur was lighting another Gitane, taking his time. Is it what Antoine would have wanted?

'What's happened to Skorpion?'

'The nest has been stamped on.'

'Have there been reports in the press?'

'It was inevitable. Hundreds of villagers were witnesses. The news agencies got wind of it.'

He told me what I needed for a decision. If it wasn't to be an exclusive about a revolution on the boil then it wouldn't be the story that Antoine would have written. It would turn into something else: how we faced the mad torturers and escaped across the burning sands. Worse, it would bring reporters down on me to probe for further morsels. I didn't want the searchlight turned in my direction. My life couldn't stand that sort of publicity.

'No,' I said. 'No story.'

'Good,' he said. He'd been watching, forgetting even to work at his cigarette.

'Why *good*, Crevecoeur? What's good about a journalist's death and my being driven ninety-nine per cent mad and nobody reading about how we escaped?'

But he'd turned his attention to a click-clack out in the corridor. A woman's shoes approaching, quick steps, businesslike, no nonsense. Another sound: the hiss of a cigarette drowning among the flowers. She came through the door, a middle-aged woman in a grey and white uniform, a frown on her face. I thought she would always enter a room frowning, expecting to find something wrong. This time her suspicions were justified and the wrinkles on her brow deepened.

'It is not permitted to smoke, This is a hospital. You should know better.'

'I'm not smoking,' Crevecoeur said.

The nurse raised her eyes to look above his head for the tell-tale cloud of blue-grey. She stood very upright and still, as if her dignity demanded it, while her eyes searched for evidence. Finding none she came and looked down at me.

'And how does one find oneself?' Her French was heavy but correct. She felt for the pulse in my wrist.

'I'm alive,' I said. 'Every part of me hurts.'

'What do you expect after what you did?'

'Is there any permanent damage?'

'One cannot be certain yet. The human body accepts a lot of abuse: tobacco, alcohol, bad diet, lack of exercise. But what you did, you understand, was of a different order. When you were brought in, the systems in your body were breaking down. You had lost so much fluid that your blood had become viscous. We have been putting the fluid back into you and the systems begin to function.'

She checked the drip bottle that fed my arm. I'd avoided looking at it. Hated the things. Some people don't like the idea of the saline drip going directly into a vein. They're uneasy about it bypassing the normal process of renewing your body through your mouth. I had a special reason to detest the drip bottle: I'd seen a man called Agate linked to one in the American hospital in Paris. He'd gone to sleep while I'd been talking to him. Someone had slipped a massive overdose of chloral hydrate into the bottle. I was the last person to see Agate alive, so I rated a visit from the Sûreté Nationale that night. My first confrontation with Crevecoeur.

He was looking at me now. I could tell that from the angle of his head while I stared at that bottle. It was passing through my head – and he was damn well aware of it – that someone could have spiked the drip solution. I wouldn't taste the chloral hydrate or smell it. There would just be a sense of growing weariness, a drifting away from the world.

I made an effort to sit upright and the nurse moved her hand to my chest. 'Calmness is needed.' It sounded better in French. The most banal things do.

'When can I leave?'

'Leave?' Her frown deepened.

'Discharge myself from hospital.'

'There is no question of that. You are gravely ill. In a sense you have had both feet in the grave. The recovery of your vital organs will be gradual.'

'How long before she can leave?' Crevecoeur pressed her.

The nurse transferred her attention to him. 'I warned you it would have to be a short visit. You're exhausting her. Smoking too. You must leave her to rest now.'

237

'Let him stay,' I said.

'There is no question . . .' she began.

'There are important things I must discuss with . . .' I eyed the military cabbage on Crevecoeur's uniform. 'With this Lieutenant-Colonel.'

Done himself well, hadn't he? Gone one better than Major Fellah.

'The army has no authority in my hospital. Particularly the French army. Armies kill. Hospitals heal.' But she click-clacked to the door. 'And do not over-excite the patient.'

'How long had you been waiting for me to surface?'

'Not long,' Crevecoeur said, which was no answer.

He couldn't have been waiting long or he would have known there was no ashtray without needing to look. I felt better about working that out. My brain could make 2 plus 2 equal 3½ and would soon be back to full measure.

'How did you know I was about to come round?'

'I didn't. That nurse consulted a doctor and they said you were in a barbiturate-controlled sleep, the dosage keeping you under for periods of six hours, and you were due for consciousness shortly.'

'You tracked me down in the middle of nowhere and sat down at my bedside to wait. You must have wanted to talk to me very badly.'

He wasn't the type to go visiting the sick with a bunch of grapes and a line in bright chat. He stared at me with bleak eyes. Go on, the eyes said.

'They let you in here alone?'

'The hospital administration was impressed by the army rank.'

'Why the army, Crevecoeur?'

'I didn't want to look conspicuous.'

He'd said something on those lines already. When he stalls like that it is to make you work things out for yourself. He likes watching you do that. He enjoys that petty power.

'You look very conspicuous.'

'Not here.'

'The army manoeuvres you mentioned were to destroy Skorpion?'

'Correct.'

'How did you discover their base was in Borj Mechaab?'

'You cannot take over an army camp and stop. A revolution must keep moving. They had set up roadblocks north of Borj Mechaab near Remada and south near Bir Zar. But instead of striking out from their base they stayed boxed in. You see you'd flown off with their weapons. The militia received reports of buses being turned back at the roadblocks, even other military vehicles being barred entry. When army HQ radioed to ask what the hell was going on, they got no reply. So they acted.'

I remembered – it was from a different life – a squadron of helicopters making south. Were those his doing, I asked Crevecoeur. Yes, he nodded. French helicopters? Tunisian helicopters? He shrugged.

'Cody, have you any idea what's involved in setting up an operation like that? I had to gain access to the French President without telling any of the bootlickers in the Elysée the real reason. I had to persuade him of the gravity of the situation, the risk to the vital interests of France. He was quick to see that. His personal approach to the Tunisian government got immediate approval for the joint military operation. That will tell you how serious it was. Units of the Foreign Legion were flown in from Corsica within hours. By chance the Colonel in charge had served in Borj Mechaab before France pulled out in 1956. Except it was called Fort Roberval when we had it.'

'Not *we*, Crevecoeur. I'm not French.'

'No,' he said. He stared at my face, even if it was hideous from a week in the Sahara. 'You choose to live in France but have none of the obligations.'

I closed my eyes. We weren't going to have that all over again: the fuss over taxes, the undesirable nature of the work I did, the threat to my *carte de séjour*. When I opened my eyes it was to see him at the door. He wasn't going. I had no hope of that. He looked both ways down the corridor and came back to his chair. He could have been playing a cheap conspirator. Perhaps just checking the nurse wasn't hovering.

'You don't mind, do you?' He lit a cigarette without waiting for my answer.

239

'What happened at Borj Mechaab?'

'We strolled it. The Foreign Legion Colonel said there would have been more resistance taking over a convent. The garrison weren't revolutionaries, just ordinary soldiers who'd had new officers forced on them. We were in command in fifteen minutes. One or two sentries were shot but then the Foreign Legion never has appreciated being challenged.'

I couldn't see it being that easy. Major Fellah would fight to the death.

'You see,' Crevecoeur went on, 'their leaders had vanished. They hadn't got a hope of success because they'd lost their weapons. Without the weapons they were no more than a bunch of thugs.'

'So you've failed. You haven't destroyed Skorpion.'

'I haven't failed. I just haven't succeeded yet. The top five men in Skorpion plus the pilot Borries took a Land-Rover and drove across the border into Libya. The frontier is less than forty kilometres away at that point. They went overland to avoid formalities at the customs post. They drove on to Tripoli, where they have been made welcome.'

'You know this?'

'We have sources in the city.'

He was quiet. I was aware of sounds from outside. There were the sudden shouts of children as if school had been let out. From a different direction came a raised voice and a slammed door. The noises were muffled and a little way off as if I'd been put in an isolation unit.

'So what is Skorpion doing now?'

'They have been looking for the weapons, like ourselves. We have been searching for the Skyvan you took and put down in the desert. We had no idea what route you took – north, south, even west into Algeria. Or how far you'd got. Our search has been too diffuse. We have had no success. But someone has. Just after seven this morning the army monitoring service picked up a radio message: "Skorpion's sting regained. Skyvan not operational. Transport helicopter necessary." The position must have been given in an earlier message and there have been no repeats so the army hasn't been able to get a fix on the transmitter. You are the only person who knows what route you took and where you came

240

down. That is why I flew here and settled down to wait at your bedside.'

Crevecoeur stopped. He said no more. He wasn't going to plead. He was watching my reactions while I took in what he'd been saying. His grey eyes were frozen on me.

'Crevecoeur, correct me if I'm wrong. Dozens of people were shot and blown up and burnt to death, but that doesn't matter. Antoine Nortier died in the desert, but that doesn't matter. I was driven mad with thirst and was on the edge of death, but that doesn't matter. A fundamentalist coup almost overthrew the government here, but that doesn't matter. All that matters is that your President gets his weapons back. The honour of France and all that garbage. You make me sick.'

Inside me was a scream of loathing but I was too weak to make it. I sank back on the pillows, pulse racing, room reeling.

'Naturally I regret . . .'

'Oh shut up.'

'Don't over-excite yourself.'

'You're impossible. You warned me to run away and now you're here like a dog begging.'

Crevecoeur looked at his watch and then away out of the window. A flicker of something passed across his face. He hated me for making him ask.

He spoke slowly. 'The President of France needs your help. The President of Tunisia needs your help. A hundred thousand ordinary people need your help. Otherwise they will die. Yes, if you demand your pound of flesh, I need your help. Who else is there who can help? If Skorpion recovers those weapons, they will strike again.'

Outside I heard a whistle and the shouts of the playing children were stilled.

22

There was a holster on his hip and the button was undone. He could draw his pistol in two seconds. If I didn't agree, would he kidnap me? He could do it at gunpoint and shoot down anyone who got in his way. He was perfectly capable of it.

In the sudden silence after the children returned to their classrooms he said: 'I can give you sixty seconds to decide.'

'Sixty seconds? Then what happens?'

'I cannot afford to waste more time.'

He was, I suppose, computing the distance from Kebili to the supposed crashpoint of the Skyvan and setting it against the time it would take to organize a transport helicopter in Tripoli to make a clandestine flight to pick up the weapons. I had a thought and asked him: 'Why don't you alert the Tunisian air force to patrol the frontier? The helicopter coming in will be slow-moving and conspicuous.'

'This is not a Tunisian problem. It is my problem. Thirty seconds.'

'But how about the joint manoeuvres?'

'Strict orders were issued that when the Skyvan was located it was not to be approached. I am the only person authorized to enter.'

'Why, Crevecoeur?'

'I haven't the time to debate with you. I need to know: are you willing to assist?'

Who said the eyes are the windows of the soul? I looked at Crevecoeur's eyes and they were the colour of arctic ice. An iceberg perhaps, with ninety per cent of it out of sight.

'You'll have to find my clothes,' I said.

I'd pressed the button. From this point events were beyond my control. Too many things crowded together. It was melodrama, farce and finally horror as Crevecoeur went into action.

He took two steps to the window and shouted outside. I didn't pay attention to his orders; I had my own problems. I put my legs over the side of the bed and the room went into orbit. For forty-eight hours I had been kept under with barbiturates and they still washed through my system. I was aware of boots in the corridor and a woman's voice raised in alarm. The door pushed open and the room was filled with men. They were part of my dizziness, swinging above me like monkeys in trees. They had blackened faces – why was that? They wore combat gear, camouflage colours in waves – or was that a drug dream?

Jesus, I must get a grip. Willpower, that's all I needed. You can impose your will on anything, bend it to your purpose.

The nurse click-clacked through the door and the frown was a great fissure down her forehead.

'Get out of here at once. What do you imagine you're doing? This patient is seriously ill. I warned you . . .' She swung towards Crevecoeur.

'Mademoiselle is leaving.'

'Impossible. She is on the danger list. There is no question . . .'

'There is no question of her staying.'

'You have no authority in this hospital.'

At her shoulder a doctor appeared and asked a question in Arabic and said: 'If you do not get out of this room immediately, I shall call the police.'

'My authority is the highest: your President.'

'This is my hospital and my patient. You have no right to say what happens to her.'

Doctors are stubborn. Crevecoeur's patience was burning on a short fuse. His right hand was curling by the unbuttoned holster. I made the effort of will and stood up and said: 'I'm discharging myself. Get this thing off my arm.'

I pointed at the drip-bottle. When nobody moved to help I tugged and felt a little spurt of pain as I broke the link that connected with a vein. That was better. Hated that bottle and the fluid going into me.

'Where are mademoiselle's clothes?'

'They have been incinerated.'

'Lemonnier, strip.'

Pure farce. There were six of these armed men. One handed over his automatic rifle and peeled off his blouson. The black of his face and neck ended abruptly in a pale chest. He looked more than naked, he looked like some flayed animal. He struggled with his boots.

'Stop this instant. It's an outrage.'

Lemonnier stripped off his combat trousers and stood in his jockstrap. He took back his rifle because he felt more naked without that than without clothes.

The nurse began screaming. One of the men put an arm round her and slapped a hand over her mouth and the scream was strangled. The doctor made a move towards the door and a man checked him.

'Put on Lemonnier's clothes.'

Do it, I ordered myself, do it. But I couldn't pull the hospital shift over my head. I turned to the nurse.

'Help me take this off.'

She mumbled and the man took his hand from her mouth. 'I expressly forbid . . .' The hand was replaced.

So it was Crevecoeur. He took a pace forward and stopped, looking in my face. A man can look in your eyes, asking, and your eyes can answer, *yes*. Michel had done it with a kiss as each button was undone. And others before him, each in his own way, fierce, tender, trembling. Crevecoeur I would never allow to take the clothes off me. He knew that and had hesitated while the seconds ticked away. But there was no other way.

I raised my arms over my head and slowly he lifted the shift off. The others were men and would be gawping at my body. Crevecoeur was himself and if he wanted to see me naked it was not in these circumstances. I think, while the shift passed over my head, his eyes were on the ceiling. I stood nude in the centre of the room and his eyes came back to my face. I must have swayed, a moment of giddiness, and he touched a shoulder. His fingers were thin but strong. In the room it was very still.

Quietly he said: 'Get dressed.'

He swung away to the circle of men. His glare spoke for him and their eyes dropped. The cloth of the uniform was rough against my skin. It smelt of cigarette smoke and sweat.

'Can you walk?'

I tried a step and the balls of my feet were on fire as if they'd been beaten with a club. Cursed my weakness. The pain was nothing. I could conquer the pain. But I was so slow.

'There's a wheelchair,' a man began.

'Carry her,' Crevecoeur ordered.

This man, whose eyes had been on my nakedness a minute ago, lifted me in his arms. I could hear his breath and sense the heat in his body.

'I will not be stopped,' Crevecoeur said to the doctor and nurse. The pistol stayed in its holster. It wasn't needed. There was conviction in his voice.

We passed a pair of nurses, a doctor, hospital orderlies. There were faces in windows and figures halted in doorways. It was a grotesque procession: Crevecoeur in his Lieutenant-Colonel's uniform, four thugs in warpaint and carrying arms, one dressed in boots and jockstrap, another carrying a woman wearing camouflage blouson and trousers and with a face ravaged by sun. We progressed through the grounds of the hospital, past a bed of hibiscus and plumbago and cannas, on beaten earth beneath a stand of stone-pines, reaching the perimeter fence. Beyond this was a football pitch, totally grassless, with netball posts at the far side of it and school buildings beyond.

Had the schoolchildren come racing across this ground during their break, breathless to inspect the helicopter that had sunk from the sky? They wouldn't have got too close. Three men stood guard, their faces blackened, rifles held aslant across their chests. I was lifted over the fence and brought to the helicopter. A car had been driven onto the pitch and a couple of militia watched us and did nothing. The only other witnesses were three youths who stood astride their bicycles and stared.

I suddenly understood something. 'Crevecoeur, this isn't a military helicopter.' There should be insignia and special radar installations.

'Let's get going,' he shouted to the pilot.

And the men weren't soldiers. I saw beneath their warpaint; their faces were a generation older than soldiers'. French Security has never been shy of using official thugs, *barbouzes*. They can torture and kill and be disowned. In ones and twos they had arrived in the country and the official at Tunis Airport had smiled and murmured *Bonnes vacances*. Then Crevecoeur had summoned them for his own purpose.

'Get going, get going.'

This was a Dauphin and the throb of its engine was louder than the Skyvan's.

'Which way?' The pilot twisted in his seat to speak back to us.

'Up, you cretin.'

The rotor engaged and the Dauphin lifted off in a swirl of dust. We went in a circle, gaining height. Kebili sank below us. At first all I saw was the football pitch, then the school and the hospital. Faces were turned up. Houses, shops, minarets and a market were added.

'Start heading south,' Crevecoeur ordered and turned his attention to me. 'Study this chart. I want you to indicate where you think you came down.'

The horizon outside tilted as we changed our heading. There was an arid landscape to the left, the glitter of a *chott* to the right. We paralleled a ribbon of road where lapwood fencing kept the dunes from drifting. Ahead a string of low houses swelled to form a village. Beyond that again was the dark green of an oasis, a hundred thousand palm trees and the grey and white of a small town.

'Tell me where you crashed.'

'Why is it so urgent?'

'I must know if we have the right heading.'

'What town is that down there?'

'Douz, where you were brought by camel.'

'South. Keep heading south.'

Just keep going. That's how it had been with Antoine and me. Lifting my eyes beyond Douz I saw desert to the horizon. We had walked across that. It was not possible. Antoine had died and I had lived. Just. Even now there was little more than a flicker of life in me.

'Do you smoke?'

It was one of the *barbouzes*. I shook my head.

There were three rows of four seats. The *barbouzes* were slouched in the attitude of men waiting for action. They were staring out at the horizon, smoking, talking among themselves, looking at me. The one who'd stripped now wore a leather jacket, unbuttoned on his bare chest. A cross on a gold chain nestled among curly hairs. He couldn't find trousers or couldn't be bothered to look.

I turned my attention to the chart. A week of pain lay hidden in its symbols. The trouble was that south of Douz there was nothing much to mark. Lines of contour followed the undulations. Small triangles marked high points. A broken blue line meant the course of a waterless *oued*. One broken black line showed a *piste*. Perhaps it was the track where I'd seen a fan belt and believed it was a snake. A blue circle was a well. Would Antoine be alive if I'd found that? It was a night's march west of our route. Anyway, suppose it was dry.

'It's not easy.'

'Try,' Crevecoeur said. 'You must tell me where the Skyvan came down.'

'Why are the weapons so important?'

'Do you want Skorpion to get their hands on them?'

I could think of no answer to that. I said: 'We left Borj Mechaab and set off north-north-west. The idea was to keep clear of Remada in case that army base had fallen to Skorpion. We mustn't run the risk of being shot down. It was twenty or twenty-five minutes after take-off that we ran out of fuel.'

'Be more precise. Five minutes could mean twenty kilometres.'

'Damn you, Crevecoeur. I'm not a genius.'

'You're not making any effort. That's your trouble.'

Bastard.

I traced a line from Borj Mechaab. 'According to the chart we passed over a road. I didn't see anything. No headlights.'

'It's only a dirt track to the Algerian border. The border's closed at night.'

'I'm sure we got past Remada. This is the best I can do.'

I sketched a circle on the chart. The circle was empty.

247

Nothing there but bad memories. He measured the distance from the Libyan border to where I indicated and it was a hundred kilometres. He measured our position south of Douz to the crashpoint and it was further. I'd estimated it as one hundred and twenty-five kilometres when we set out to walk. Crevecoeur spoke to the pilot and there was a slight course adjustment, the rays of the sun moving until they struck my hand.

The sand-sea stretched in front of us. Directly below it was flat. Towards the eastern horizon were low escarpments softened by heat haze. It was a world without definition. The colours were dun, muted grey, dirty gold.

What did Crevecoeur intend?

I understood the man. I must have known the answer. But I was mentally, emotionally and physically drained. My energy had been dried up by the Sahara. I felt like a passenger, controlling nothing.

I stared out, struggling to make sense of the ground below and recall the features of the place where the Skyvan had crashed. Rocks flashing past on either side, its nose ending against a hillside, the view from the top showing nothing but the hardpan, isolated rocks, a scattering of desert weed, the dried-up course of a *oued* to the south, a patch of sparse bushes.

The colour below changed. It became beige and was pock-marked like a cheese-grater. We had passed over the dividing line between the shifting sands and the hardpan. That had happened on the second night's march. We were drawing closer.

Skorpion's sting regained.

'Crevecoeur, are those weapons going to be any danger to us?'

'God forbid.'

He looked at me a moment and turned back to the *bar-bouzes*. They were preparing for battle, checking the clips in guns, opening boxes of grenades, stacking canisters of teargas. No one joked. Talk had dried up. Cigarettes showed like white scars against their warpaint.

The engine note changed. We tipped over into a swooping

descent, levelling off forty metres above ground and turning towards the east.

Crevecoeur raised his voice: 'We have entered the target area and are beginning the low level search. It will be a grid-search across a ten kilometre front, each sweep being one kilometre further south.'

'If we go higher,' someone said, 'we'll see better.'

'If we go higher,' Crevecoeur snapped, 'we risk being seen. To succeed, surprise is essential. Tell them what we're looking for.'

The *barbouzes* lifted their faces to stare at me, as a pack of wild dogs will.

I said: 'It's a Skyvan that force-landed. The terrain is similar to this: flat with rocky upthrusts and isolated low hills. Not much vegetation: sparse weed and désert grass. Bushes indicate a dried-up river bed. Specifically we are looking for a hillock sixty or seventy metres high. Where this has eroded, the rocks have rolled onto the plain. The aircraft ended in a "U" formed by the hill and a rockfall. It's hidden on all sides except the south. Crevecoeur, we won't see the Skyvan until we overfly it.'

'It's for you to recognize the hill and the rocks. That's what you're here for. The rest of you look too. Use your damn eyes.'

He was jumpy. He was a security cop and now he was trying to lead a commando raid and his nerves were stretched until they twanged.

Desert, mounds of rocks, weed, a ridge, a lone shrub. The helicopter leant into a turn, went south, turned to make a parallel course heading west.

Beige and tan and fawn and grey and rust. My eyes searched for the right configuration of low hill and rocks, the flash of sun reflected off metal or glass, movement. There would be men about and the transport they came in.

'Did the people who found the Skyvan come by plane or Land-Rover?'

'No information.'

Skorpion could have had a light aircraft doing a grid-search, as we were. In a week they could cover a large area, a great arc with Borj Mechaab at its hub. Or they could have know the rough area where we had gone off some radar screen but it had taken them this long to get a Land-Rover into the area. There was no wind today, no sandsweep. Tyre tracks would stand out in this drab landscape. There was nothing.

I closed my eyes. They ached. All of me hurt. There were stabs in my chest and belly, throbbing in my feet, itches all over my face and arms. I should be in a cool white room in hospital.

'Over there.'

I opened my eyes and one of the *barbouzes* was pointing. Rocks tumbled at the bottom of a low hill. It checked. I nodded.

'Gillot, Timbaud,' Crevecoeur ordered and two men slid open the doors of the helicopter. They cradled automatic weapons in their arms.

The hillock was about a kilometre to the south. The Skyvan was hidden from this side. There was no sign of a Land-Rover or light plane. But I was sure this was the right place. Three giant rocks were on top of the hill and in the distance was the dark patch of the *oued*. Our pilot reduced height until we hugged the ground. The downdraught from the rotor raised a miniature sandstorm.

The pilot called back: 'I'll take the left hand approach round the hill. The sun will be above and behind us.'

'Agreed,' Crevecoeur said. 'All right, once we're in sight of the Skyvan, speed is vital. Don't give them a chance to fight. Do you understand? Gillot, Timbaud, shoot anyone who moves. If they take cover, pin them down. The rest of you will jump . . .'

That was as far as he got.

They were staring at the hill, all of them, fascinated by what lay hidden behind it. They were amateurs. They were bully-boys and murderers but they weren't professionals. Not one of them thought to watch our backs.

Skorpion came from the blind spot behind us, out of the sun as our pilot planned to do. The first we knew was the shattering of glass and the whine of ricochets and screams from one of the men. Our pilot reacted at once, putting the helicopter into a right angle turn and racing towards the north, away from the danger area.

Crevecoeur was twisted round, squinting into the sun, and then he yelled at Timbaud to shoot up, shoot *up*, but the man folded in half and toppled out of the door. The pilot was throwing the Dauphin from side to side, zigzagging like a terrified hare. The desert was a blur underneath but I could see spurts of sand, sometimes to the left, sometimes to the right, sometimes ahead, as the bullets chased us.

'Give it all the power you've got,' Crevecoeur screamed, 'get us away from the hill.'

Seconds passed. A minute passed. We were escaping, I was sure of it, when the glass by the pilot shattered and he cried out, heaving up from his seat, collapsing again. He slumped over the control column. His last action was to cut the ignition and the helicopter slammed into the ground with a violence that jolted every bone in my body.

'Gillot, Lemonnier, Maufoux, use your submachine guns.'

It did no good, Crevecoeur yelling. Our Dauphin was engulfed in a swirling sandstorm and a roar from above. It was impossible to see what was in the sky. It grew dark as dust blotted out the sun.

'Cody, get out, run for it.'

Crevecoeur was at the door. I was on my way to join him, hobbling, painfully slow. There was no strength in my legs. I had walked all the stamina out of them. He disappeared from sight. By the time I reached the door he was twenty metres away, running in a crouch. He stopped and turned to look, his hair blown every which way, his clothes flapping, his face screwed up by sand.

A tiny tot could have jumped out but to me the earth looked a long way down. There was the sound of gunfire everywhere. One man was standing his ground, aiming up in the sky. Tough but stupid, the way of *barbouzes*. I couldn't see what he was aiming at. But he must have been visible to the enemy above. He threw his arms up and staggered back as bullets plucked at his combat jacket.

'Give me your hands,' Crevecoeur said.

He'd come back for me.

The sound of shooting went on and on while Crevecoeur carried me. It was the clouds of sand which saved us. The powdery stuff billowed into the air and hid our retreat to a boulder that lay stranded on the desert. It was huge, almost the size of a bungalow. Crevecoeur dumped me on the ground and stood above me. I had never seen him shake before. No particular fear showed in his face. It was just his nerves danced to a different tune. He screamed abuse up into the sky.

Hovering in the air was the transport helicopter the radio message had asked for. It was one of those aerial gunships the Soviets field-tested in Afghanistan and now supply to anyone who thumbs his nose at Uncle Sam. There was paint slapped on the side to cover the markings. They're ugly brutes that look welded out of Meccano. You need a heat-seeking missile to bring one down. Rifle fire bounces off like peas.

A *barbouze* whose name I didn't know jumped from the Dauphin and began a suicide run towards a heap of stones. He was shot down. He began to crawl, leaving a slug-trail of red. A fresh burst of gunfire caught him and he lay still. The gunship hung in the air like some giant hawk hovering for prey, but nothing moved. Satisfied, the gunship lurched higher. It could carry thirty troops fully laden with battle gear. The crates in the Skyvan would be no problem. Its pilot checked back over his shoulder once, the sun lighting up his blond hair, and then the gunship headed off towards the distant hillock.

'*Dieu.*' It was a hiss through Crevecoeur's teeth. Dust lingered in the air like bonfire smoke. Crevecoeur was peering into it. 'Maufoux,' he shouted. 'Timbaud. Pelletier. Brugger.' There was no answer. 'Is there *anybody*?' There was silence. '*Bon dieu de bon dieu.*' He began to move, turned to say: 'Wait here', and moved again, breaking into a jog. He detoured by the last man who'd been shot down and stood for some seconds staring at the figure. He didn't kneel down, feel for a pulse, check if there was a flicker of life. Hopeless, I suppose. He carried on with long strides towards the Dauphin. There should have been a grubby raincoat flapping round his knees; that is how I saw him at Sfax Airport. He disappeared inside the helicopter and my first thought was he'd gone to radio a Mayday message. But in a matter of seconds he was out and scampering back to the rock. He'd gone to fetch his attaché case.

He knelt down beside the case. From the breast pocket of his uniform he removed a piece of plastic like a credit card but with a broad metallic strip. He inserted this into a slot under the handle, opened the case and pulled up a metal rod. The case was of matt black but it wasn't what I'd thought it was. On the inside of the lid was the legend in French: *Ministry of Defence. Authorized personnel only. Observe all screening procedures.*

He said: 'Turn your back and keep under cover.'

'Turn my back?'

'On that hill.'

There was no sign of the gunship. It was rendezvousing with the Skyvan. I stared and stared at the hill until Crevecoeur lost patience. He leant across and hauled me down into the shelter of the rock and jammed my head between my knees.

'Keep down.'

He slumped on the ground beside me with the case on his knees. From his pocket he dug out a mini-cassette and locked it in position over twin sprockets. He flicked a switch. A dial was illuminated and a green light winked on.

'You see nothing. You hear nothing. You forget everything. Understood?'

'What are you talking about? What mustn't I see?'

'And don't ask questions.'

He could have been on the last lap of a marathon. He panted through an open mouth. His face had lost all colour and swam with sweat. We stared at each other. There was a force inside him as powerful as gravity. I saw it in his eyes.

'There is no other way. Believe me.'

He drew a deep breath and turned his attention to the case. With his thumbs he depressed two large square buttons. The green light went out. A red light came on. An electronic tone pulsed out the seconds. Crevecoeur's face gripped me. His eyelids twitched to each bleep. His lips moved, mumbling the seconds to himself. Thirteen, fourteen, fifteen. The electronic tone became continuous and then stopped. The desert round us, which had been the colour of raw cane sugar, flashed white and as the roar began the white faded back to

tan. The ground tremored under my body. A rumble went
on and on. Some huge force had been released and it wouldn't
go away. I'd imagined Niagara, when the sun had got to me.
This was more powerful than a thousand suns in the desert.
On and on and then subsiding. I jerked upright. Half the hill
seemed to have disappeared. The top of it had been blown
clean away. Boulders were scattered in every direction. Some
had tumbled frighteningly close to us, rocks as big as a car.
Stones still pattered back to earth. Dust soared. A mushroom
boiled up into the sky.

'You've *murdered* them.'

'*Putain!*' he screamed at me. 'How many thousands was
Skorpion planning to murder. Did they tell you? What targets
had they chosen? The medina in Sfax? The Mosque in
Kairouan?'

That's what Skorpion will do – provoke terror. I heard the
hoarse voice. *We shall strike and strike again. Out of chaos
comes creation.*

'That isn't just "war material" taken from a factory.
They're not guns or grenades. You lied to me.'

The noise had died away. The earth gone still.

'Disguised the truth perhaps,' and he shrugged. 'Out of
date stuff. Free-fall bombs that can be activated by atmospheric pressure – that would have been Skorpion's way. Also
they can be radio-detonated provided you have the code-tape
– my way.'

'Skorpion had got hold of nuclear weapons?'

'Impossible? I thought so too. God, the lack of security –
it's unimaginable. That something so terrifying could be
stolen . . . That fixer PDS had worked it out. You've watched
television news. When cruise missiles are deployed there are
thousands of demonstrators and thousands of police. Right?
But when nuclear weapons become obsolete and are taken
away, who cares? There's no one. PDS knew that. Shrewd
bastard. These were being returned to the *Commissariat à
l'Energie Atomique* for disarming. There was one guard on
the train and he was found drugged in the morning. Something in his coffee flask. Somewhere along the line there was
an unscheduled stop for a red signal and the crates were
unloaded.'

254

You had to know the timing, you had to know the route, you had to buy contacts. That was why PDS had always been so expensive.

Crevecoeur got to his feet. 'It is intolerable that a man like Fellah should have such weapons in his hands. These would have been the first nuclear weapons exploded in anger since 1945. After the first, the second soon follows. The third seems routine. Then comes the holocaust.'

'You exploded them in anger.'

He patted his pockets until he found a squashed pack of Gitanes. He lit a cigarette and watched the smoke drift out of his nostrils.

'You exploded them in anger, Crevecoeur.'

His face wore a mask of white. 'I exploded nothing. Do you understand? Skorpion never had those weapons. They were part of the joint exercise.'

'You can't get away with that. The French and Tunisian Presidents will never agree.'

'Oh? Do they have a choice?'

Snap went the lock as he shut the lid of the radio-detonator. You can see a thousand black cases like that on the metro every morning. I even gave one to Michel on his birthday. Look closely at the man carrying one. Make certain his eyes aren't the colour of spit. Crevecoeur took half a dozen steps, tucking the case under his arm, and stopped to look over his shoulder.

'What are you waiting for? The fall-out? We must hurry.'

'Is this what I tell Ella Borries? Her husband was incinerated in a nuclear explosion in the Sahara?'

'Idiot.' He came back and stood very close. 'You tell her nothing. Can't you grasp that, Cody?' He stared. His eyes never blinked. 'Nothing. Now we have to get out. You've got work to do. Check the Dauphin hasn't been too damaged to fly.'

'I have to do *what*?'

'Get the helicopter started.'

I took a step back. You keep your distance from a mad dog.

'Crevecoeur. Listen. I cannot fly a helicopter. I don't know how.'

'You piloted the Skyvan. I have never flown anything. Don't tell me you're afraid.'

He couldn't know about my beating pulse. Or the sweat that had broken out in a dozen secret places. 'Crevecoeur . . .' But I couldn't think what to say.

'Come on. I'll carry you to the helicopter.'

'Don't touch me.'

He raised an eyebrow and turned round and walked away.

Antoine, I need you. I need your help.

I followed in Crevecoeur's tracks. He made straight for the helicopter. He didn't waste so much as a glance on what lay beyond the hill. What point was there? Nothing could be left alive – not a man, not a weed, not a dung beetle.